PENGUIN BOOKS

Every Christmas Eve

Emma Heatherington is the *Irish Times* and international bestselling author of seventeen novels, including UK number one ebook *This Christmas*, as well as Amazon Top 10 and USA Kindle hits *The Legacy of Lucy Harte*, *One More Day*, *The Promise* and *Secrets in the Snow*.

Her novels are set in Ireland, each exploring life-affirming issues combined with heart-warming love stories. Emma's distinctive style, full of poignancy and warmth, has developed a loyal and ever-growing fanbase.

Every Christmas Eve

Emma Heatherington

PENGUIN BOOKS

PENGUIN BOOKS

UK | USA | Canada | Ireland | Australia
India | New Zealand | South Africa

Penguin Books is part of the Penguin Random House group of companies
whose addresses can be found at global.penguinrandomhouse.com

Penguin Random House UK,
One Embassy Gardens, 8 Viaduct Gardens, London SW11 7BW

penguin.co.uk
global.penguinrandomhouse.com

 Penguin
Random House
UK

First published 2025
Published in Penguin Books 2025
001

Set in 10.4/15 pt Palatino LT Pro
Typeset by Six Red Marbles UK, Thetford, Norfolk
Printed and bound in Great Britain by Clays Ltd, Elcograf S.p.A.

The authorised representative in the EEA is Penguin Random House Ireland,
Morrison Chambers, 32 Nassau Street, Dublin D02 YH68

A CIP catalogue record for this book is available from the British Library

ISBN: 978–1–804–95337–2

Penguin Random House is committed to a sustainable future
for our business, our readers and our planet. This book is made
from Forest Stewardship Council® certified paper.

 MIX
Paper | Supporting
responsible forestry
FSC® C018179

For Jim and our children Jordyn, Jade, Dualta,
Adam and Sonny.

With thanks and love for your strength,
bravery and for all you do.

Then

Christmas Eve, 25 Years Ago

'We did it,' said Ben. 'We really did it! I think you might be magic, Lou Doherty.'

The brand-new life we'd just delivered moments before lay within touching distance, covered in a blanket to protect her from the elements. She was all long legs and wide blinking eyes, while her skin was still damp and downy and her ears twitched and flickered as she adapted to her whole new world.

A world I was now a big part of at the tender age of sixteen.

With the newborn baby foal beside us, Ben and I knelt together in the shelter of the stable, the smell of damp hay and horses filling the air as the snow fell gently outside the open door.

It was already a Christmas Eve like no other, even if I'd no idea how this moment would end up shaping both of our lives forever.

'I don't think I've ever seen anything so beautiful in my

whole life before,' I said, staring at the tiny foal, 'or had a Christmas gift so special. That was amazing. It was like something from a movie.'

He laughed at my wide-eyed enthusiasm, but it was true. I'd never witnessed anything like it and believed I never would again.

'We make a good team, Lou,' he told me. 'You handled every bit of that so calmly, so coolly. I'd have you on my side any day of the week, and twice at weekends. Same time next year?'

Even then, although I hardly knew him, Ben Heaney had a way of making me feel like I was the only girl in the world.

'Same time next year, Ben,' I joked in return. 'I think we make a great team too. Thanks for making me help you out instead of running in the opposite direction like I was so tempted to.'

We sat for what felt like ages in comfortable silence as thick flakes of snow fluttered down on to the roof of Ballyheaney House in the distance, covering its sprawling lawns like a thick, white blanket.

Not far from the stable where adrenaline kept us warm and the baby foal purred under the watchful eye of her mother, the Ballyheaney House Charity Afternoon Tea was in full festive flow inside the Heaney family home, a stunning eighteenth-century house which was inspired by St Peter's Cathedral in Rome.

But we had escaped from all the celebrations for just a little while.

'I wonder has my mother noticed I'm gone yet,' Ben

muttered, though I knew deep down he wasn't bothered, considering what we'd just achieved with Sally, their adored mare.

'Maybe we should go back?' I suggested.

'No, it's fine. We can relax for another few minutes,' he told me. 'They're all going to be so impressed when they hear of the new arrival. And besides all of that, I'd much rather be here with you than lifting glasses from tipsy guests who tell me how handsome and grown up I am since they saw me last year.'

It was exactly the reply I'd been hoping for. With Ben by my side, I wished I could bottle up that moment and savour it forever.

It had been twelve whole months since I had last laid eyes on Ben Heaney. A shy, awkward introduction and a brief conversation with instant chemistry was as far as we'd managed at last year's party, but I'd dreamed of him ever since.

Yet nothing could have prepared me for this incredibly special, intimate and unexpected first chance to spend one-to-one time together, so far away from everyone else.

Back inside his magnificent stately home, fine bone china cups would be clinking on matching saucers in a magnificent blue ballroom as chatter and laughter formed a symphony alongside a string quartet playing Christmas carols in the corner. Right through the centre of the room, a mouth-watering buffet was spread on a long table covered in crisp white linen, with silver candelabras circled in green holly and bright red berries foraged from the hedges close to nearby Lough Beg.

The Christmas Eve party was an annual sweet escape into a way I imagined my life could be one day. And if I'd the chance back then to travel the world or stay in that stable with him, I'd have chosen him every single time.

He was dashing, with intense green eyes and a bird's nest of tousled dark auburn hair I longed to touch at any given opportunity. His body was lean and muscular, defined from seasons of training on and off the rugby pitch, but his most engaging feature was his tenderness, which defied his seventeen years. Most of all, to me he was a mystery, whether hidden behind the gates of Ballyheaney House, or far away at boarding school, or packed off to Europe on exchange trips throughout the summer.

To get a glimpse of any of the Heaney family was always a source of village gossip. They were different from us in so many ways, yet he and I were starting to form a bond that no one would know about for a very long time.

'So, when do you leave for school in Dublin again?' I asked, feeling silly for the ache in my heart I already felt for what was to come.

'Don't tell me you're missing me so soon?' he sighed. 'You've got it bad. I knew it.'

I felt my cheeks flush.

'I'm jesting,' he continued. 'Ah, look at your little face. I'm joking, I'm sorry.'

'It was a very simple question,' I reminded him, wishing the pink flush that always let me down would go away.

'Well, school starts again in early January,' he said, 'so I imagine I'll be sent off on the train as soon as the holidays are over. Packed off and packed away, never to be seen again until half-term, when I'll be off to help Uncle Eric on his farm in Wicklow as he embraces the weird and wacky world of fast cars, faster women and fine cigars.'

'I see,' I gulped, feeling very ordinary in comparison.

'He isn't like that at all. It's rather boring actually, so I'd much rather come back here,' he said, fiddling with a piece of straw. 'I'd much rather be at Ballyheaney House so I can hang out like this with you.'

His eyes were sad for a moment, and once again I was reminded of how I lived such a different life, far away from the twinkling lights and the Christmas carols and the plush ballroom that had brought us together that day.

Ben's home was an impressive former bishop's manor tucked away in the rolling countryside, while mine was a modest bungalow close by the banks of Lough Beg. His school was a posh boarding establishment two hours away in Dublin where ambition was high and everyone's business was kept to themselves. Mine was the local comprehensive down the road where everybody knew your name, your address and what you were having for dinner.

And because of this, an invitation to the annual Charity Afternoon Tea on Christmas Eve at Ballyheaney House was a huge treat for all the village – and now so much more than that to me. It was a chance to sit close to him, to talk to each other, to flirt and smile, to feel that maybe, just maybe, there might be a true connection between us that would one day defy the odds and bring us properly together.

'Will you really miss me?' I asked, knowing that the

thought of him thinking of me would keep me smiling for many, many nights to come. 'Or was that just another jest?'

'I will really miss you,' he replied. 'Truthfully, I mean it. Today has been very special.'

I thought my heart was going to burst when his hand found mine and he squeezed it, closing his eyes for a few seconds.

'I'd like you to name her please, Lou,' he said to me eventually. His suggestion almost took my breath away. 'If you don't mind?'

'Me?'

'Yes, you.'

A rush of excitement filled me from head to toe, and I could barely think straight.

'But – but are you sure? Won't your parents . . . ?'

'My parents would agree that it's the least I can do, given how much you've helped me today. I'll tell them all about how you brought her into the world with so much calm and sensitivity while they were entertaining half the village,' he said with confidence. 'So, I'd like you to name her. Please.'

I gulped hard, unable to hide my beaming smile. We'd been talking earlier by the swing under the oak tree when we'd heard a cry from Sally the mare in the stable. I'd wanted to run in the other direction for help, but Ben had convinced me to stay. He'd told me we could do this together, and we did.

'Are you sure it's a "she"?' I asked him.

He raised an eyebrow.

'We once had a cat called Pat with a swollen belly, who

later became Patricia when a vet told us that "he" was having kittens,' I told him.

He threw his head back with laughter. Oh, how I savoured every ounce of him.

'And there I was, singing your praises for how natural and calm you were,' he said. 'While you, on the other hand, question my ability to sex a foal. Now, what would you like to call her? Take your time.'

I did exactly that and he waited, tending to Sally as I thought of a name for this beautiful creature. I'd never been so close to nature in this way before.

And then it came to me.

'Little Eve,' I declared eventually, my eyes wide with excitement. 'Maybe it's a pretty obvious choice, but I like it. She's so little. And she was born on Christmas Eve.'

'Little Eve,' he said, looking up at me with a smile. 'I like it. Little Eve, the Christmas foal of Ballyheaney House.'

I felt a shiver running through me. My breath lingered in the cold air as I waited for him to say more, but then the most wonderous thing I'd ever witnessed with my own two eyes occurred.

Not even thirty minutes after I'd helped with her birth, the tiny foal shook her head, then leaned her weight on her brown, spindly front legs. My mouth dropped open in astonishment as she slowly found each of her back feet, one after the other. She stood up, wobbling at first, but her mother licked her tiny legs to encourage her until she stood tall.

'Wow! Well done, Little Eve,' I whispered with quiet admiration. 'You are amazing! You really are!'

I looked at Ben as his green eyes glistened. Mine did too.

'Little Eve, I love you already!' he said with a warm smile that could have melted the snow outside. He stretched out his hand and Little Eve stumbled towards us, before falling on to the soft hay.

'I'm so in awe of her,' I cried. 'What a little star. A Christmas star, that's what you are, Little Eve.'

I leaned back on the cold stone wall in wonder at the blinking foal as she took in her new world.

'And I'm in awe of you,' he said to me.

I shivered again and he quickly fixed a blanket round my shoulders, then tilted my chin towards him.

'Can I kiss you?' he asked. 'I've been wanting to do it for a whole year now.'

I did my best to play it cool, hoping my cheeks wouldn't let me down again by flushing pink.

'Um, yes. Yes, I'd like that very much,' I replied, feeling like my heart might explode, then I slowly closed my eyes as his lips met mine. It was lingering, it was perfect, and it made my insides glow. I had dreamed of this moment a million times, I had longed for it, and now it was really happening.

'We'd better get back inside, but before we go, please tell me something I'll remember forever,' he asked me. 'Something I can think of when I'm learning Latin and French in a cold Dublin classroom in a few weeks.'

I turned towards him. Our gaze locked. I didn't have to think fast. I knew exactly what I wanted to say to him, so I sat up straight and looked into his soul.

'That's easy,' I said softly, feeling tears prick my eyes at the thought of him being so far away from me once more. 'Every Christmas Eve, let's always think of this moment, and of our precious Little Eve, no matter where we are, for the rest of our lives.'

He pulled me close again, and I melted into the safety of his strong arms.

'You, me and Little Eve.'

As we walked our separate ways minutes later, back to the sticky heat of the tea party where no one else knew of our bond, I don't think I'd ever smiled so much in my life. Ben disappeared to tell his father the news of the foal's unexpected arrival, and I joined my parents, who were already tipsy on the fizzy wine.

As small talk surrounded me and laughter filled the air, I knew in my young heart I could easily love him forever, but I also knew that life would have very different plans for us.

The youngest Heaney boy was worldly, whereas I was naïve and protected in my small family circle. He was gentle and kind but wild and carefree, and led such a different life from me.

Yet he'd agreed to our promise, and although we only had a few wonderful Christmas Eves together after that, before a final, heart-wrenching goodbye, I've never forgotten that very first kiss in the stable where we brought new life into the world before our very eyes.

These days I think of him just like we agreed to every Christmas Eve.

And I can't help but wonder, wherever he might be, if Ben Heaney still thinks of me too.

Chapter One

Lou

NOW

Sixteen Days to Christmas Eve

I hold my lukewarm mug of hot chocolate with both hands and stare up at the azure late afternoon sky, its crescent moon hanging above Jupiter, just over the steeple on Church Island in Lough Beg.

'A sign of positive decisions, perhaps,' I ponder, swaying slightly in the cutting winter breeze. 'I *have* made the right decision coming back here, haven't I?'

Maybe the more times I say it, the sooner I'll end up believing it.

It's been a bitterly cold day in our village, yet reasonably calm for December, with only the odd drizzle of icy rain now and then. Nana Molly, who is due here any minute, is delighted there's no snow yet despite the reports, but I can't help wishing for some proper frosty weather to get us all in the Christmas mood.

More Christmas spirit means more shoppers, which is better for all of us in this tiny corner of the world.

The festive tree is standing proud in the village, there's a huge crib in the local church and I've spent the entire afternoon busting my guts to decorate Buds and Beans, my florist's-cum-coffee bar, with lights and candles on anything that will hold them. And with only half an hour till Monday's earlier closing time, I'm already thinking of how I'd murder a foot rub and a glass of something bubbly back at my cosy new cottage as a reward for all my hard labour.

The glass of bubbles I can sort in a heartbeat. The foot rub – well, that part's a bit trickier to arrange unless I do it myself.

'You always were a daydreamer, even at school, Lou Doherty.'

The older man's raspy voice stirs me at first, but I smile as I recognise one of my favourite locals. 'Caught again,' I say, feeling a rush of heat go to my cheeks at being discovered waffling aloud, and not for the first time today. I hope Master Campbell didn't hear more than he needed to. I really should stop talking to myself, at least in public places like the main street of our village where everybody likes to know your business.

'Are you still open?' he asks me, his words holding the weight of time in every syllable. 'I believe there's a cinnamon latte and a chocolate treat with my name on it if it's not too late?'

'I'll always make time for you, sir,' I reply to the dapper, recently retired schoolmaster. 'Isn't the crescent moon stunning? It looks like it might scoop up the old church ruins on Lough Beg and take her away.'

But Master Campbell doesn't even glance up to the sky in response. Instead, he steps across the threshold, mumbling to himself about how he thinks it's now cold enough for snow, and follows me over to the coffee dock.

His tailored, knee-length navy overcoat matches his once sparkling blue eyes, and his voice never fails to bring me back to my days at primary school when my only worry in life was how soon I could press fast forward and get a job in the real world.

And now here I am, right bang *in* the real world, where I sometimes wish I could go back and start it all over again. Only this time I'd do it very differently, avoiding all the challenges and pitfalls I've faced, having just about survived to tell the tale.

Or would I?

Never in my wildest dreams did I imagine that at the age of forty-one I'd be back in the village I grew up in, serving coffee to faces both familiar and new, soothing weary souls and aiding celebrations of people I don't even know with a bright bouquet of fresh flowers delivered to their door.

'This place is becoming more like a church confessional every day,' Mum likes to remind me at every opportunity, but I know she loves it here at Buds and Beans since she left her job at a local engineering firm to help me out. 'You must have one of those faces, Lou. You know the type. You don't even have to utter a word and, within minutes, locals and strangers are spilling their hearts out to you over an oat cappuccino.'

She is spot on with her observations, and Master Campbell is a case in point.

'I was dreading turning the page on the calendar this morning,' he says as I serve him his cinnamon-laced drink with his favourite *pain au chocolat*. 'Another day closer. Ah, I used to say I hated Christmas, but now I realise how much I loved it when Agnes was with me. What a difference a year makes.'

He puts his head into his hands, so I pull out a chair and sit with him to hear him out, thankful that it's almost closing time and the place is quiet except for the sounds of Wham's 'Last Christmas' softly lilting in the background.

'Agnes would have to drag me around town to shop for the grandchildren,' he tells me, wiping his nose on a freshly pressed handkerchief. 'Bless her, she'd panic-buy for the two of them then send me to the post office that very same day, making sure we didn't leave it too late so the parcels would get to our Eamonn and the wee ones in New Zealand on time. I complained far too much, but I secretly enjoyed it, especially when we'd hear the gifts had arrived on the other side of the world.'

He pauses to gather his thoughts.

'If it's any consolation, my dad used to moan about Christmas shopping more than the government and that was a lot,' I tell him, feeling a pang in my own gut for days gone by when my father's one-liners were legendary. 'Some people don't enjoy this time of year, and that's fine, sir. I have to say I can think of a million things I'd rather do than bump into strangers while we all spend more money than we can afford to.'

But Master Campbell is still silent, lost in his own trip down memory lane.

My heart breaks for him, but just when I'm about to attempt to offer some more unsolicited advice, he takes a second crisp white handkerchief from his pocket, dabs his eyes and sits up straight.

'Anyhow, that's enough of my maudlin,' he declares, sniffing and wiping his nose. 'I'm sure you've got far more important things to be doing than listening to an old man like me yearn for times past.'

'You can always find an ear here with me,' I tell him.

He smiles, his bushy white eyebrows meeting like two thick caterpillars in the middle. I'm not sure if it's my imagination, but his eyes look brighter already.

'We're all so very lucky to have you back in the village where you belong,' he replies, tucking the hankie back in his pocket.

'That's nice to hear,' I say quietly. 'Even if I still doubt if I've made the right call by leaving New York.'

'You *have* made the right call,' says my mother gliding past, broom in hand. 'It's still early days, Lou. Be patient.'

I only wish I had her confidence in my decision. There's so much I love about being back here on my home turf, but the loneliness engulfs me sometimes when I think of my daughter so far away.

'Ah, Christmas will be different for both of us this year,

that's all,' says Master Campbell. 'Is Gracie coming over from New York to see you? That's something to look forward to.'

I meet my mother's eye, wondering if she is thinking what I'm thinking.

'Yes . . . Gracie will be here for Christmas,' I reply, but my voice is tinged with uncertainty. 'At least, I'm hoping so. At twenty years old, my daughter doesn't believe in laying down roots yet. She has the travel bug well and truly alive and kicking inside her, but who am I to argue with that?'

Master Campbell nods with a smile.

'Like mother, like daughter,' he says with a hearty chuckle. 'And travel far you did, and brave and buoyant you were, Lou, but more like the swallow than the swift. I knew you'd one day find your way home.'

'I think you know me too well, sir,' I reply, patting his hand.

'A teacher knows his pupils for life,' he responds, delighted to have said his piece. 'Your Gracie will come home for Christmas, just you wait and see.'

'I only hope you're right,' I mumble.

It's been six long months since I left New York and everything I'd built there within a leading interior design company, and not long after, Gracie set off for her final year at college. For months before I'd been pondering my decision to move back home to Bellaghy, the tiny Irish village I'd grown up in, but when the gorgeous Katie's Cottage came up for sale, my mind was made up instantly.

'Well, look who it is!' I hear from the front door as the bell rings at the arrival of my always charming Nana Molly.

'Good afternoon, handsome Edward. Now don't you cut a fine vision on this December day. Oh, and Lou, I simply adore your decorations. I'm glad you took my advice on the coloured lights instead of those boring plain white or gold ones. The whole place is so cosy and festive. Well done!'

Nana Molly, as usual, is like a ray of sunshine from the moment she enters the room, even on this chilly afternoon. At almost eighty, she defies her age, living her life with zest and energy – and sometimes against doctor's orders.

Her secret? A shot of brandy every night and her daily walks around Longpoint Wood by Lough Beg.

'Seeing you all has made my day,' chuckles my old schoolmaster, almost dizzied at the sight of Nana Molly. My late grandfather used to joke how he felt invisible in her company. I can easily see why.

'I bet you say that to all the girls,' Nana Molly says with a cheeky wink as she pats Master Campbell's shoulder. 'Once a charmer, always a charmer. We need more of that round here. Thank you, kind sir.'

I catch a fleeting glance of the former schoolmaster, whose solemn frown now suggests he might feel he has said too much, but soon he is smiling again as Nana Molly keeps everyone's spirits up.

She lifts a mug and taps it with a long teaspoon.

'So, I have news,' she announces.

She makes her way behind the counter, helps herself to a coffee and pops a few pound coins into my cash box as she does so. A statement like this, especially from her, is enough to make all of us sit up and listen.

'Is it gossip or news?' I tease. 'There is a difference, so be careful, darling grandmother.'

Nana Molly ponders my question for a few seconds.

'Both,' she replies with an almost wicked smile. 'Oh, you're not going to believe this. This is big news. This is *very* big news.'

Master Campbell is all eyes and ears as Nana holds up one hand theatrically. She is wearing a faux-fur beige coat, a bright yellow polo-neck jumper and a pair of flared light blue jeans that belong back in the seventies, where they probably came from. A blinding, potentially awful combination, yet it suits her to a tee with her slim little figure and short, curly, dark brown dyed hair with a tinge of red.

We wait with bated breath.

'The village Christmas Fayre will have to be cancelled this year due to venue constraints,' she announces. 'And the lead sponsor pulled the pin, so they're completely screwed. With just over two weeks to go, they don't have the time or the contacts to make it happen.'

'Ah, now that's a crying shame,' says Master Campbell.

My mother, who takes off her green apron and reaches for her coat, is much less sympathetic.

'Is that it?' she cries. 'Is that the news?'

Nana raises her pencilled eyebrows.

'What do you mean, *is that it*?'

'The Christmas Fayre is cancelled?' says Mum, in mock fluster. 'Is that it? Sure, we can go to the one in the next village, or the next, or the next. I thought it was going to be something more exciting, that's all.'

'Well, I hadn't *finished* my news,' says Nana Molly with her hand on her hip and her lips pursed tight. 'Honestly, it's hard to have a conversation with you two declaring disappointment and interrupting me constantly. At least you've the grace to pretend to look disappointed, Master Campbell.'

My old schoolmaster shifts in his seat, doing his best not to laugh out loud.

'I haven't said a word!' I plea.

'Tell the truth, Lou. You don't give a toss either,' Mum says, doing her best not to give in to a fit of the giggles.

Master Campbell chuckles in his chair by the window. I'm so happy to see him smile.

'OK, so what's the punchline, Nana Moll?' I ask as I dry up some cups and place them on the wooden shelf on the wall. 'The Christmas Fayre is cancelled and . . . ?'

She lets out a deep sigh.

'The punchline is that Mrs Quinn from the Christmas Fayre committee has written a pleading letter to Tilda Heaney.'

She pauses for effect, knowing our mouths have now dropped to the floor, including Master Campbell's.

'Tilda Heaney?' asks Mum, puzzled. 'Why on earth would she write to Tilda Heaney?'

Nana can't help but smile at the look on our faces now she's got the reaction she expected.

'She has written to ask the Heaney family to help raise spirits within our community this year by bringing back . . .'

'No,' I whisper.

'The Christmas Eve Charity Afternoon Tea Party at Ballyheaney House.'

'You're joking!' says Mum.

'I'm not,' Nana replies.

My stomach goes to my throat. I grip the small counter, feeling faint. I might be sick. My eyes glaze over.

'Can you believe it?' Nana continues, her voice now shrill in my ear. 'I mean, talk about setting yourself up for a fall! Christmas Eve Afternoon Tea with the Heaneys! As if that's what we need, and as if that family would ever dream of bringing it back. Sure, there's only Tilda and eccentric old Eric left. Well, I know I won't be going, that's for sure.'

I glance at my mother, who seems to have drifted off to another planet. She certainly isn't on the same one I'm on right now.

'Gosh ... wow!' she says at last, clasping her hands together. 'I think that would be just what we all need. Oh, I can't help but picture it all. Their home is so beautiful. This is wonderful news! A party at Ballyheaney House on Christmas Eve is something to look forward to.'

'I totally agree, Liz,' says Master Campbell, who is rubbing his hands and grinning, but I don't respond. I can't. And I'm glad that none of them have noticed how my cheeks are burning, or how beads of sweat are forming on my forehead as I look around for a place to hide.

I fear I might be sick.

'Wonderful? Why exactly?' exclaims Nana.

'Wonderful and exciting and everything else along those lines,' says Mum with glee as she dances around the florist's with a tea towel as her partner. 'Oh, those really were the good old days in this village, right up until it all came to a very abrupt ending with no reason, rhyme or explanation.'

Master Campbell clears his throat. 'Wasn't it because Mr Heaney died?' he suggests.

'He was a dead weight for years before that,' says Nana Molly.

'Nana!' I cry. As much as I'm in a state of shock, there's no need for that. 'Mr Heaney died years after the last Christmas Eve party, so it was nothing to do with him.'

I'm glad they don't quiz me any further, knowing I probably have inside information from those days.

'Ah, the exquisite live music,' continues Mum. 'The fairy lights on the trees, the delicious food in the blue ballroom, like a banquet. The fashion sense of Tilda Heaney and her gorgeous family. The glitz and the glamour . . . not to mention the money raised for charity. I can see it all happening! I can feel it already! Am I there yet? I wouldn't miss it for the world.'

Master Campbell pipes up from behind his coffee cup. 'I wonder would the son and daughter come home for it if it did happen?' he ponders.

I fear I might choke.

'Now, wouldn't that be something else?' says Mum. 'Our Lou and Ben had quite a thing back in the day.'

I raise my eyebrows.

'He hasn't been seen much in this village for ages,' Master Campbell continues. 'And his sister lives in Spain, I believe? Or is it Portugal? I often wonder about them both. It would be a fine homecoming for them too.'

'Do you think they would?' I ask, unable to hide the tremor in my voice. 'Do you think they'd come back?'

My legs are playing a blinder by still managing to hold me up now the conversation has got this far.

'Wouldn't that be crazy seeing him again after all these years,' says Mum. 'Your old sparring partner, Lou! You used to live for your days at Ballyheaney House. Wasn't it so incredibly sad what happened to Ben's poor—'

'Mum, please stop,' I say, finally showing my face from behind the coffee machine.

My mother's mouth drops open.

'You two were never that serious, though?' she says.

'No,' I mumble. 'No, we weren't serious at all.'

I feel bad for lying and for cutting her off mid-sentence, but I can't disguise my fears as the past comes back to haunt me all over again. Serious? We were very serious until it all came crashing down, but Mum and Nana don't know the half of it. I couldn't bear to talk about it for a very long time.

But now, all I can see with such clarity and beauty, and all I can feel from the deep clench of my gut, is the face of the man I loved more than anyone I've ever known.

He was the man who broke my heart the worst. The man I really did think I'd marry one day, in so much more than just a young girl's dream. The man who said he'd never marry another, and that he'd wait for me, even if it took forever.

I knew deep down that by moving back here our paths might cross again one day, but I'd blanked it out as highly unlikely and carried on with setting up my new home and my new business, saying I'd cross that bridge if or when I came to it.

And now the bridge is being built as we speak.

The highly unlikely is sounding quite likely, and with even a whisper of it happening, I already want to run away back to New York and never show my face around here again.

Chapter Two

Ben

'It's OK, sweetheart. You can cry it all out. Take your time. I'm right here.'

I sit on the edge of my daughter's double bed, doing my best not to show how with every tear she sheds, Ava's heartbreak is quietly killing me inside. There are photos of yesteryear strewn across her duvet and pillow while she clutches a framed favourite in her hands, her fingernails painted a deep shade of pink just like her mother used to do for her every Christmas when she was very little.

Fairy lights hang around her headboard, a bookshelf which needs reorganising reminds me of how fast she is growing up, and a miniature lit-up tree sits on her bedside locker – a last-minute addition at her request as she battles to embrace December and all it brings.

It's been six years since we lost Stephanie, yet since the turn of December and as Christmas comes closer, it's like the reality of not having her mother is suffocating Ava all over again. There's very little I can do, except to stay close to her when she wants me, and step back when she needs some space.

I'd been warned about this from other parents in a similar situation to mine, especially as Ava is an only child, with no siblings to lean on. I was told it would come in waves, but that after a while those waves would get lower and the time between them would increase. That is happening for sure, but today it's time for another wave to hit the shore, and we'll have to go with it until it passes again.

'I just get so angry sometimes, Dad,' she sniffles, clasping a wet tissue now in her fist. I offer the palm of my hand. She passes me the tissue and I hand her a fresh one in a routine that has become all too familiar. 'Freya said something in school about her mum taking her into Dublin city to see the lights tonight and do some Christmas shopping. They're having a girly day. It totally set me off. Like, why did she have to die, Daddy? Why did my mum have to die?'

I picture the happy families who will make their way into the city this month for some festive treats and Christmas shopping under the sparkle and shine of all the decorations lighting up the night sky. I can already hear the buskers as they stand on Grafton Street, their hands bright red with the cold and their warm breath filling the air as they belt out 'Fairytale of New York' on every corner. I can smell the street food, the sticky chocolate, the crêpes sizzling on hot griddles and the swirls of cream that melt before you take your first bite.

I can hear the children's laughter. I can hear the arguments too. All part of the hustle and bustle that makes some of us love Christmas and others dread it.

'Life can be so unbelievably cruel, baby,' I whisper to my only child, pushing her thick auburn hair out of her eyes. 'I so wish I could take all your pain away, Ava, I really do. And I know it's not the same, but I'd love to take you to Dublin to see the Christmas lights. We could go up this evening if you want to? I'm not the best at shopping, but we could . . .'

She glances at me, a look of both pity and disgust on her scrunched-up face.

'Dad, thanks but . . .'

'OK, look, erm . . . forget I even said that. How about we take Roly out for a run on the beach at Sandycove with our torches?' I suggest instead, wide-eyed with a sliver of hope that this might be a goer. 'We can wrap up warm and watch him run riot on the sand until he tires himself out like he always does?'

'I dunno,' she mutters, twisting the tissue in her hands. 'I'm not sure I'm in the mood for a beach walk.'

'We could get fish and chips on the way home?' I suggest, doing my best to think of what we could do on what's essentially a school night. 'And eat in the car down by the pier before homework? Roly would love some fish and chips, I'm sure.'

Our golden retriever bounds into the bedroom at the sound of his own name. I'll swear that dog has super senses I'll never quite understand.

'Thanks, Dad, but I think I'm going to just have a lie-down for now and watch some animal YouTube videos to take my mind off things,' she tells me, gathering up the photos before our dog destroys them. 'Will you put these away, please? Sometimes her pictures make me happy. Sometimes, like now, they make me sad.'

'Sure,' I tell her, as a million questions flood my mind on grief and how it all works. Ava was so young when Steph died. My biggest worry at the time was whether she'd even remember her mother, and after the shock of the first few months it seemed like my biggest worry might be coming true as our daughter readjusted her sails and appeared to be adapting much quicker than I was. But since she went to big school last year, it's like the old wounds have opened all over again. I'd hoped last December was a one-off, but here we are once more. So this year I'm going to do something about it. I can't just stand by and watch as she goes to pieces in the run-up to Christmas.

'I hate this time of year so much,' she announces. 'And I hate that I hate it, because we used to love Christmas when she was here, didn't we, Dad? Didn't Mum love Christmas? Didn't she love decorating the tree and cooking lots of nice things for us?'

I nod in agreement. 'She did, baby,' I say. 'She loved it all.'

Roly whimpers in what sounds like support but is probably his way of letting us know how he'd love to be up on the soft duvet, casually tearing apart the photos Ava has taken from an old family album.

I gather up the photos, doing my best not to look too closely at the smiling faces that stare back at me. Our first Christmas as a family of three, then four when Roly came along as a puppy a couple of years later. It was Stephanie's idea to get a dog, insisting that Ava had the love of an animal in her life the way I had back at home in Ballyheaney House when I was a boy. I wasn't so sure back then, but now I couldn't be more relieved that we have him to look after, because otherwise there would still be days when neither Ava nor I want to get up out of bed.

Roly, with his acrobatics that got him his name and his big dog energy, keeps us sane more than he could ever know it.

'You sure you'll be OK?' I ask when I get to the bedroom door, but Ava is already tucked under the duvet, curled into a ball with the comfort of her iPad for company. 'I'll take that as a yes, then.'

'Everything still feels so empty here, no matter how much I try to fill the house with noise or decorations or people at this time of year,' I explain to my business partner, Matt, when he pops by on his way home from playing a game of squash after work. 'I know that Ava feels it too, no matter how hard we try to make it work without her mother.'

'But you've both been doing so well,' he reminds me.

'I suppose we have,' I reply. 'I think we're doing well, until something like Christmas comes along and we're back to square one. This house is never going to feel like home again, I fear.'

Matt is usually a great listener, but he seems engrossed in my new Christmas decor as I spill out my guts to him.

'I hear you, buddy, but this house isn't empty. It's modern and it's magnificent,' he tells me as he absorbs the elaborate gold-and-green colour scheme that embraces every room on the bottom floor of my south County Dublin home. 'It doesn't look empty, nor does it feel empty to me. You've done a pretty neat job on Christmas this year, Ben. I'm going to have to keep Vic away from here until I manage to make more of an effort at our place.'

'What can I say, I do my best,' I reply, wondering if he really believes I'm fully responsible for all these decorations. 'Preparing for those parties at Ballyheaney House served me well in my youth.'

There's a spectacular tree in the hallway by the red front door, another splendid display in the sitting room and an extra-large bushy tree sits twinkling by the floor-to-ceiling window in the dining area just off the kitchen, where we chat over a home-made smoothie.

'I suppose that makes sense, but I didn't know you were all *that* creative, Ben,' he says. 'I'm genuinely impressed. I mean, with our vet business, and your daughter, and the fitness regime, where did you even have the time to find your artistic streak? It's a prize-winning display, man.'

'I'm very much a *part-time* vet in our practice these days,' I remind Matt, which makes a change from him reminding me about it since I decided to cut back my hours to a three-day week. 'I'm a part-time vet and very much a full-time dad, but come on, surely you don't believe I chose all of this myself?'

'Ah!'

'I'm good, but not that good, I'm afraid,' I confess as a look of relief takes over Matt's face.

'You could have got away with that,' he laughs. 'Am I always this gullible?'

'Hmm.' I laugh. 'I won't answer that. No, I hired a company from the city who promised to create *a festive atmosphere in your home that will fill your heart and soothe your soul*. I'm not sure I got my full money's worth on the last bit. It is pretty, though.'

Matt shrugs his shoulders. 'It's all very impressive to me, but I hear what you're saying,' he replies. 'I don't think companies like that can change how you feel, no matter what they promise.'

We sit for a short moment in silence, staring at the lights and the colours as I wonder why I ever thought it would make Ava feel better.

'Ah, I dunno any more,' I say, putting my head in my hands. I rub my face, then lean back on the kitchen chair with my hands behind my head. 'No matter what I do, it never feels like it's enough to make Christmas special again. Even after all these years it feels like something or someone's missing, and that's because she very much *is* missing. Steph is gone, and she isn't coming back.'

I curse myself for how I can say her name now without feeling the sting that used to pierce my heart so badly. I hate that it's getting easier. Part of me wants to make it all better for Ava, yet another part of me wants to wallow in the loss forever, because that's what I feel Steph deserves even if it's the last thing she said she wanted.

'I've been thinking that maybe I should sell up and start

again somewhere brand new, Matt,' I say suddenly. 'What do you reckon?'

Matt almost chokes on his smoothie. We've both been on a no-alcohol, gym-going kick for three months now and the results are showing, even if it will all no doubt go down the drain come Christmas.

'You're kidding, right?' he says. Matt shakes his head and looks back at me with concern. He and his wife, Victoria, have been best friends with me and Steph right from the start, when we set up home here in south County Dublin fifteen years ago as newlyweds without a care in the world and with no idea what the future had planned for us both.

'Ah, it's so hard to be happy when your kid's unhappy,' I say, wondering if I should go upstairs and check on Ava, or leave her to scroll through her favourite videos like she said she wanted to do for a while longer. 'I feel like we need a change or something new. Fresh energy, you know? It's been six years and right now I'm worn out, Matt. I'm exhausted. But I promised Stephanie I wouldn't wallow forever, nor would I let Ava do so. It's time for us both to decide what we want in life and really go for it.'

Matt raises an eyebrow. His eyes light up.

'You mean . . . do you think you're ready to get back on the dating horse again?' he asks me.

'I didn't say that.'

'I might be putting words in your mouth, but I'm right behind you if you are, mate,' he continues. 'The last time with the English girl, Kelly, wasn't a *complete* disaster.'

'Oh, it *was* a complete disaster,' I correct him. 'Yes, it may have been a great date which led to another and another, but in case you've forgotten, Kelly overheard Ava asking if I'd found her a new mother. The poor woman ran for the hills, probably back to England if the truth be told.'

But Matt has an answer for everything, it seems. 'Ava is older now,' he reminds me. 'She'd handle it much better these days. We always knew it would be hard, and that it's entirely your business when you want to try again. And at the same time, if it never happens then that's OK too, so—'

I put my hands up to stop Matt in his tracks. He claims to know me the best out of anyone, yet the dating scene couldn't be further from my mind.

He's on a roll though.

'Hey, how about the cute teacher who keeps giving you the eye at parents' night?' he says, his eyes dancing with excitement. 'Or – or the blonde lady, Ciara, who brings her pet poodle into our practice at every turnaround. She *so* has the hots for you, Ben. Most of the time that dog is absolutely fine!'

'Matt!'

'Or, you know Vic has a single friend, Jenny. We always joke she'd be a perfect match for you. A bit older than you, maybe, but she's—'

'Matt!'

'Or how about – yes, remember the Christmas Eve girl you told me about one night when we were both hammered on Jack Daniel's?' he says, his eyes dancing with excitement now. 'The one back home up north? What's her name again? I know you said she lives in Chicago.'

Oh God.

'She lives in New York, actually.'

'New York, that's the one,' he repeats. Jeez, I shouldn't have encouraged this conversation by correcting him. 'She seemed to have got under your skin big time, back in the day. You could look her up out of curiosity just to . . . ?'

'OK, slow down, Matty boy. Slow way down, please,' I say quickly as my heart burns in my chest. He didn't even have to say Lou's name to almost knock me over. The very idea of her is enough. 'I'm not sure why you're bringing that up again.'

'Still a sensitive subject?'

'No, not really, but I told you before how I never want to . . . anyhow, you're barking up the wrong tree entirely,' I tell him swiftly. 'I didn't say I'm ready to date again. I've tried it a few times already and the last one was a car crash.'

'Whoops, that was my fault too,' Matt remembers.

We both laugh as we recall my blind date from hell, orchestrated with great intentions by Matt and Vic, where the lady turned up drunk and spent the entire dinner on her phone, texting her ex.

'Someday I will get back on that good old dating horse,' I say with a slight shudder, 'but for now there must be more life for me and Ava to live, that's all. Much more than this.'

Matt has the grace to look embarrassed.

'I'm so sorry I mentioned the girl from Christmas Eve,' he says. 'I shouldn't have even hinted at your past relationship with the one who must not be mentioned.'

'It wasn't a relationship in that way.' I close my eyes.

'Your love story, then.'

'It wasn't a . . . oh, for God's sake, Matt! Why did you bring this up?'

'Too far, sorry,' he says. 'OK, that's my cue to go. I'm going to mooch out past these wonderfully expensive decorations that you don't even appreciate, through the hallway of the house you once loved and now hate and into my car, which I'll drive in the direction of my own home, which you know you can call at any time, and I promise I'll never bring up such a touchy subject again.'

'Thank you.'

It's too late though. She's already stuck in my mind, and Matt has no idea how hard it is for me to shake her off when that happens, even after all these years.

When Matt leaves I flick through channels. I scroll on my phone. I do my best, but I can't relax, nor can I switch off to concentrate on what's on the telly.

Why did he have to bring up Lou Doherty of all people? I haven't thought of her in so long. I've even managed to skip thinking of her for a few Christmas Eves as the years have ticked by. So, why is the very thought of her managing to distract me so much right now?

And when I accidentally fall asleep on the couch, I see her in my dreams, which I'm not sure if I love or hate any more.

My phone rings, waking me up from my early evening slumber after what feels like just a few moments. It's my sister, Cordelia.

35

'How is my way-too-handsome, talented and wonder-fully kind big brother?'

I sit up on the couch and rub my eyes.

'OK, what do you need?' I ask her. 'Business advice? Relationship advice? A loan? A Christmas miracle like I do?'

'Ouch, no. None of the above. Just a chat,' she tells me, but I have an inkling already that she's up to something. 'I swear, Ben, my flat is like the bloody North Pole! Would you believe I've a burst pipe? Again! I'm going to ask for my deposit back when I move on from here. Like, it's Spain for crying out loud, not the Outer Hebrides! But enough about me. How are you? How's our girl and what's the story with needing a Christmas miracle?'

Cordelia has lived in different European countries since she left home at eighteen, always city-hopping, job-hopping – and boyfriend-hopping too if the truth be told. I've never known anyone with a bee in her bonnet or itchy feet like my only sibling, but I wouldn't change her for the world. I update her on Ava, before she launches into the very real reason she has called me this evening.

'You'll never believe this, but Mum got a letter from one of the locals today. Now, don't freak out when I tell you this, but guess what?'

My stomach is a bit queasy at the sound of this. I'm in no mood for stress or worry on top of what I already have on my plate, but I'm not sure why someone from the village would feel the need to write my mother a letter unless it's something serious.

'Has Uncle Eric said something?' I ask. 'Is there trouble?'

'No,' she laughs. 'It's nothing to do with Uncle Eric. You won't believe this, but a local committee has written asking that Mum and the Heaney family – that would be you, me and Uncle Eric, by the way – would consider bringing back the Christmas party at Ballyheaney House this year.'

'Ha!' I spurt out, reeling in utter shock.

'What?'

'Is this a joke?' I ask her. 'It's nearly two weeks until Christmas, sis. Why would anyone in their right mind think we'd want to do that again? We live in different times, Cordelia. There's no way.'

My sister is far from impressed by my reaction.

'OK, don't hold back on your opinion, Mr Cynical!' she exclaims. 'Can you at least try to think about it without snorting or laughing or dismissing it entirely, please?'

I stand up and walk around my sitting room. Then I sit back down again as I stare at the floor with a million thoughts and memories racing through my mind.

'I think it's absolutely ridiculous,' I splutter, standing up now to pace the floor again. 'It's not just something that can be arranged at this late notice anyhow, but even if it was possible, how or why would we want to do that all over again? I can't even imagine it. Who wrote to Mum?'

'A president or chairperson of some sort.'

'Who is she?'

'I don't know,' says Cordelia. 'I haven't lived at Ballyheaney House in donkey's years, and Mum hardly leaves the house these days unless it's for a doctor's appointment, so I don't think she knows either, but it's a legitimate request.'

'And is this committee going to organise it?

'No, Ben,' she says with a sigh. 'Don't be silly. *We* would organise it. Our family, at our home. Why are you being so negative?'

Negative? Realistic, more like.

'I don't often say this, but catch a grip, Cordelia. The answer is no.'

'I can do the catering,' Cordelia continues, as if someone has lit a spark inside her. It's like she hasn't listened to a word I said. 'You can help get the house ready practically and we all know you're a great organiser, Ben. Remember Dad's sixtieth birthday party? You and I took full charge of that, and it was epic!'

'He hated every minute of it,' I remind her.

'He hated almost everything,' she reminds me. 'Except his walled garden. Oh, come on.'

'No.'

'It could be so much fun,' she rambles on. 'It could also be just what our family needs this year to inject some energy into Ballyheaney House as well as into our own hearts this Christmas.'

I pause and do my best not to laugh but a loud cackle escapes.

Has my sister softened suddenly? She doesn't do hearts and feelings. She's a fly-by-the-seat-of-her-pants kind of gal who, and I mean this in the most endearing way, thinks of no one but herself as she has absolutely zero responsibility in her life.

'Cordelia, please slow down,' I say to her, pinching the bridge of my nose, feeling more serious about it all now. 'You've got to admit this is totally unexpected and not something any of us would have dared to as much as consider after the fiasco of the last one, when Dad pulled the plug for good. A party at Ballyheaney House is not what we need this Christmas. In fact, a party at Ballyheaney House is the very last thing anyone would want this Christmas. There's no way Ava would agree to it.'

'I think it's a great idea,' my daughter says.

I swoop around to see her behind me, dressed in a padded yellow jacket and a cosy blue hat, as if she's now ready for that walk on the beach after all.

'Wait a minute! Have you two been in cahoots behind my back?' I ask.

Ava shakes her head while Cordelia goes into full-throttle denial all those miles away.

'A Christmas Eve party for charity would be so much fun,' says Ava.

'You think so?' I ask her, noticing how her previously tear-filled eyes are now trimmed with mascara, which gives me a gut-thump reminder of how she's almost a teenager.

'Grandma has told me all about those good old days, and I've seen some photos too,' she tells me. 'I can help organise it if you'll let me. And maybe I could help pick the charity? Say yes, Daddy, please! I dare you to be spontaneous for once in your life.'

My sister bursts out laughing.

'It would mean us uprooting for Christmas and I've just spent a clean fortune on fancy decorations for this place,' I plead, hoping that might be a start in my defence. 'I can't waste all that.'

'Take them up north with you,' suggests Cordelia. 'They'd look magnificent in Ballyheaney House, I'm sure.'

'And we'd need to work out a budget and see what work needs to be done to the house before we fling open the doors to the general public,' I remind my sister, who will no doubt swan in at the eleventh hour when all the hard work has been done and declare afterwards how easy it was to get the big house ready. 'I'd need to resurrect my DIY skills, which to be honest I've missed quite a lot recently.'

'Yes!' they both cry in unison.

'You're the best!' shouts Cordelia. 'It's going to be the best thing you've ever done, wait and see.'

I shake my head, feeling very much like I've been pushed into something I'm not quite prepared for. I also fear that in more than one way this evening, I've allowed the Pandora's Box of Lou Doherty memories to be prised open again.

Thank goodness she lives in New York now.

'So, you'll go to Ballyheaney this weekend then and make a start?' says Cordelia. 'We only have two weekends before Christmas to pull it all together.'

'I love how you say "we" when you're not even in the same country,' I remind her. 'But yes, I'll give Mum a call and we'll see if she's up for giving it a go.'

I'm not sure how this has happened, but it seems I've

agreed to organise a once legendary party at my childhood home with about two weeks to do so.

In many ways, I'm doing it to distract Ava. And I suppose it's an excuse to get out of this empty, soulless house for the holidays.

It could be a blessing in disguise or a complete disaster. Only time will tell.

Chapter Three

Lou

THEN

Christmas Eve, 24 Years Ago

I lay under my duvet, flipped open my red Motorola phone and said a quick prayer I'd already have a message from Ben now that our big day was finally here, even if it was still only 8 a.m.

It was Christmas Eve again at last. I had turned seventeen recently, and most importantly it was the day of the big Ballyheaney party.

I could almost breathe in the excitement from the moment I opened my eyes as I thought of the guests arriving at the big house, the crisp call of winter in the air and the romance on everyone's lips, as we all succumbed to the charm and glamour of the Heaneys and their unrivalled hospitality.

But this year was already different, because this year I had an inside view of it all. I was part of the team, and it felt so good.

Downstairs, I could hear my mum and dad laugh over breakfast. It was one of my favourite sounds in the world. Life was good for me and my family, but the big day at Ballyheaney was going to make it even better. I just knew it.

My heart lifted when I read the brief text message from Ben. I imagined he had woken up full of butterflies for the day that lay ahead, just like I had.

Let's rock it 2Day, Lou. Can't w8 2CU later.

If he couldn't wait to see me again, I could have doubled that feeling right back, even if it had been less than twenty-four hours since we'd parted ways.

We'd spent the evening before arranging tables for the party in the blue ballroom, blowing up balloons for a display in the hallway where a photographer would capture guests on arrival, and ferrying boxes into the kitchen where Ben's sister, Cordelia, was helping the usual hired chef to prepare canapés.

But I wasn't only helping out as an excuse to be with Ben.

I was involved officially that year, as I'd been helping at Ballyheaney House all summer after I'd got the holiday job for a student helper there, which had been advertised on the bulletin board in our local supermarket.

I took it as a sign of our destiny to be together when I was the successful candidate, but in reality the decision was no doubt influenced by my assistance in the delivery of Little Eve the year before, as well as by my obvious fascination with the home's magnificent design.

No matter how many times I visited, I viewed everything at Ballyheaney House with wide-eyed marvel.

The high ceilings, the ornate teardrop chandeliers, the decorative floor tiles and intricate woodwork, the huge oil paintings, the centuries-old tapestries, the luxurious upholstery on the curved mahogany chairs: I was both deeply inspired and in awe every time I discovered something new.

It was like a dream. But at Christmas it was even more special. It was a place that made me dance around a floor brush or sing into a feather duster. It was a place where I felt right at home, and where I felt like I'd found my tribe with Ben's mum Tilda, Cordelia, Uncle Eric, Little Eve of course, and even Jack, Ben's grumpy father, who loved to show me around the red-brick walled garden with its climbing white roses.

'You know this house almost as well as I do now,' Ben told me when I clocked in at Ballyheaney House as soon as I'd got showered, dressed and ready for the day ahead. 'I must say, my mum is a super fan of yours now too. And don't even start me on Uncle Eric. He thinks you're the greatest thing since sliced bread. He doesn't take to many people, believe me.'

I blushed as I polished bundles of silver cutlery, while Ben folded red napkins at a round table in the drawing room. We'd found our own private little corner, away from the madness and rush of the other parts of the house, and barely paused for breath as we caught up on what had happened in each other's lives since we properly saw each other last.

Which was on Christmas Eve a full year ago.

'I missed you in the summer,' he said to me as we worked side by side. 'Imagine, the only fortnight I was home in July, you were jetting off with your family to Spain! That really was a bummer.'

'I know, I felt the same, Ben, believe me. It was a last-minute arrangement for my family to go to Santa Ponsa,' I explained to him. But what I hadn't revealed was how it had only happened because my dad won a few quid on a lotto he was involved with at work.

However, Ben or no Ben, my summer days in Bally-heaney House were some of the very best of my life as I emerged into young adulthood. As well as mucking out the stable where we shared our first kiss, my job also involved grooming Sally and Little Eve, walking them round the grounds and helping to clean the amazing rooms in the house; and on my lunchbreak I'd read in the sun by the roses in the walled garden, which gave me the kind of inner peace that I feel like I might have been searching for ever since.

I was devastated when September came round and I had to give up my post at Ballyheaney House so I could focus on my chosen subjects for A level with a view to making the grades for university.

Ben too was knee-deep in preparing for his Leaving Cert in Dublin by then, so he rarely made it home, but as soon as December came, I made a point of offering my services for the biggest event on our village's social calendar, with the ulterior motive of an infatuated seventeen-year-old.

'We've been texting each other almost every day this year,' I reminded him as I buffed up the cutlery to the sounds of 'Merry Christmas Everyone' from the CD I'd brought with me especially. 'I don't think my phone has ever been so busy, but yes, it was a pity we missed out in the summer. Ships in the night, that's what we are, Ben.'

'Yet here we are again,' he said. I didn't need to look at him to know he was grinning from ear to ear, because I was too. 'I feel very lucky to be back in the company of my bestie.'

'Ahh, that's sweet,' I replied.

'I was talking about Uncle Eric,' he joked, so I gave him a playful nudge in return.

It was such a thrill to be behind the scenes with the Heaney family on Christmas Eve as they welcomed in musicians, caterers and the local media, including a very fussy photographer and a representative from the nominated charity who had arrived far too early and was now vacuuming the stairs while Tilda Heaney applied her make-up in her bedroom. Her husband, Jack, was off shopping for extra fairy lights as the decorator had brought faulty spare bulbs for the hundreds of lights around the garden, and Uncle Eric had just arrived from his fancy townhouse in Wicklow, dressed like someone from a period drama.

I adored Uncle Eric (which everyone called him, even Tilda Heaney), so I was very glad to hear that he liked me too.

'Ah, there you are,' he said when he found us tucked away in the drawing room. 'My two shining stars of Ballyheaney

House. But don't tell Cordelia I said that. As her godfather, she'd be very upset and rightly so.'

'Rather you than me admit that in public,' said Ben, shooting me a glance as if to say *I told you so*. 'She'd send you to the Tower for that, Mr Darcy.'

Uncle Eric looked down at his very elegant, navy knee-length jacket, white frilled shirt and cream dandy-style trousers. The corners of his lips curled up at the comparison to Jane Austen's famously dashing hero.

'A gentleman always dresses to impress on occasions like this, especially when I live in hope each year that my secret one true love might walk through those doors,' he declared. 'Surely you aren't wearing that, Benjamin? Haven't I taught you anything in your eighteen years?'

Ben patted at his scruffy T-shirt and jeans with a shrug. I thought he looked extra sexy, especially in the bottle-green tee, which complemented his dark auburn hair and light stubble.

'Women, beer and poker, that's what he's taught me,' Ben said with a nod in my direction, which I knew couldn't be further from the truth. 'Everything bad, I've learned it from my Uncle Eric. He is the definition of a rebel, or the black sheep of the family if you want to put it bluntly.'

Uncle Eric threw his head back and laughed so heartily, I thought he might explode. He was a handsome man in his late fifties, and like his nephew – who I was by now totally besotted with – he oozed charm and good manners and was a treat to be around. But he certainly wasn't a womaniser in any shape or form. He'd told me about his secret one true love one morning in this very room when we indulged in coffee and scones smothered in jam and cream while putting the world to rights.

'I stand over all of my bold behaviour with pride,' he said, keeping the joke going. 'On that note, have I told you about the new lady in my life? A barrister from Malahide called Sue with the most beautiful set of—'

'All right, Uncle Eric!' I said quickly. I wasn't sure if this part was true or not.

'Teeth, I was going to say, Lou,' Uncle Eric continued without so much as a pause. 'Honestly, I've no idea what you thought I was going to say.'

I was mortified at that, while Ben chuckled beside me. Uncle Eric was on a roll.

'Her late husband was a dentist, so she has a smile that would light up any room.'

'Is Sue a real person, though, that is the question,' Ben said, which made me giggle. Uncle Eric could give out banter, but he could also take it. 'Cordelia and I have this long-held idea that our dear uncle might not be telling us the whole truth about his love life. How would we really know? Mary the former beauty queen was never to be seen in real life, Maggie the actress disappeared into thin air, and now there's Sue the barrister with the perfect set of teeth. Sometimes we think they're all a figment of his imagination. We've never actually seen or met any of them. And don't get him started on his secret one true love.'

'Oh, I'm totally up to speed with that one,' I chirp in. 'Though her identity remains a mystery to us all.'

'As if I'd bring any of my lady friends here to Bally-heaney House,' joked Uncle Eric in return, rubbing his hands together again. 'I'd never hold on to them if they met my crazy family.'

'Crazy?' said Ben. 'Look who's talking!'

'I'm kidding, Lou, you do know that?' Uncle Eric declared. 'My niece, my nephew and their parents are my actual favourite people, and you, my darling, are right up there too. You earned that place when you brightened up Ballyheaney House all summer. And now it's Christmas Eve. How blessed are we to have you on our team.'

'Thank you,' I said, pursing my lips with pride.

'And she's my favourite too,' said Ben, which made me drop a silver spoon right out of my hands and on to the round mahogany table. 'I may be dressed like I've been dragged out of a ditch, but doesn't Lou look stunning in her red, Uncle Eric?'

'Truly scrumptious,' said Ben's uncle. 'Absolutely splendid and with all the grace of her dear . . . all the grace of a swan gliding along the still waters on Lough Beg.'

I wondered if Uncle Eric was going to say something else and then changed his mind, but I didn't have the courage to ask so I quietly accepted the compliment instead. I'd bought a new woollen red dress especially for the occasion, one which both my parents and even my grandmother complimented without me even having to ask. I'd worn lipstick to match and applied an extra layer of mascara to emphasise my brown eyes.

'I mean this earnestly when I say that without Lou during

the summer, I don't know how your parents would have managed,' Uncle Eric said, clasping his hands together as he spoke. 'And that is no exaggeration. Little Eve is like a baby to her, isn't that right, duck?'

Uncle Eric had affectionately called me 'duck' since a day in the summer when I'd had a run-in with Ballyheaney House's flock of mallards which left me in hysterics. Once I'd got over my shock and embarrassment, I too saw the humour in it, and I named him 'goose' in return.

'Little Eve holds a very special place in my heart and always will,' I replied, much to Uncle Eric's satisfaction. 'It's her birthday today, of course, so I've brought her a gift. It's a new blanket, so I'll slip off and give it to her later when everything is up and running.'

Ben put a friendly hand on my shoulder while I polished the last batch of knives, forks and spoons. They were heavy and were stamped with a silver hallmark, a bit like the fancy set my parents used for special occasions only.

'Well, in that case I'll let you both get on with it,' said Uncle Eric. As much as I had come to adore the older man, I was more than happy for him to read the room. I was keen to have Ben all to myself as much as possible. 'I'll see you on the dance floor later, eh, Lou?'

'That's a date,' I told him as he strode out, leaving me with a huge smile on my face and what felt like an orchestra of crickets in my tummy.

'As long as you save the last dance for me,' said Ben, moving his chair closer to mine. 'I can't tell you how glad I am to be here with you at last, Lou.'

I carried on polishing the cutlery, unable to wipe the grin off my face. If happiness was a person, it would have looked exactly like me.

'Same, Ben,' I whispered. 'This is cosy, isn't it?'

I could hear him breathe beside me, then we both sang along to the Christmas songs on my CD like we were the only two people in the world.

When our first set of chores were done, we made a point of slipping off to see Little Eve at the stable, feeling like Romeo and Juliet hiding their attraction out of plain sight, though I didn't stop to wonder why.

Ben had been very open and honest with his uncle when he said I was his favourite, and that was good enough for me. After all, I hadn't told my parents how close he and I had become either. I feared they'd warn me off, that they would be concerned that someone like Ben Heaney would never be serious with someone like me.

So I said nothing to my family. And Ben, it seemed, hadn't said anything to his either.

'Hey, Sally. Happy birthday, Little Eve,' I cooed as soon as we reached our hiding place. It was warm in the stable – well, warmer than outside, where the morning dew had frozen crispy and white at the lawn's edges. 'Look what I have for you.'

I opened a carrier bag to unveil the burgundy blanket I'd bought in Belfast a few weeks before when Dad and I were Christmas shopping. It was warm and fleecy on the outside, with satin quilted lining. Best of all, it cradled over her back like a hug.

'Oh wow, she really suits it,' said Ben from where he stood in the doorway with one hand resting on the stall door, his cold breath visible in the frosty air.

'I think so too,' I agreed, smoothing the blanket down and patting the horse's flank while feeling his gaze on my every move.

Little Eve snorted in approval, which made us both laugh, and when Ben walked towards me with a hunger in his eyes, I thought I may have died and gone to heaven.

We kissed on the warmth of the hay with a passion so fierce it almost frightened me, but before we could get any further, I heard the voice of Jack Heaney coming towards the stable.

Ben and I sprang apart, our cheeks flushed and our hair tossed from the brief encounter that may have been a whole lot more had we not been interrupted.

'Ah, you beat me to it,' said Jack when he reached the open stable door. 'I was bringing the horses some fresh blankets, but as always, Lou, you're one step ahead of us all round here. What would we do without you?'

'How do you know it wasn't my idea?' quipped Ben, winking at me behind his father's back.

'Because I know my son,' Jack guffawed. 'Now, how about you go and change into something smarter before the guests arrive? Lou, you'll need to brush down your clothes too. We can't have our staff smelling like horse hay and manure.'

Our staff.

Well, that was me put firmly back in my place, even

though Ben rolled his eyes as if to tell me not to take his father's words too seriously.

I was more than 'staff' to Ben, I knew that for sure.

I was seventeen years old. I was falling in love at the speed of lightning in his presence. And I'd a strong feeling that Ben might be falling in love with me too.

Chapter Four

Lou

NOW

Fourteen Days to Christmas Eve

'It would be great company, that's all I'm saying, Lou. A Pomeranian is a good companion, though maybe a little bit yappy. How about a tiny little Yorkie? Oh, imagine a cute little puppy to snuggle up with you every evening.'

My mother is in one of her very persistent moods today. Subject: puppies. Theme: not taking no for an answer.

We are making up ten poinsettia centrepieces for the local Women's Institute Christmas dinner, while debating the merits of getting me a pet of some sort so that I'm not alone in my beautiful new cottage.

'That all sounds very tempting indeed,' I agree, 'but I don't think it's fair to have a dog when I'm at work all day, six days a week. It would break my heart to say goodbye every morning and look at its sad little face as I leave. I couldn't do it.'

Mum rolls her eyes and hands me a lovely little gold-sprayed pot. I must admit, aside from days like this when she seems to torture her own mind with how she can make my life better, we do work quite well together when it comes to creative combinations for our customers.

'Get a cat, then,' she suggests, clipping a piece of gold ribbon to match our beautiful pots at lightning speed. 'Cats are much more independent. You know, when your father passed away, I was so glad your grandmother came to stay with me. She's so independent too, coming and going, but it's nice to have her company as long as I let her have the remote control.'

'Are you comparing Nana Molly to a cat?' I tease. 'What type of cat? I think she'd be a very elegant Persian.'

'I was thinking more of a cranky old alley cat.'

'Mum! You're bad!'

'I'm joking, but I've no doubt you can't wait to tell her that and sink me right in it,' says Mum with a smile. 'Your father used to do it to me all the time. He'd land me in trouble with her at every opportunity, just for fun.'

We go on about our business in comfortable silence, though I can't help but glance at her once or twice while she stays on autopilot, caught up in the quiet ache of remembering my father, who was taken from us so suddenly, far too cruelly and far too young.

'Oh, I can't wait to have Gracie home for a few days over Christmas,' she whispers, slowly coming back to the present. 'Has she booked her flight from New York yet, Lou?

Imagine the four of us together at Christmas! You, me, Nana and Gracie.'

I feel a familiar knot in my stomach tug tighter and tighter with dread.

'Having all four of us together at Christmas has never been an easy thing to organise,' I say as my mind and body go into protective 'just in case' mode. 'What I mean is, I don't want you to get your hopes up, Mum. I've an awful fear Gracie isn't going to make it. I've offered to book her flight, but she always hurries off the call when I mention it.'

'Nonsense,' Mum replies, pushing back her latest masterpiece and tilting her head in admiration. 'She'll be here. There's no way we can do Christmas without her. Tell her I said that. Now, are you sure we've made the right call with the red and gold combination on these pots? Maybe the ladies would have preferred silver pots instead? Or just plain black may have been nice too?'

'Gold is prettier,' I say, pushing my hair out of my eyes, glad of the distraction from chat about Gracie. 'Yes, I'm sure we made the right call with the gold pots, Mum. I asked Bridie from the WI committee and she said gold is good.'

'Good as gold,' Mum whispers, then hums her way through the next pot while I go to fetch a parcel from our delivery man. 'Good as gold.'

By the time I get across the store, passing our growing collection of festive delights such as velvety red roses and soft silver willow, the regular delivery guy, Declan, whistles and drums his fingers by the coffee dock as if he's been waiting forever.

'I could have left this outside in the snow, but I'm a gentleman so wouldn't do such a thing, Lou,' he says, holding out a small screen for my signature.

'Ah, my order of cellophane,' I declare. 'Yes! Christmas has come early for me.'

Declan looks like the cat that got the cream, but I'm not exaggerating. A speedy delivery like this for the florist's makes life so much easier, especially as a Christmas rush is just beginning.

'Oh, could I get a quick cappuccino to take away, please, Lou?' Declan asks me, pushing his black glasses back on his nose. 'Extra cinnamon?'

He jiggles in his pocket for change as I fix up his drink.

'No problem, Declan. Have it on me,' I tell him. 'It's a cold one out there, so I hope this warms you up. Thanks, Declan.'

His face lights up like a Christmas tree, making me warm and fuzzy inside, but it's the least I can do. One of the things I adore the most about village life is how everyone pulls together like one big team, and I couldn't operate my business without someone like Declan.

'How about a turtle?' Mum asks me, deadly serious, when Declan leaves. 'You always wanted one of those as a child.'

I throw my head back, let out a deep sigh and hand her a new bunch of poinsettias.

'How about accepting that I'm perfectly fine the way I am?' I tell her, setting down a pair of scissors a little more firmly than I intended, but my mini strop is halted by Declan's return.

'Sorry to interrupt. I forgot to ask earlier,' he says all a fluster and slightly out of breath as if he's run a marathon. 'Would you mind displaying one of these in the window, please?'

'Of course,' I reply, taking a rolled-up poster from him.

'Tilda Heaney asked if I'd pass a few of these posters around, when I was dropping off a parcel to her earlier,' he tells us. 'Hot off the press, I believe. I wouldn't usually agree, but I said yes as it's for charity, plus, let's face it, the Heaneys are hard to say no to, aren't they? Such lovely people. I only hope my boss doesn't find out. I could get the sack for this, so say nothing!'

He laughs, which tells me he's enjoying his moment of rebellion, but when I unroll the poster and read what it says, I'm certainly not laughing, that's for sure. And his comment about how it's hard to say no to the Heaneys is stuck in my gut. Yes, they are lovely people. I know that more than most around here, and there lies the problem.

'Oh my . . . so it's happening, then.' I feel the colour drain from my face, but I quickly change my expression into a forced smile when I see the look of confusion on Declan's face. 'I mean, wow. That's all. That was quick.'

'Well, yes, that *was* quick!' Mum repeats after me as she leans over my shoulder and reads aloud from the poster. '*Christmas Eve Charity Afternoon Tea Party at Ballyheaney House, Wednesday 24 December 2025 at 12 noon. Admission £25. All proceeds to Daffodil Cancer. Everyone welcome.*'

'It's for an excellent cause,' Declan sings, as if he's chief organiser and not just someone delivering posters on the quiet to keep sweet with the Heaneys. 'Close to my heart like so many others, as my own mother is recovering from cancer.'

'Ah, Declan, I'm so sorry to hear that. Does it say where we can buy tickets?' Mum asks as she squints to read the poster again. 'I imagine this will sell out quickly.'

Declan swiftly points to a QR code on the bottom left-hand side.

'Very modern for the Heaneys, so they must have someone young helping,' he says. 'Thankfully, those of us who are more technically challenged, like me I admit, can get a ticket from the post office in person.'

I scan the QR code, then bury my face in my phone.

'Christmas Eve is a busy day, so I'm not going to be able to go, unfortunately,' I mumble as the info on the event pops up on my screen. 'But I'll buy tickets. As you said, Declan, we've all been affected by cancer in some shape or form. I hope your mum is feeling better these days?'

There, I've redeemed myself and my earlier negativity by opening up a conversation about the well-being of his mother, who I've never met. But Declan isn't hanging around this time. In fact, he's already hotfooting it towards the door.

'She has good days and bad days, but mostly good, thanks,' he calls back in our direction. 'I can't stop to chat any longer, sorry. I'm on the clock with the boss, but see you again soon.'

'Bye, Declan!' I shout with far too much enthusiasm. 'Yes, see you soon. Love to your mum!'

I look at my mother, who is tutting and shaking her head.

'What?' I ask, handing her the poster as if it's burning my fingers. 'I said I'd buy tickets, didn't I? I'm not that hard-hearted.'

Mum licks her lips slowly, staring over her glasses, then shrugs with nonchalance.

'You seem nervy, Lou. Or jumpy. Or hyper, maybe. What's going on?' she asks, with a look that reminds me of when I was in trouble as a child. 'Is it due to the slight possibility that Ben Heaney might make some magical appearance like Santa Claus on Christmas Eve? Was there something between you two you've never told me about? Something deeper? Something more *serious*?'

'God, no!' I exclaim, cursing myself for telling my mother a white lie, but I have my reasons. The main one being I still can't bear to think about it, never mind talk about it. 'I'd hardly recognise him if he walked through the door.'

OK, that was more than a white lie. In fact, it was veering much closer to an out-and-out black lie, if there's such an expression. I'd know Ben Heaney from a thousand miles away. I'd pick him out of a line-up in a heartbeat.

'I can't help but think you're being negative about something extremely positive in our community because of an old boyfriend,' she mumbles. 'Really, Lou. I do expect better from you on this occasion.'

Now, that stung. Both of those statements stung.

'Mum, he was never my real boyfriend.'

'Your lover, then,' she says.

'He wasn't only my lover either.'

Oh, my heart. Oh, how he was so much more than that.

'You're very close and intimate friend, then,' she says in exasperation. 'Deny all you want, but I've a hunch that you two had something very strong going on, whatever you want to call it. But it was a long time ago, so it's probably a good idea to be a lot more mature if you can manage it at all.'

My stomach twists and turns. My throat goes dry.

'Mum, we were no more than kids back then, so of course it isn't about Ben Heaney,' I say, wishing we didn't have to talk about this. 'Now, pass me those scissors, please. Bridie from the Women's Institute is picking up her centrepieces in less than half an hour. We've been held back and distracted for far too long as it is this morning.'

It's almost walking distance to the village from my house, but it's a very busy road and since I've been known to take copious amounts of foliage and flowers home with me to keep me busy in the evenings, and since the weather here isn't exactly tropical in summer, never mind in December, it's much more sensible for me to drive back and forth.

That's not to mention the personal bouquet deliveries, which was intentionally part of the service I brought to Buds and Beans since I opened in the summer, straight out of a very creative world in New York City, thinking all my dreams would come true when I finally got back home. There's nothing to beat seeing someone's face light up when an unexpected bunch of flowers is delivered to their door and into their hands.

A surprise birthday gift, a way to say *Congratulations*, or

I'm sorry, or *I love you*. A bunch of flowers can brighten up anyone's day, and it's an honour for me to witness it on an almost daily basis.

But what *are* the dreams I'm chasing by coming back here? I often wonder. What am I searching for? Is my mother right? Do I want company? Do I need something or someone to go home to in the evenings?

Should I get a puppy?

No, I don't need an animal to comfort me. I don't need anyone or anything. I've always been more than happy with my own company, and I'm well used to that by now, even in New York when Gracie moved across the state to study English three years ago. My small business here is ticking along enough to keep the wolf from my door, and I've the most beautiful home I could ever have imagined, tucked away in a rural haven with my mother and grandmother close by.

But I miss my daughter. God, I miss her so much.

I don't have a definite date yet, but I'm counting down the days until I see her for Christmas.

If I see her for Christmas.

The sight of Katie's Cottage coming into view lifts my heart like it always does, and I feel a tiny bit better by the time I've pulled up outside my bright yellow gates and left the engine still running and the lights on so I can see where to open the latch.

No matter how many times I've done so, this place never fails to excite me when I get back here. It was never expected to reach the market, having stayed in the same family for generations, so to say it was a catch is an understatement.

Gracie wanted to show her boyfriend, Sam, where she originally came from before we escaped to New York when she was a toddler. Up popped Katie's Cottage for sale, as if it was meant to be. I thought she was winding me up at first when she called me over to come and see it on her laptop.

'It's like something from a chocolate box, Mom,' she cried out with delight. 'Look at the thatched roof, oh wow! And it dates way back to 1820. Imagine how steeped in history it must be. Aww, it's like stepping back in time. I love it. I really do!'

And I love it too. There was no need for Gracie to tell me its history. I'd been waiting on this moment to arrive since I was a young girl.

Katie's Cottage is my very own little slice of heaven. It's a rustic blend of old and new, with whitewashed walls, terracotta-tiled floors and even a fully functioning fireplace in my bedroom, which could be highly romantic in the right circumstances. For me, though, there's simply nothing more I love than slipping into my most comfortable clothes, putting a match to the fire in the sitting room and reading a good book in the old-fashioned floral armchair left for me by the former owners.

My Celtic harp, a gift to me from my late father on my sixteenth birthday, sits proudly in a corner by the window, though I don't play it at all these days. I used to find such solace in playing music, but these days it's more like an ornament than an instrument, which makes my lip tremble if I think about it too much.

'Your dad used to say his heart lifted higher than he even knew possible when you played the harp,' Mum told me while we wallpapered the living room together in the summer. I chose a subtle violet and cream design which turned out nicer than I could have hoped for. 'Maybe you'll find your mojo again one day soon, even if in his memory.'

I know I will. I don't know when, but I'll play it very soon. I know I will.

Gracie FaceTimes me before bedtime. I've cleansed and moisturised my face, I've lit an organic cedar candle, and I'm convincing myself that I'm positively peaceful after a very strange day.

I don't need a puppy or a cat or a turtle. I'm fine.

'So, after all that, praise the Lord we got the pots all finished and delivered, but not before Declan came back to deliver a poster for the revived Charity Afternoon Tea Party at Ballyheaney House,' I tell Gracie.

'That's the big fancy house you worked at when you were younger?' she asks me.

'That's the one, yes.' She is on her lunch break at university and eats a sandwich while we catch up, as we try to do a few times a week. 'It was one of those days when I couldn't catch my breath at all. I was running around in circles, but we got all the orders out, then I delivered a birthday bouquet to a local lady who turned one hundred years old today. Now, that was special, especially when I gave her a hug and her old eyes glistened with delight. But I really wasn't expecting to hear about events at Ballyheaney House, was I? I mean, I'd enough chat about that with Nana Molly on Monday when she first heard it on the grapevine. As if I'm going to that, charity or not.'

I imagine Gracie is only half listening as I rant and rave about a place she doesn't really know an awful lot about, apart from what I've told her and what she's learned through brief holidays here throughout her twenty years.

'I don't get it,' she says, scrunching up her perfect face. With her freckled nose and almond-shaped eyes framed with dark, wavy hair a mirror image of mine, she is my past, present and future all rolled into one, yet we can be as different as chalk and cheese on a lot of things too. 'The lovely old birthday lady with tears in her eyes is beautiful. I get that. But what's the big deal with the charity thing? Who cares if you go or if you don't?'

I hold up my mug of tea as if it's a shield, already in a state of defence.

'You're absolutely right, Gracie. Who cares about it? It's no big deal whatsoever,' I reply, wondering too why I'd felt the need to mention the party to my daughter who lives on the other side of the Atlantic.

'Well, you do, it seems.'

'Erm, well, I guess it was . . . yeah, I suppose I was being nostalgic, that's all. Ballyheaney House and the Christmas Eve party was once a big part of my late teenage years,' I say, doing my best to explain without explaining the whole truth. 'It was a coming-of-age thing, I suppose, and quite a treat back in the day. Maybe you could go with your gran, eh? That might be nice for you both. I don't think it's Nana Molly's thing, but your Nana Liz wouldn't miss it for the world.'

I'm rambling as I always do when I'm either nervous or trying to paper over the cracks of a conversation.

My daughter pushes her face closer to her phone screen in a comical way that makes me only able to see one of her huge brown eyes. She slowly pulls back again, her eyebrow arching and her lips pursing tight.

'So, you're not going?' she asks.

'No,' I reply.

'And it's no big deal?'

'Right.'

'Yet you felt the need to tell me about it not once but twice this week,' she reminds me. 'And you think I might like it?'

'Maybe?'

'So, why don't you go too?'

Jeez, I sometimes forget how my own daughter can read me like a book even through a tiny screen when she's thousands of miles away. I wonder how she manages to tell exactly what I'm thinking just from my face, my tone of voice, or some totally unrelatable piece of useless information about a charity event in a tiny village in Ireland which has absolutely nothing to do with either of us.

'Forget I even mentioned it.'

It's the best I can come up with, other than give her a complete history lesson on happenings from before she was born.

'Mom?'

'Gracie?'

I'm ready for her to pry and quiz me some more, but instead, when I look at her properly, I'm almost sure I can see tears well up in her eyes. My daughter may be able to read me well, but I will always be able to read her better.

'Oh my gosh, what's wrong, baby?' I ask her as I set my

mug of tea on the coffee table. I swoop my phone into my hand from where it was balancing. 'Was it something I said? What's going on, love? Are you in some sort of trouble?'

She looks away and rolls her sleeve over her hand, then holds it up to her face.

'No, it's nothing you said, and I'm not in trouble. I wasn't even going to tell you today but now I feel I should,' she says without looking at the camera. I swallow hard, hoping that whatever comes next isn't as serious as she thinks. 'Mom, I'm so torn. I don't know what to do.'

'Oh, Gracie.'

'I know how much this Christmas means to you,' she says, 'especially with it being your first one in Ireland, but if I leave Dad then I'll feel so guilty too because the little ones want me there and they're growing up so fast. They're so excited for Santa.'

My heart bleeds for her while a wave of mum guilt rips through my veins.

'I haven't booked a flight yet because I am torn between Nana Molly getting older, and being with you of course, but then Charlie and Lily are at a magical age that won't last forever either,' she continues. 'They really want me to stay, Mom. I don't know what to do.'

As upset as I know this is going to make me when it all sinks in, I can breathe again knowing my daughter isn't in any sort of danger, that she isn't sick and that she isn't going to come to any harm.

'Gracie, darling, you don't need to cry, honey,' I whisper, shaking my head as I try to reassure her. 'I totally understand how hard this must be for you, but if it's upsetting you this much then just go with what your gut tells you and stick with it.'

'But, Mom.'

'There are no buts in all of this,' I tell her, even though my insides are brewing up an earthquake of disappointment. It's something I'm going to have to discuss with her dad so we can both ensure she doesn't feel she has to be split down the middle between us at any time of the year. 'You are an adult now, and you are entitled to make up your own mind with every decision that comes your way. But at the same time, sometimes being an adult sucks, and we have to make decisions we don't really want to.'

'It sucks big time,' she says, looking relieved already.

'As long as you know that I'm always here for advice or to brainstorm any problem you ever have,' I tell her. 'And never forget I'll support you every step of the way. Whatever you decide, me and your dad will run with it. End of story.'

I can almost see the stress lift from Gracie's face when I finish, which makes me happy even though deep down I am engulfed with sadness. I'm not mad with her, I'm sad at the situation we're now in. A situation I created by upping sticks and moving so far away from her, even though she was the one who convinced me to make it all happen.

'You're the best, Mom,' she tells me.

'I know, I know,' I say, hoping it will raise a smile. 'What can I say? I'm fully schooled in matters of the heart, and I may as well be a guru when it comes to parenting. I learned it all on the job, with no formal training whatsoever, but that doesn't matter because I know *everything*.'

She laughs and rolls her eyes on hearing a phrase I've said to her many times, especially throughout her teenage years when I used to remind her how it's my first time on this planet too, yet I'm always only ever going to do my best for her even when I'm winging it.

'I have to go now,' she says, sounding like a weight has been lifted off her young shoulders. 'I've a lecture on Linguistics for two whole hours, but I'll be able to concentrate on it a bit more now we've had this conversation. I'll make a proper decision really soon. Love you!'

'I love you too, Gracie,' I reply, before we wave like maniacs and debate over who will hang up first, just for fun.

But there's nothing fun about the possibility of facing Christmas in a different country, far from your only daughter, is there? And I must understand that as much as I could jump on the phone now and ask John if he's been stirring things up, his family has a right to want to spend Christmas with her too.

So I'll just have to take it on the chin if she decides to stay stateside this year, something which is much easier said than done. I love my gorgeous cottage and my wonderful job, and being so close to my mum and my grandmother is the best in so many ways, but there are still times like this when I ask the universe why it brought me back here after all these years.

Or why the hell I ever chose to listen to it in the first place.

Chapter Five

Ben

Twelve Days to Christmas Eve

Ava is almost levitating with excitement when I pick her up from school at lunchtime on Friday before we embark on our first party-planning journey to Ballyheaney House.

She has already taken off her school tie by the time she gets into the car, chatting ten to the dozen.

'Careful Roly doesn't jump out!' I remind her, but she's an expert at manoeuvring our ten-year-old canine friend by now. 'He seems very excited to be on a road trip, but we'll have to stop at all the usual places to let him stretch his legs.'

'And pee, Dad,' says Ava, leaning in to pet his furry face. 'We don't want any accidents on the new leather seats, do we, Roly? Dad would go mental, wouldn't he?'

I'm not sure I've heard such joy in her voice or seen such a grin on her face since we won Meet and Greet tickets to see some cool indie band she was into a few months ago. Apparently, they're already 'so last year', but at the time she was like the cat that had got the cream.

'It's one-thirty now,' I say out loud. 'I want to get to Bal-lyheaney House in daylight if possible so I can check over as much as I can before we leave again tomorrow. But next weekend, I'll be driving there after school finishes, and we'll stay for Christmas.'

My daughter is barely listening to my terms and condi-tions, nor does she care that we only have two weekends to plan this whole thing.

In her twelve-year-old mind, I imagine all she cares about at this very moment is that school's out early and that I did indeed bring her phone charger, her iPad and the bag of clothes she packed meticulously last night with enough to last a full week, never mind a quick one-night visit up north.

As I drive with the company of Taylor Swift and my daughter singing at the top of her voice, with intermittent howls from Roly in the back seat, I want to shake myself for not thinking of this earlier.

I don't mean this unexpected party plan.

I mean, how did I miss the joy going to Ballyheaney House brings to my daughter? Or what it brings to myself, for that matter? But then, we do live almost three hours away. I have the major issue of a veterinary business to keep going, which I already feel I've been neglecting, and Ava has school Monday to Friday and activities on most weekends, so it's not like we can pack up and go on a whim very often.

'I wish there was still a pony at Ballyheaney House,' Ava announces as we drive across the Mary McAleese Boyne Valley bridge at the medieval town of Drogheda. I've always felt a rush of excitement when I cross this famous bridge, ever since I was old enough to drive rather than get the bus or a train home from boarding school. 'Did you know, Dad, that the last pony was called Little Eve because of the day she was born? Uncle Eric said she was the most beautiful foal he'd ever seen.'

Hearing my young daughter speak with such familiarity of what went on at my family home long before she came along almost takes my breath away. She sounds so much more invested than I've ever noticed before. Have I really been so distracted to know she was interested?

'Yes, Little Eve was a beautiful foal and an even more beautiful mare,' I agree, feeling the tug of nostalgia once more. To be honest, it hasn't really gone away since I agreed to go ahead with my sister's crazy suggestion. Old memories have been flooding my mind like a tsunami morning, noon and night since our first phone call about it on Monday.

'Uncle Eric says you delivered Little Eve when you were only seventeen,' says Ava over the sound of a Taylor ballad. 'You never told me about *that*!'

My eyes widen as I search for a response.

'Maybe because I do that type of thing now for a living, I never thought to,' I say, doing my best to explain, 'though I must admit it was very special when it happened.'

My eyes mist over at the memory. It was more than special. I do my best to focus on the road ahead as the events of yesteryear come back to me like I'm watching an old movie. It was a day I'll remember for the rest of my life, because in that moment I knew I was falling in love for the very first time. I also remember the grip of fear, knowing Lou and I were destined for heartache. I also knew that I'd never forget her, no matter how much I tried.

I can still smell Lou's perfume when she turned up at the party that day. It was a clean, crisp, citrus scent, but it's her touch I remember the most. The way her hand fitted into mine, the way she laid her head on my shoulder in the stable even before we'd kissed.

We fitted. We just fitted.

'Is that when you decided to become a vet, Dad?'

'Sorry?'

I turn the music down a little.

'When you delivered the baby foal?' she says. 'Is that when you knew you wanted to be a vet?'

I'm very glad that Ava's questions are getting me back on the right train of thought.

'I think I knew I wanted to be a vet before then,' I tell her, fully back in the moment. 'One of my favourite things about being at home in Ballyheaney House was looking after the animals.'

She shifts in her seat. 'Go on.'

'Well, we had horses,' I explain, 'but we also had three dogs, some very cheeky ducks, some chickens, and a flock of sheep who grazed down by Lough Beg. Your grandma even had a prized peacock called Cleopatra who was poached one winter morning. It broke her heart into pieces.'

I shudder, realising I've just unlocked a memory about the peacock and how much my mother loved her. I don't think

I'd ever really seen her cry until the day Cleo was taken, and it frightened me to see her so upset.

'Did she ever get another one?' Ava asks me. 'Poor Grandma. I don't think I've seen a real peacock before, but I'd love to.'

'Sadly no, she never did get another one, but Cleo left her mark on all of us,' I reply, trying not to giggle as I recall how Cordelia used to bring the peacock into the drawing room while she studied during the school holidays. 'She used to greet me at the very front gate when I got home from boarding school. I always wondered how she knew I'd be back, but she did.'

Ava turns down the music a little more. This could be a Christmas miracle already. I don't think I've had her full attention like this for a very long time.

'Why on earth did she call her Cleopatra?' she laughs. 'That's a bit of a random name for a peacock.'

'After Alexander the Great,' I say, delighted with myself for remembering this all now. 'He was a famous king of Macedonia who loved peacocks so much, he banned anyone from killing them. His sister was called Cleopatra. Mum always said she'd have loved a male peacock to name Alexander to bring more beauty to Ballyheaney.'

'But she never got another one?'

I let out a sigh.

'Sadly not, Ava,' I reply, silently acknowledging how I'd been so caught up in my own life then, I'd hardly thought of looking after my mother's interests. 'I sometimes wish she had.'

Ava is all ears. I'd forgotten how much bonding we can do when driving somewhere together. At home, we tend to exist alongside each other, with too many distractions on our devices to have a regular, proper conversation.

'I love hearing your stories about Ballyheaney House,' she says, and when I glance at her, I see a sense of contentment on her beautiful face that I haven't seen in ages. 'Tell me all about when you delivered the baby foal on Christmas Eve, Dad. You've never told me before, but I think that will be my favourite story of them all.'

'Of course I will,' I say with pride, but my mind goes blank, and I find myself starting and stopping. No matter where I go in my mind, I can't seem to find the words because the whole event is blurred with memories of Lou.

'Erm, well . . . let me see. It was such a busy day,' I begin at last, knowing I'm on a road to nowhere because no matter how I try to recall the day in question, all I can see is her. The way she wore her dark, wavy hair round her shoulders. Her fingerless gloves. Her pink duffel coat and chunky boots. 'Cordelia was busy in the kitchen helping the chef to make all sorts of delights for our guests. Gosh, she was only fourteen years old and already she was stunning us all with her cooking skills. I think you take after her in that way, Ava. She was so creative. She still is.'

Ava looks at me, puzzled.

'And the baby foal?' she says, waving her hand in a bid for me to get to the point.

'Oh, yes, well, soon all the guests arrived,' I mumble, 'and things were up and running, so I thought I'd take a break by going for a walk in the gardens, even though it was so cold outside. It was a white Christmas that year, so the snow was thick on the ground.'

'And the baby foal?'

'I must have had some sort of instinct that Sally was about to foal,' I say, 'even though we'd predicted the birth would be the following week. So anyhow, I knew I would probably be missed back at the house. You'll see for yourself how much work it takes at these parties. You'll be given all sorts of jobs from serving drinks, to clearing tables to . . . erm . . . and then . . . well, then . . .'

Ava reaches across and turns up the volume again.

'Oh, Dad.'

'What?'

'I think I'm going to ask you some other time to tell me about it, because it seems you've either lost your memory or else you've become really boring and bad at telling stories. Uncle Eric is the best. He remembers everything.'

I couldn't be more delighted at the 'get out of jail' card I've just been presented with.

'I was just warming up and setting the scene, but fair enough,' I tell my daughter, but she is having none of it. 'I was giving you a back story. Doesn't Uncle Eric waffle on more than I do when he tells stories? I hope so.'

'Your turn for music,' she tells me, scrolling through her Spotify app again. 'And please don't say any of that weird nineties dance music.'

'There's nothing wrong with my nineties dance music!'

'There are a few good tunes, but you play them way too often,' she tells me. 'Can we have some AC/DC instead?'

'Oi, what happened to it being my turn?' I ask her, loving how giggly she is as she scrolls to find a song that we'll both like. 'I think we'll stop soon to stretch our legs and have a warm drink. What do you say?'

We both drum with our hands as the opening sounds of AC/DC's 'Thunderstruck' blasts through the car's sound system, while Roly howls along from the back seat.

'Yes, and you can use that time to jog your memory about the day you helped birth Little Eve,' Ava shouts over the music. 'No setting the scene needed. Just cut to the chase. I want to hear all about it.'

'Sure,' I reply, as pictures of Lou's beautiful face fill my mind once again. They play out in slow motion, in flashbacks of the years that led to the biggest turning point of my life. Christmas Eve after Christmas Eve after Christmas Eve until there were no more.

The signs for my home village at this time of year warm my soul in a way I wasn't expecting, like a quiet anticipation running through my veins. This hasn't happened since I was a boy.

Three miles from the Castledawson bypass, then two miles, then one mile, then none.

'When were we last back here?' I ask Ava, almost embarrassed to hear the hard truth. 'Was it October?'

'Well, I wanted to come here in October for my birthday,' she reminds me. 'But you and Matt had to go to that conference in London, so I had to stay with Vic and the boys. That was so unnecessary.'

I roll my eyes at her indignation. Ava has grown up with Matt and Vic's family. They're the closest things to siblings she'll ever have, yet she pretends the boys annoy her a lot more than they do from what I can see.

'And I was here in the summer for a weekend with Cordelia while you went to Spain to stay in her apartment for some time out,' Ava continues. She really does have a much sharper memory than I do. 'That was so much fun. We went swimming in the lough. Oops, I wasn't supposed to tell you that.'

'I'm going to pretend I didn't hear it,' I say as the village I once called home comes into view. The first thing I notice in the near distance is the lofty spire of St Tida's Church. 'But when was I last here? I suppose that's what I'm trying to figure out. We've had Grandma and Uncle Eric down to stay a few times, but when did I last come to Ballyheaney House?'

'Easter,' Ava says straight away. 'Remember, we came here at Easter for Grandma's birthday, but it turned out to be a disaster because Uncle Eric fell in the courtyard, and you had to take him to hospital. That was so scary.'

I nod my head and shiver as I figure out that I haven't visited here in eight months. How can time pass so quickly? How could I have let it go this long?

'He was a lucky boy,' I recall, remembering how I had to almost bribe my dear uncle to have his shoulder X-rayed when he slipped on some moss. 'I hired in some groundsmen after that to give the courtyard a good blasting, but it should have been done earlier.'

I let out a sigh, much louder than I intended to. Cordelia and I really do need to talk about Ballyheaney House and its future before the place crumbles around Mum and Uncle Eric.

We drive into the village and pass the Seamus Heaney HomePlace, a proud homage to our Nobel Prize-winning poet. Then comes The Taphouse Bar, where I once sneaked out to meet Lou for an afternoon pint when I was supposed to be mucking out the stable; Doc's Bar, where Lou and I would put party plans in place by the fire over Guinness, red wine and salted peanuts; and the aptly named Poet's Corner café, which I remember doing a mean cappuccino.

'You're not superhuman, Dad,' Ava tells me.

'What?' I reply. 'Well, I know I'm not superhuman, but what do you mean?'

'I mean, you can't be there for everyone all the time,' she says. 'Oh, look! Can you please slow way down, Dad? I want to see the Christmas tree up close. Isn't it pretty? I think this is even nicer than the ones in Dublin.'

I fear my daughter may be ever so slightly exaggerating.

'Stop, Dad,' she says. 'Please. I need to take a photo.'

I slow down to a stop to let Ava take some pictures of the village Christmas tree with her iPad. What a difference a few days can make in this wonderful world of lone-parenting a bereaved child.

'Freya is going to be well impressed,' she says as she clicks and zooms with expertise. 'Maybe she could come here with us sometime. Could she? I'd love for her to see the cows, and the swans on the lough. I don't think Freya has ever seen a swan.'

'In summer, yes, of course she can,' I say to Ava, making a promise to myself as well as to my daughter. 'We'll make a point of coming here more often if that's what you'd like to do, and you can bring a friend, no problem. Now, let's move on as Grandma will be watching out for us coming.'

Ava clambers into the front seat again and I'm just about to turn off towards Ballyheaney House when I notice a striking new shopfront on Castle Street. It says *Buds and Beans* on the sign above a generous-sized window that's dressed like nothing I've ever seen before. Not around here, anyhow.

A tall and tasteful old-fashioned Father Christmas stands in the middle of the window, surrounded by reindeer and tiny white lights, but what makes it burst with colour and class is the array of fresh flowers in reds, greens and golds. Whoever put this all together could give the company I paid a fortune to in Dublin a run for its money. It's quirky, it's clever and it adds so much warmth and character to the street.

'Look at this cute little nook! Let's get Grandma some flowers,' I suggest, bringing the car to a stop at the kerb-side. 'I think that would be a nice gesture. Gosh, this place looks so pretty, doesn't it, Ava? It's something different, that's for sure.'

Ava, as always, is a few steps ahead of me.

'Yes, me and Cordelia got the best hot chocolate here in the summer,' she says, her eyes dancing with excitement. 'It's a florist's *and* a coffee shop, Dad. The little old lady who works there didn't really know how to make hot chocolate, but I taught her how. It was so funny. She even gave me an extra flake and said I'd taught her something new, and that her granddaughter, the real owner, would be so impressed. Dad, she was like eighty or something but so cool. We had such a good laugh.'

I'm intrigued even more now. Whoever this lady is, she has more taste than I've seen in all my time living close to Dublin city. It's almost giving me American vibes with its lush greenery and soft twinkling lights that make the interior glow.

'Well, now you can test her out again,' I say to Ava. 'Let's go inside and see if she remembers you. I quite fancy a hot chocolate now that you've mentioned it, but I'll pass on the flake. I'll save all that extra chocolate for Christmas Day.'

I take a moment to look more carefully at the window dressing as a light dusting of snow falls on to my shoulders. I button up my coat and pull my scarf close, glad to have put them on when I got out of the car, and admire once more the spectacular winter wonderland in front of me. Tall vases hold long-stalked trumpet-shaped flowers I don't know the name of, but their elegance draws me in, as does the huge holly wreath decorated in silver, gold and red ribbon.

Ava is already inside, no doubt charming her old friend while reminding her of that day in the summer when she taught her everything she knows about hot chocolate.

'Sorry, I don't mean to get in the way,' I mutter, when one of the staff comes outside to rearrange some pots that hold miniature Christmas trees. She hunkers down and I can see from the side of my eye how she checks the lights on each little tree with such care and attention before switching them on.

'No, honestly, you're fine,' she mumbles in a local accent which is casually transatlantic. 'I can work around you.'

'I can move,' I say, stepping aside to the left. 'But if you don't mind me saying so, this window display is something else. If this is anything to go by, I can only imagine what's on the other side.'

She sounds a little out of breath.

'Oh, thank you. That's very kind. It's a labour of love, that's for sure,' she says. I hear her wipe her hands repeatedly on her apron as she stands up behind me. I can see her reflection in the window now. 'Six months of hard graft but I've loved every minute of it. Well, most of it. You're very welcome to have a look inside.'

A shiver runs through me. There are goosebumps on my neck that are the size of golf balls and it's nothing to do with the cold and the snow. Her wavy, dark hair is slightly shorter than it used to be, and it's partly covered with a red headscarf tied at the top. I can't see her face clearly, but I'd recognise that voice anywhere, even if the accent has slightly changed.

No one else might notice that detail, but I do. Only because I once knew that voice so well.

'I guess I took a little bit of a long career in New York interiors with me and used it to my advantage,' she tells me. 'I used to work in a—'

I can't wait any longer. I turn around slowly to face her.

She doesn't finish her sentence. Our eyes lock for the first time in more years than I can count right now.

She takes a step back and her hands go up to the sweet face I used to know every inch of. A face I kissed a thousand times. A face I never tired of thinking of. A face I once thought I'd look at for the rest of my life.

My voice cracks as I take in the sight of her and it hits my heart like a bullet.

'Lou, it's me.'

84

Chapter Six

Lou

THEN

Christmas Eve, 23 Years Ago

My parents cooed with delight as they watched me serve up canapés to delighted guests in the blue ballroom when the next Ballyheaney party came into full swing. But no matter how much I tried to put on a brave face, my stomach was in tatters after an earlier conversation with Ben as I was putting the finishing touches to the tables.

Because he was now studying in Paris, his social circle was rippling even further while I was still at school in our home village, feeling like I lived in a puddle to his grand ocean. And no matter how much I tried to deny it, hearing of his many adventures stung me much more than they should have done.

I was jealous, and I could barely hide it.

'Let me introduce you to Lou,' I heard him say to Shaheer, a fellow student who had travelled from Paris for Christmas

85

with the Heaney family. 'Lou, remember I told you about Shaheer? He's going to be a haematologist when we grow up.'

'If we grow up,' said Shaheer, extending his hand to greet me. 'We're too busy having fun in France.'

'It's so nice to meet you,' I replied, brushing my hair out of my eyes with the back of my hand. 'Ben has told me all about you. He and I are good friends.'

'Friends?' said Ben. Shaheer looked out the window, suddenly distracted or pretending to be so.

'Very good friends,' I said, hoping that might sound better. I wasn't intending to hurt him, but the word 'friends' seemed to have hit him hard.

'Buddies,' he said, raising an eyebrow. 'Shaheer, let's go grab a beer. It's hardly too early, is it? I'll see you later then, my friend.'

As much as I was still besotted with Ben, I wasn't sure how else we could describe our relationship. I was hardly going to tell Shaheer that, despite our distance, Ben and I talked most days or at least texted, and when we did get the chance to meet up it was like thunder, lightning and stars colliding all at once.

Ben seemed to be trying to avoid me after this though, so as the ballroom filled up I focused on the job at hand by pouring fizzy wine into narrow flutes, carrying trays of glasses back and forth to the kitchen and making sure everyone had a drink, as per the rules set by Tilda Heaney.

She was the epitome of old Hollywood glamour, with her captivating presence and vintage style. Her husband was grumpy and aloof with most people, in comparison, while Cordelia bore no resemblance to either of them, choosing to bend every rule in the book according to Uncle Eric, who bombarded me with so much information that the Heaneys almost lost their veil of allure for me.

But Ben was definitely like something heaven-sent, a lot like his mother with his elegance and confident manner, yet he had a soft and tender side that made him even more attractive than his stunning good looks.

And now I had unintentionally offended him on the one day that meant more to us than any other.

'Ladies and gentlemen, we have an extra-special treat for you today,' said a rather tipsy Uncle Eric from the makeshift stage in the corner. 'Please welcome, on Celtic harp, our very own Lou Doherty.'

Though I was expecting this, my heart jumped into my mouth. I took off my apron and handed it to my mother, then made my way towards Uncle Eric, whose face was red and beaming.

It was at Tilda Heaney's request that I'd brought my harp to the party. I'd even noticed a few tears in her eyes earlier that morning as I practised on my own in the ballroom.

My legs shook like jelly as I pushed through the crowd, my head dipping down in fear of making eye contact with anyone I knew.

I wasn't really used to performing in public, at least not out of the school assembly hall, but it was something I planned on doing more of, especially if I could make some spare cash out of it with university just around the corner.

This was not your average audience though. It was half my home village, it was the Heaneys, and mostly it was Ben Heaney, the permanent subject of my dreams.

The audience applauded as soon as I took up position, but I was still too afraid to look up, mainly in case I caught my dad crying, which was very probable. As I adjusted the microphone slightly and strummed across the strings of my harp, suddenly the room fell silent. I swallowed hard, hoping the beads of sweat that formed on my forehead weren't visible to the naked eye.

When I dared to glance in a different direction from where my parents stood, I saw Ben giving me an enthusiastic but subtle thumbs up. Then he stretched his strong arms up to open the top part of a window, as if he'd read my mind. I smiled at him to say thank you, knowing right then I couldn't have loved him more if I tried.

I closed my eyes, feeling the joy of my parents urging me on as I played the opening of 'The Holly and the Ivy'.

You could have heard a pin drop.

I allowed myself to become instantly lost in the soothing sounds as I plucked the strings, feeling at ease instantly. I sometimes believed my harp whispered back to me, and I never failed to find comfort in its company when I felt lonely or afraid. The strings were so familiar under my fingertips, and each pluck felt like a step towards a place of sheer happiness, of Christmas days gone by and of many more to come.

Even before the tune came to its gentle ending, I was greeted to the sounds of raucous applause with requests for more which made my heart skip a beat. I was suddenly aware that all eyes were on me, but instead of being afraid like I had been, it felt like I was floating. It was a strange mix of adrenaline, pride and humility knowing I'd shared something I loved so much, and that they felt it too.

I looked up to see my parents both wiping their eyes, but it was Ben's face that stood out from them all. He was nodding, his eyes glistening, while he clapped his hands, unable to disguise our connection. Uncle Eric stood with his chest out like a proud peacock, landing a supportive hand on Ben's shoulder.

'Well done,' he mouthed in my direction.

I finished with a soft, melodic version of 'Silent Night', and when the whole room sang along it turned out to be one of the most moving and memorable moments of that year's party.

'Ladies and gentlemen, the talent and beauty that is Miss Louise Doherty on harp,' said Uncle Eric into the microphone when I was done, as a glass of whiskey in his hand threatened to spill over. 'This year's party is even more magical because of the touches she's brought to it. We all love you very much, Lou.'

'Thanks, Uncle Eric,' I whispered when he gave me a very tight hug. 'I hope you're not in too much trouble with Cordelia for saying that.'

'Ah, she knows she's my ultimate number one behind it all,' he said, giving my shoulder a squeeze. 'You were fantastic. Well done, Lou.'

I felt tears of joy sting my eyes as I milled through the crowd of well-wishers, all gushing with hands on chests or pats on my back. What seemed like hundreds of faces blurred in front of me. I'd no idea where I was going. To my parents, probably, for reassurance and comfort as overwhelm took over from the adrenaline I felt while playing.

'You are incredible,' I heard a deep voice say. I stopped in my tracks and looked up into Ben's face. Just the sound of his voice took my breath away. 'That was more wonderful than expected, if that's even possible.'

'Thank you,' I stuttered. 'Wow, I think it's going to take me a moment to come back to earth after that. I've never performed to such a big crowd before.'

'Am I allowed to say I'm proud of you?' he asked tentatively. 'As your friend.'

'You are very much allowed, thank you,' I said with a wry smile to acknowledge his dig in my direction.

We both laughed, but then I was serious again.

'Ben . . . the truth is . . .' I stammered. 'I think I'm so afraid of you—'

'I sincerely hope you aren't afraid of me,' he interrupted.

'I hadn't finished,' I replied, wishing I could melt the frown from his strikingly handsome face. 'What I mean is . . . Ben, I'm trying to protect my own heart because I'm so afraid of it being broken. We talk and text all the time, we laugh all the time. I know I can tell you anything because I feel like you know me better than anyone else in the whole world.'

'I think I might do,' he agreed. 'So why do I feel like there's a *but* coming after this?'

'But we rarely see each other, Ben, so how can we ever

be anything more than friends? It's so hard,' I whisper, 'and now you're in Paris to study for four whole years, and you've all these new friends and soon there'll be girlfriends too. I imagine there are already.'

He glanced around the room then took my hand, which was still clammy from playing music to what had felt like the masses.

'Look at me, Lou,' he said softly. 'Just look at me for a moment.'

I did what he asked me to, feeling my knees go weak in a way I'd never believed was possible.

'You are eighteen, I am nineteen. How about we forget about the bigger picture for a while?' he suggested. 'How about we enjoy every second we have today and every day until I have to go back to Paris, and after that we take everything as it comes?'

His brow furrowed at the thought of what I might say in reply, but he had no need to worry. In a very tricky situation, it was all we could do.

'I think that's a very good idea,' I said, smiling.

He touched my chin. 'Good. So what do you want right here, right now? Not later today, not tomorrow, not in ten years' time. I mean at this very moment?'

We stood so closely our foreheads were almost meeting, and while I was very aware that we were in a crowded room, I didn't care.

All I cared about in that moment was him.

Us.

Whatever *us* meant.

'You,' I told him, feeling my stomach flip as I said it. 'I just want to be with you.'

His eyes lit up.

I'd never wanted to be around anyone as I did Ben Heaney, so to know he felt the same made me feel like we were standing on the edge of something very special. It both frightened and excited me in equal measure.

Maybe we didn't need to put a label on it or make any big long-term announcements.

There was no denying it. When we were together, there was an electricity, a pull, a magic if you like, and it filled me up more than I'd even thought was possible.

From that day on, I wanted him more than ever.

Chapter Seven

Lou

NOW

I know it's juvenile and somewhat ridiculous, but after the unexpected encounter with Ben Heaney outside under a flurry of snow and the glow of a street light at dusk, I run back inside and find myself in my tiny storeroom, where I shut the door, lean against the wall, close my eyes and remind myself to breathe.

But my breath catches in my throat. I cover my mouth for fear of letting out a loud and uncontrollable gasp. My hands are trembling as old feelings threaten to choke me. Memories swirl around my head, filling me full of regret and nostalgia.

'The red amaryllis used to be my favourite, but I love the white ones more now,' I hear his little girl say from the other side of the door. 'It looks like a trumpet, but it represents strength and beauty and determination. My grandma told me that.'

'Well, I had no idea. What a clever young girl you are,'

Nana Molly replies. 'As the saying goes, every day is a school day.'

I had no idea of that either. What I do know is that it's going to take me more than a few minutes of hiding in a poky storeroom to get over the shock of my life.

The years have been kind to Ben Heaney.

Too kind, almost. The chiselled jawline is still there. The wavy hair, damp from the light snowfall, the piercing green eyes and the striking presence that never failed to make my legs buckle and my heart soar.

I hear the doorbell ring, announcing what I assume is his arrival into my shop. Oh God, this is insane.

'What I'd give to have had those beautiful auburn locks back in my day,' Nana Molly coos to his daughter. I decide to count to ten, then I'll step out. No, twenty, actually. No, there's no point denying it, I'm going to need to allow myself another few minutes before I leave my little cocoon of safety to face the music. 'How old are you, Ava?' Nana Molly asks.

'I'm twelve,' Ben's daughter replies. 'I was twelve in October.'

Ava . . .

What a beautiful name. I wonder did Ben choose it or was it his late wife's favourite? I wonder does he still love the name Rose, which we'd once playfully decided we'd call our own baby girl after the white rose he picked for me one day from his father's garden? I wonder did they know Ava would be a girl, or did they let their first baby's gender be a surprise like John and I did? I wonder did they decorate the

nursery together, making it perfect for their precious first-
born? I wonder did they plan to have any more children?

Most of all I wonder how he is coping without his wife
and Ava's mother. Her name was Stephanie. She was only
thirty-five years old.

'Lou? Lou, darling, you have customers?'

Nana Molly threatens to blow my cover before my personally designated minutes are up.

'I'll be right there, Nan!' I call as quietly as I can. 'I'm –
I'm looking for some red velvet ribbon. I know it's in here
somewhere.'

'Just there's a very *handsome* customer waiting to be
served,' Nana calls in to me with the subtlety of a sledge-
hammer. I thank God that my own mother has gone to the
hairdresser's to her usual Friday appointment. I dread to
think of how she'd react to the prodigal son's return.

'Can't you see to him?' I say through gritted teeth when
she steps it up a gear by opening the storeroom door, almost
revealing where I am. I peep out to notice how Ben is taking
in his entire surroundings, running his hand along the woodwork of the coffee bar, gazing at the small chalkboard where
I've written out my modest offering of hot drinks.

He touches one of the small square tables I painted with
such care. He admires some Christmas wreaths I spent
hours and hours making at home with silk blue ribbon, fresh
holly and shiny red baubles. My shop was only intended to
be a florist's to bring together my passion for people and
colour, but with a few mismatching small round tables by
the window, a basic coffee machine, a wooden bar decorated

95

with blackboards, local honeys and jams, and a selection of traybakes and treats, it has quickly become a hub of activity. With plenty of craic and gossip, I'm told it was just what the village needed.

'I thought you might like to serve him,' Nana whispers. 'He's quite a dish. Look!'

I signal for her to join me in the storeroom and pull the door slightly closed behind her.

'Nana, that's Ben Heaney and the little girl is his daughter.'

'Ben Heaney? Is it?' she asks, her neck craning. 'Are you sure? I don't remember him being so handsome. But then again, his uncle and father were always fine-looking men too. Pity they didn't have the personality to go with it.'

I hold back from telling her how I definitely *do* remember.

'Nana, please keep it all very cool,' I beg her, but it's too late. She's gone.

'Ben Heaney!' she exclaims at the top of her voice, walking back on to the shop floor. Oh, how I wish I could disappear. 'I don't believe it! My goodness, what a lovely surprise to have you pop by!'

So much for my grandmother's nonchalance towards the Heaneys. She's practically salivating at the sight of him, much to my despair. I blow out a long breath, do my best to fix the strands of hair that have fallen around my face, and fish a lipstick from my apron pocket, giving my lips an extra layer of red, which has always been an instant mood-lifter.

I close my eyes and say a quick prayer, then tentatively make my way into the shop where the man I never stopped loving stands only a few feet away.

My gut instinct told me this day would one day come. I often prayed it would, and I've played this scene out in my head so many times over the years. Would it be when out shopping one day in a busy town that we'd find ourselves in the same place at the same time? Would it be in a strange city, or in a local park, or maybe we'd see each other somewhere that meant something to us both? But I'd never, ever dreamed they'd bring back the event that had brought us together in the first place, here in our home village.

When I'd finish daydreaming about seeing him in real life again, I'd wrestle with my feelings, doing my best to convince myself that my love for him would subside one day. I've kept it all to myself, because after all, who would believe that someone could still hold your heart more than two decades later? No one would.

To my friends and family, Ben Heaney is simply an old flame from yesteryear, if even that. He is someone I used to know, the son of a family I worked with during the summers when I was a schoolgirl. To them he's only a closed chapter of my life story, to be looked back on with a faint smile and a fond but faded memory.

But they don't know the secrets of our Christmases past. They don't know the heartache or the pain we both went through when saying goodbye one bitter, cold Christmas Eve.

They don't know the truth.

'Mrs Molly Cooke,' Ben says to my grandmother, who curtsies before him when he says her full name. My chest pulls tight. I feel like I've been punched in the gut when I hear his voice again. 'It's been a long time, but I remember meeting you in The Taphouse many moons ago. You were singing the song "Peggy Gordon" by the fire in all your glory. I must say, you're as alluring now as you were back then.'

She puts her hand to her chest and lets out a sigh.

'Ah, how kind. You know, that's still my party piece, Ben,' she replies, gazing up at him. I only wish I'd your sharp memory, but I'll take that compliment, thank you very much.'

His shoulders look so inviting, so strong. His posture is confident, yet there's deep pain in the way his voice shakes when he speaks. Maybe he is as taken aback as I am? I don't think he knows I'm standing here yet, which helps me gather a little composure.

'I was just having a very enlightening conversation with your daughter about amaryllis,' Nana continues, her voice dropping down a few notches at last. 'Isn't she wonderful. I'm sure her precious mama would be very proud of her.'

Nana looks like she might cry for them both, but Ava isn't within earshot now, thank goodness. She has made her way to the far end of the florist's, intrigued it seems by the festive miniature train set I took with me from New York, just like most children who visit this place are, no matter their age.

I do my best not to stare in her direction, but my first thought on seeing Ava is how I'd love to give her a hug and tell her everything is going to be OK. I was only a few years older than she is now when I lost my dad suddenly, and although I appreciate that everyone's grief is different, I do understand how it can have extra bite at certain times of the year.

'Hello, Lou,' Ben says gently.

My heart stops for a split second when I hear him say my name.

'Hi, Ben,' I reply, meeting his eyes slowly while doing my best to keep breathing. 'I'm sorry about just now. I ran back inside because I—'

'It's OK,' he says. 'No need to explain.'

His voice to me is as soothing as it ever was.

'Thank you.'

'I would apologise for taking you by surprise out there, but I'd absolutely no idea you were back home. Believe me, I'm a bit shaken too. The last person I expected to see in this village is you.'

'Lou has been back here for a whole six months now,' Nana chimes in.

'This is . . .' Ben continues. 'I'm a bit lost for words. Lou, you look wonderful.'

The little coffee corner of my shop is now empty after a busy day, thank goodness. I'm also thankful that Nana has the sense to make her way across the shop floor to talk more flowers with Ava. I know I'll be quizzed intensively about this later, but that's the least of my worries.

Apart from the joy of bringing up Gracie and loving every single part of her childhood and teenage years in America, it's almost like the past twenty years of my life hadn't existed.

Physically, Ben hasn't changed that much, apart from perhaps how his hair is greying a little at the temples. His eyes are intense and observant, yet full of life experiences I know nothing about.

I have so many questions I don't know where to start.

'Your daughter is beautiful,' I whisper, feeling my voice tremble. Tears sting my eyes, even though I had promised myself for years that if our paths ever did cross again, I wouldn't be emotional. 'How is she?'

He licks his lips and brightens up at the mention of Ava. We both glance in her direction, where she is talking ten to the dozen about roses now.

'She's very excited to be back here,' he says. 'I'd forgotten how this place gets under your skin. I fear it may have already had an impact on my daughter too. I might have a battle on my hands to get her to come home.'

I feel that old familiar pull, like a magnetic force between us. I see a familiar hunger in his eyes and all I want to do is touch him or hold him tight. His broad shoulders taper into a trim waist beneath his black woollen coat that lies open to reveal a fine beige jumper. As always, his style is timeless, refined and classy. I want to stand closer to him, but he isn't mine any more.

I'm not sure if he ever really was.

'I feel the same about being back home, even though I sometimes question my decision to come back for good,' I reply. 'It's my first Christmas here in a very long time. I'm excited for it too.'

He beams, but his eyes tell a different story.

'I hope it all works out for you,' he tells me.

'Me too.'

My mind goes blank, and I feel his has also. We don't know each other any more. We are simply strangers with a bank of old memories, with nothing more to say. I had this all so well rehearsed, but now that we're under the same roof again for the first time in forever, it's like my mind has been erased and only a wave of deep sadness is left.

But then he whispers, 'It's so, so good to see you, Lou.' He bites his lip. 'I've thought about this moment many, many times since we said goodbye.'

'So have I,' I reply immediately.

Suddenly I've so much to say, like my brain has finally caught up with my tongue, but Ava and Nana Molly come waltzing back in our direction, armed with flowers and looking very pleased with themselves, just in time to burst our bubble.

I wish my heart rate would slow down, or that I could press pause on what's going on around us so I can say what I want to say.

But I can't do that in front of an audience.

'I've chosen a bouquet of amaryllis for Grandma, Dad,' says Ava. 'Red ones even though I prefer white, and Nana Molly thinks Uncle Eric might like a holly wreath for the front door of Ballyheaney House. She says it will be right up his street.'

I marvel at how most children who meet my grandmother are invited to call her Nana Molly, just like back in the day when everyone referred to Ben's Uncle Eric as so.

'Very well chosen, Mrs Cooke,' says Ben, more than impressed. 'My wonderful uncle has always had a love for holly at this time of year, but he doesn't have the energy to gather it from the gardens the way he used to. He'll be delighted with this.'

'I sometimes think my grandmother has a sixth sense,' I say. 'Ava, it's so nice to meet you. My name's Lou and I'm an old friend of your dad's.'

Ben's eyes catch mine as the phrase brings back an old memory. Neither of us can resist a smile.

'You're very pretty,' Ava tells me. Now that she's closer, I can see her beautiful heart-shaped face and her haunting brown eyes, which are a duplicate of her mother's, if my memory serves me right.

I'd never met Stephanie Robinson Heaney, but my mother couldn't wait to send me a photo of their wedding when it made the newspaper.

'She's a doctor from Castlebar in Mayo, if you don't mind,' she told me over the phone after sending me the press clipping by email. 'Apparently, they met on a train when travelling across Europe! How romantic! I'd say that dress cost the price of a small car! She reminds me of the actor in *Pretty Woman*. What's her name again?'

I had to dig deep to find any sign of happiness for Ben within me, while resisting the urge to be physically sick on my own behalf.

How did we get it so wrong?

'I like your red headscarf,' Ava continues. 'My teacher wears one of those too sometimes. We think she fancies Dad.'

Ben throws his eyes up to the heavens.

'Well, that's very kind of you to say so,' I tell Ben's very charming little girl, doing my best to appear calm like this is an everyday occurrence and not like I'm looking at a life I once thought was mine. 'Are you looking forward to Christmas in Ballyheaney House?'

She glances up at her dad as if she is gauging his reaction first. Ben gives her a nod of approval.

'Sometimes it's not much fun where we are,' she says, scrunching up her nose. 'I'm going to bake cookies with my grandma this weekend. Then, when Cordelia gets back from Spain, we'll do karaoke and I'm going to help organise the big Christmas Eve party.'

Ben's eyes meet mine again for a fleeting second. We exchange a wry smile which makes me want to stop the clock again.

I'd give a million to know what's going on in his mind right now. And by the same token, I'd give a million to make sure he can never know what's going on inside my own head. I'm so far down memory lane, I'm not sure how I'm going to make my way back.

'How about I wrap these beautiful flowers up?' Nana Molly says, coming to the rescue. 'I've a little something for you behind the counter, Ava. Did I hear you say you like cookies? And we still need to rustle up those hot chocolates.'

Ava takes the bait and follows Nana over to the coffee dock. Neither Mum nor I thought she'd ever enjoy helping at Buds and Beans at her time of life, but every day she does, I see her enjoy it even more, especially on a day like today when we have customers like Ben and Ava Heaney unexpectedly arrive just before closing time.

'So . . .' I say to Ben, not knowing where I'm going next.

My mind is in a flurry as I wonder if he thinks I've changed much, or does he only see me in the very same way he used to, like I do him? I run my fingers through my hair then pat down my green apron. Ben's head is dipped but his eyes are fixated on mine.

'So,' he replies.

A heavy sense of longing for the past lingers in the air. I wonder if we could both turn back time would we do things any differently? But then I wouldn't have my darling Gracie and he wouldn't have little Ava.

'It's so nice to see you again, Lou,' he tells me. 'You look . . . you look like I've always remembered you. Which is very, very fondly.'

It's like he just read my mind. It's like some things never change.

A wave of grief both drains and exhausts me at the thought of another goodbye. A chill runs through me, yet I feel suddenly flushed. Is this it? Is the moment I've been dreaming of forever over already?

'Now that I can breathe again,' I say, hoping to lift the weight of tension that hangs in the air, 'I can say it's been nice to see you again too, Ben. I hope you and Ava have the most wonderful Christmas and that all your preparations go smoothly for the big event on Christmas Eve.'

He swallows hard. He looks quickly at Ava, then back at me.

'Maybe you'll be there?' he asks me.

He holds my gaze.

If my heart could possibly break any more, I fear it may have just shattered into a thousand little pieces.

I shake my head.

'That would be too . . . that would be way too *hard*,' I say, choking on every syllable. 'I hope you're doing OK, Ben. I hope you and Ava are doing the best you can. I'm sorry.'

He rolls back his shoulders, clasps his hands together tightly and nods repeatedly like he too is trying to find the words.

'We are good,' he replies. 'We are really good, mostly. Thank you for asking.'

'I should go.'

He laughs.

We both laugh. Oh, this is like turning back the clock. It's a blend of cruelty and sheer joy rolled into one.

'I think you mean I should go?' he says, tilting his head in the direction of the door. 'I only ever wished the best for you. I hope you know that.'

I really do want him to go now. I'm not sure I can hold my real tears back for much longer.

'What do I owe you?' he asks Nana Molly, then makes his way towards the counter.

As 'Silent Night' plays on my carefully selected festive playlist, I lift a bucket of twigs I plan on spraying with silver paint only to give my hands something to do.

'Isn't it crazy,' I hear Nana Molly say to herself not long after Ava and Ben have said their repeated thanks and good-byes to the sound of the bell above the door, 'how some old wounds are as fresh as the day they were opened. Life is strange. Wonderful and strange.'

I lean up against the storeroom door, pausing to hear if she has any more words of wisdom to share, if only to herself. And then it dawns on me.

Nana Molly has no clue what happened between Ben and me all those years ago. She paid absolutely no attention to my friendship with him back in the day. In fact, she avoided any mention of him almost deliberately, it sometimes seemed.

So what old wounds might she be talking about? Yes, life is very strange indeed.

Chapter Eight

Ben

As I drive away from Lou I make a promise to myself I'll never venture back into Buds and Beans, no matter how many times I need to come back to Ballyheaney House to help get this stupid party ready.

And I will never give in to the urge to look her business up online, because that would lead me down a path I never want to be on again. Our brief conversation was enough to rip open old wounds, so why would I want to put myself, or Lou, through that all over again?

Roly barks in recognition when I follow the tarmacked driveway and turn off on to the gravelled private lane that leads to the bright white front of Ballyheaney House. It's a sight which never fails to take my breath away, under the lighting that makes it visible right across Lough Beg and the famous Church Island. Long Georgian windows line each of its three storeys, and the steps that lead up to its huge pale grey wooden door are almost regal in their welcome.

'Yippee, we're here,' says Ava, already scrambling to get out of the car.

I knowing I'm breaking the house rules already by parking by the front door.

'Yes, yes, before you say it, I'll move the car when I get my breath back,' I call out when Mum reaches the top of the steps beneath the huge stone pillars that frame the entrance to our family home. 'It's been quite a day already. It's good to see you, Mum.'

She looks tired and frail in her pale pink pullover and grey slacks, but she still radiates beauty in every way. I fear sometimes for her loneliness, far removed from village life and friendship when she still has so much more to give.

What does she do all day except argue over politics or what's going on in world news with Uncle Eric? Do they keep to their own private quarters these days? Maybe this party is what she needs after all. Maybe it's what they both need.

'Grandma!' Ava calls, bounding ahead of me with Roly on her trail. 'Oh, I forgot your presents in the car. And I forgot my hot chocolate.'

'Come in out of that sleety drizzle, both of you. We can get all that in a minute,' she says, kissing Ava's forehead when my daughter wraps her arms around her waist in a tight squeeze, but her eyes are on mine. 'Never mind where you parked, my love. I'm so glad you got here safely in this weather.'

We shuffle into the huge square hallway, one after the other, and I feel a welcome blast of warmth in an instant. One of my father's greatest legacies is how he kitted the whole house out with a heating system that always makes every room cosy, no matter how high the ceilings are and no matter what time of year, though I know Uncle Eric turns it off in the bigger rooms that aren't used any more to cut back on costs.

It feels like I've been holding my breath since we left Lou and her grandmother only a few minutes ago, so I let out a deep sigh, which of course doesn't go unnoticed by Mum, who is taking in my every movement with concern like she's always done since Stephanie died.

'What are you thinking, dear mother?' I ask, doing my best to tease her rather than worry her. 'Too fat? Too thin? Not enough vegetables? Or is it protein? Do I need to exercise more? Or less? Go for it.'

She stands on her tiptoes and playfully pinches my cheek.

'Nothing wrong with your tongue, Ben Heaney, you handsome devil, she jokes. 'Save all that craic for your Uncle Eric. You know, if he asks if I can find the horse racing again on the TV today, I swear I might be done for murder in the first degree.'

'I bet Ava could find it for him in approximately twenty seconds.'

'I've no doubt she could,' Mum says, holding Ava close by her side. 'But Ava and I have many other fish to fry while you two get busy.'

'Two?'

'You and your uncle, if you can drag him off that armchair,' she tells me. She has got to be kidding. Uncle Eric is good at many things, but at eighty-two his DIY days are limited, or so he says. 'We are going to have the best evening reading books in the library room or baking in the kitchen, far away from his ranting and raving in front of the TV, aren't we, darling? When it comes to Uncle Eric, I'm having a break. It's all over to you.'

I hold my hands up.

'No way, José,' I tell her. 'I've far too much to be doing around here to have him holding me back, so he's going to have to entertain himself for another while on his comfy old armchair.'

'Is Uncle Eric's armchair as old as he is?' asks Ava, giggling behind her hand. She knows my uncle and his humour far too well.

'I'm not deaf, you know,' calls Uncle Eric, which makes us all try and stifle our laughter even more. 'No need to gang up on me, young Ava. I'll be quiet as a mouse if you just find my feckin' channel.'

'We'll be with you soon,' I shout back to him. 'Whatever you do, don't come out here to greet us. No, no, don't budge. We'll come to you. As usual, Your Highness.'

I wink at my mum, who tilts her head.

'It's so good to have you both here,' she says, her smile contradicting the sadness in her eyes.

'Are you OK, Mum?'

'Of course I am, now you're here. Do I tell you enough how fine you are to me, Ben?' she asks me. 'You're so like your father, but nowhere near as moody, thank the Lord. I hope he doesn't haunt me for saying that.'

I nod towards a family portrait that hangs on the wall. It's from the late nineties, our whole attire is abysmal, but I love it because every one of us has laughter and boldness in our eyes. It took ages for my dad to stop blinking every time the photographer took a shot, which led to his frustration, which ultimately made the rest of laugh before he joined in with the giggles too.

'He's never too far away, is he?' I say with a smile. 'Which is both comforting and frightening at the same time. What do you think he'd say about us bringing back the party on Christmas Eve?'

My mother's eyes widen. She takes a deep breath.

'Funnily, I think he'd rather be where he is now than face all that again,' she says. 'If there's such a thing as turning in his grave, he'll be spinning.'

'I have a feeling you could be right,' I say, following her into the kitchen.

'What about you?' she asks. 'Do you think this is a good idea, or are you still on the proverbial fence? That local committee was very persuasive, Ben. I'm sorry if it's putting you under pressure. Two weeks isn't a long time to organise a party.'

'I just hope and pray that the committee has plenty of members who are as keen on the day itself, when we need all hands on deck,' I tell her. 'Ah, I've mixed feelings about it all, Mum, but we've made our call now, so I guess we run with it and pray it's not a big fat disaster like the last one.'

Mum closes her eyes and shudders.

'Let's not even go there,' she whispers. 'I could have a heart attack just thinking of it, but these rooms have been too still for too long. Ballyheaney House wasn't built for that.'

She looks away. I couldn't agree more. It's exceptionally

beautiful but it has been so quiet here in recent years, it's almost ghostly.

'This Mrs Quinn lady who wrote to you,' I say to her. 'Perhaps we could meet with her to see if her people can help us in advance with the planning since it was their grand idea?'

'No,' Mum replies, then a little more softly. 'No, Ben. I don't think that will be necessary. I don't want anyone involved who wasn't involved before. Let's keep our circle small and surprise them all with a wonderful day at the most wonderful time of the year.'

'Point noted and taken, loud and clear,' I reply.

'Do you have a Christmas tree up yet, Grandma?' Ava asks, wandering around and looking for even the slightest sign that Christmas might be a stone's throw away. There's nothing as far as I can see.

'I don't yet, but that's a job for your dad this weekend,' she replies. 'I don't fancy going into the dusty attic and there's no way Uncle Eric will be of any help, so it's over to Ben, I'm afraid. Oops, I don't think he knew about that!'

'But we're only here for one night,' I remind her. 'That can wait until next weekend, surely. One step at a time, ladies. I'm only one person.'

'You're our real-life hero,' says Mum, while Ava nods in agreement. I've a feeling there could be a lot of jobs ahead I didn't know about.

'Any chance of some help with the horse racing at Sandown, Ben, before it's bloody bedtime?' Uncle Eric comes waddling into the kitchen, speaking at the top of his voice. 'I've been flicking through all afternoon, and I simply cannot find it. There's nothing smart about this TV. Codswallop, that's what it is. Bring back analogue, for crying out loud!'

'Come on, let me figure it out,' I reply, as my mother goes to lead Ava off in the opposite direction. 'But I told you on the phone last week. You need to be smart to use a smart TV.'

'Ha, flaming ha!' he chuckles in return. 'Well then, we're all feckin' goosed, aren't we!'

'Welcome home,' whispers Mum over her shoulder. Her eyes meet mine, and I feel my heart soar.

I say this every time I come here, but I should really do this more often.

With my uncle tucked up in the sitting room watching his beloved sport at last, and Roly at his feet by the fire, and with Ava happy and content with her grandma in the kitchen, I leave them all to it as I carry in our overnight bags from the car, followed by the bunch of flowers and holly wreath, and finally the two hot chocolate drinks which will need a blast in the microwave by now.

'Why don't you give mine to Uncle Eric for his sweet tooth,' I say with a wink to Ava. 'Between that, the horse racing and the holly wreath, we should be off to a very positive start.'

Uncle Eric's mood changes remarkably when we show him the holly wreath. In fact, if I'm not mistaken, I can almost say he gets emotional.

'Ah, I've always said it never feels like Christmas until I see the holly,' he says, his aged voice cracking. 'Now, that brings me back. I'll hang this on the front door, and we'll all

113

have a prosperous season. In fact, Ben, you can do that now that you're here. I can keep my feet up and pretend I'm a man of leisure for a little longer.'

The amaryllis are a similar hit with my mother. She takes her time to admire the flowers in the kitchen, then catches my eye with what I believe to be a knowing smile as she slowly smells them.

'This is all very cute,' she says, peeling off the small sticker on the wrapping paper that bears the Buds and Beans logo. 'Isn't that the new place in the village? I keep meaning to do so, but I haven't managed to pop by just yet.'

But she doesn't fool me.

'Oh, and while we're on the subject, thanks for the heads-up about you know who. That was a bit of a shock, to say the least,' I say to her. 'Why didn't you tell me she was back here? I could have been more prepared, and don't say you didn't know. You may be tucked away in this big house, but news travels very fast around here.'

Mum pops her flowers into a tall vase.

'I have no idea what you're talking about, Ben,' she says, then turns her attention back to Ava, who already has her apron on in preparation for their baking session. 'But the flowers have brightened up this place no end. Thank you both.'

I carry our bags up the heavy red carpeted stairs, past tapestries on the walls that date from different centuries and magnificent oil paintings depicting generations of Heaney men and women from days gone by. As I do so, I already notice some parts of the house that are going to need a freshening up over the coming weeks. Despite my mother's best efforts to keep on top of it all, there are cobwebs in high corners, chips of paint on woodwork here and there, and the blue room, fondly known as the ballroom even though its nowhere near as big as it sounds, smells musty and damp. Uncle Eric has dabbled with the heating system in there for certain, so my first job will be to make sure it stays on as much as possible between now and Christmas Eve.

I find my bedroom for the night, where I drop my overnight bag and fall on to the bed to gather my thoughts for a moment, even though it isn't even teatime yet. I put my hands behind my head as a million things run through my mind. There's simply so much to do, I feel suffocated already. Are we crazy to think we can coordinate all this in just two weeks?

What if no one shows up? Now, that would be a disaster. We haven't even asked if it's what the public wants. As far as we know, it's just one tiny committee who wants it, so I hope it's got a big voice.

Maybe we need a proper guest list so that we can invite people personally to bring the public in, rather than depend on posters. I'm thinking social media types, community representatives and local businesses who aren't afraid to show up to support charitable events, especially at this time of year.

I can feel your panic all the way from here, my sister texts me, just as I was about to secretly curse her up and down for getting me into this in the first place. *Remember, you don't have to do it all by yourself, brother. Mum has the contact details for Mrs*

Quinn and her posse, so we need to use them if only from afar. Then you can make one of your famous lists and delegate.

I raise an eyebrow. Knowing Cordelia, she is no doubt texting me from a fancy wine bar or restaurant in southern Spain, where she is being treated like a queen by God knows who. I always said if she fell in manure, she'd get up smelling of roses.

Mum says this is entirely a family affair, sis, I reply. *She's happy for the committee to help on the day, but she doesn't want a group of strangers traipsing round Ballyheaney House like they own the place before that. Only those involved in the olden days need apply.*

Where's Lou Doherty with her creative genius when we need her? Cordelia texts back immediately.

I choose not to even go there.

Did it really happen? I need a bit of time to process it all, so I go back to when I first saw her reflection in the florist's window and replay it all in my mind.

My heart beats faster when I think of the utter surprise I felt, and smile when I think of her hiding away from me at first. I have goosebumps when I hear her voice in my head, saying my name, telling me she'd thought about a day when we'd meet again just like I had so many times.

Most of all, I feel a deep sense of pride for her ballsy return here, for building her business in a short space of time and for all she has already brought back to our community from what I can see so far. Her shop front is stunning, and her taste is as impeccable as it always was.

Right now, she is within walking distance from where I

lie here this evening. Right now, she is at home in this very same village.

The distance and its layer of protection no longer exist, so as if I've already lost all sense of self-control when it comes to Lou Doherty, I do what I promised I wouldn't do.

I lift my phone from where it lies on top of the bed, and I search for Buds and Beans on Google. Within a millisecond I have her business social media page and her picture on my screen, which makes me short of breath but also full of adrenaline.

I almost wish this wasn't so easy. I *could* send a message to her page, but instead I tap her number into my phone and save it, then I send a text as quickly as possible before I change my mind.

Despite my earlier bravado, I know there's simply no way I can drive back to Dublin without doing something.

Chapter Nine

Lou

'A new-build bungalow, yellow door, third house from the end of the lane. Yes, yes, I hear you, messages,' I say to my bleeping phone as I drive along a very windy country lane, searching frantically for number 137 Old Forge Lane. 'So much for Apple Maps taking me right to the door.'

It's my final delivery of the day. I'm very conscious that I'm running behind on this one, and time is of the essence, according to the customer. I thrive on meeting deadlines for my small but growing customer base, but it's fair to say the events of this afternoon have delayed me somewhat.

My tummy rumbles, and it dawns on me that I don't have a lot in the fridge for dinner. I'll stop and get some groceries on the way home, but firstly, I need to find this house.

After Ben and Ava left Buds and Beans about forty minutes ago, I managed to pull myself together and made every excuse under the sun to Nana Molly for my reddened eyes. She eventually decided it had to be an allergy to the pollen from a new delivery of flowers, which I ran with, thankful to get off the hook.

Ben and I don't need closure. We don't have unanswered questions. We weren't engaged to be married, nor were we ever an official couple to the outside world, so why did seeing him again upset me so much? Perhaps it was how I saw myself in little Ava, now growing up with a huge hole in her heart for the parent she lost far too soon. Perhaps it was for Ben himself, for navigating the storms of life without the woman he'd pledged to be with forever. Or perhaps it was the truth. Perhaps it was because the woman he'd married, the one he'd planned a future with, wasn't me, like we both somehow thought it would be a long time ago.

Maybe because, now that it's almost Christmas in the Irish village we both grew up in, I'm being reminded once more that my hurt over him still stings.

'For someone who suffers from hay fever almost all year round, I will never understand why you opened a florist's, Lou,' Nana Molly told me earlier as I pretended to sneeze into a tissue to conceal my puffy face. 'There's no way you can go out on deliveries looking like that. Sit down by the window and have a warm drink. I know it's cold out, but if we open the door for even a couple of minutes it should hopefully pass.'

'I'm fine,' I told her. 'I need to keep going or I'll be late, and we can't have that in this business. Timing is everything.'

'Five minutes won't make a huge difference,' she said, physically plonking me down at a table. 'Your health has to come first, Lou. End of story.'

I felt bad for lying to her, especially as she fussed over me like she has done since I was a child if I as much as whimper. She even called in next door to the mini supermarket to fetch me some over-the-counter medication, which I then pretended to take. She was so proud of herself when I eventually looked better, but it was her kindness, a little time and the soothing taste of a warm, milky decaffeinated latte that really did the job.

With the heater blasting in my car and a good old-fashioned country-music playlist keeping me company, I am more than glad to have this personal delivery to get me out and about.

The young lady who ordered the flowers was adamant that I left it to this time to deliver to make sure her husband was home from work. She herself was due home at around five-thirty today, and he was usually home a little earlier, and it was essential I give him the flowers before she arrived. As usual, I got much more information from the client than I needed. All I had to do was find the house, a mere ten-minute drive away, then turn up on the doorstep with a bunch of flowers – on time. Or so I initially thought.

'We had a row, if truth be told,' she confided over the phone this morning. I could hear what sounded like a busy schoolyard in the background. 'We've never had a row like it before in all our six years together, especially not since we got married in June, so I don't want to be going home this evening for more. It's our first Christmas in our new home too. Aw, do you think a bunch of flowers will make things better?'

At first the hairs on the back of my neck bristled at the thought of what exactly she might be dreading going home to, but when I heard the rest of the story, I knew I'd nothing to worry about.

'It depends on what it is you're trying to mend,' I replied. 'I could give you a whole lecture on how I believe flowers can create intimacy and connection, making not only the receiver but the giver feel instantly uplifted. I could say how the scents and the colours brighten up someone's world, even in the darkest moments, and I could also say that they can provide joy and well-being that lasts for days. But then I would say that, wouldn't I, but I don't know what it is you're trying to fix.'

I hear a school bell ring then, suggesting she'd have to go very soon, but she seemed in no hurry.

'This is embarrassing, but you see, there's this TikTok thing my little sister said I should do,' she told me. 'She said it was fun.'

'Uh-huh,' I replied, putting her on loudspeaker so I could arrange my latest holly wreath masterpiece as she rambled on. 'And I'm guessing it wasn't fun after all?'

Mum, who was clipping fresh holly branches beside me, was rolling her eyes again at how I always heard the sad stories. I'd no doubt she had a point.

'No, it wasn't fun at all. In fact, it was an absolute disaster,' the young lady, whose name was Beth, told me. 'Do you know what an "ick" is?'

I had an idea where this was going. Mum was making faces as she did her best to keep up.

'Yes, I do know what an "ick" is,' I said with a smile. 'I have a daughter who keeps me up to date with all the modern-day lingo. It's something that irritates you or puts you off a person, is that right?'

Mum makes an 'ooh' sound and nods along. I must admit I never could comprehend the point of this so-called 'trend' either.

'Exactly, that's it in a nutshell,' she continued. 'Like, how was anything to do with an ick for me *ever* going to end well? He was so super offended when I said his dress sense didn't really do anything for me, so then he told me that the Ralph Lauren shirt I bought him last Christmas, which cost me an arm and a leg, was now listed on his Vinted page because he'd never wear it in a month of Sundays! I had to stop recording the TikTok. I thought I was going to blow a gasket. The cheek!'

I had to tell my mother to stop laughing out loud beside me.

'I totally lost it,' she continued. 'I called him every feckin' name under the sun and told him he could spend the night in the spare room, which he ended up doing even though I didn't *really* mean it. Don't get me wrong, I'm still mad at him for putting the shirt on Vinted, but I'm also sorry for starting the whole thing and for listening to my sister in the first place. No wonder she is single! Her and her stupid ick game. So anyhow, this is my attempt to say sorry. With flowers.'

I admired her efforts already. I was also very relieved her situation wasn't a serious threat to her recent marriage.

'You know, I'm not exactly one for dishing out relation-ship advice, Beth,' I told her. 'But I have an extra idea that might help? Along with the flowers, of course. You may or may not like it, but hear me out for a second.'

'Go on, I'm all ears,' she told me as a second bell rang in the background. 'I swear I'll do anything. Imagine telling someone what you don't like about them! It doesn't even make sense.'

I fully agreed and we set to work once she'd assured me that she wasn't risking her job or abandoning her pupils while we talked it through. She was on a free period. Phew. And by the time we were finished, both of us were delighted with the end result.

'I was going to say you're wasted in that job, Lou, but no, you're perfect for it! Totally perfect,' she said. 'I really need to get back to work now, but I'll be recommending your flor-ist's to all my friends this Christmas and I'll share on all my socials. Thank you!'

Even Mum was impressed.

'You are wonderful,' she told me, giving me a light hug on her way past. 'You always did have a knack for seeing the bigger picture, Lou. I'm proud of you for that.'

So now here I am at a brand-new bungalow on a dark country lane, armed with a bunch of red roses and a card for a puzzled-looking young man who answers the door holding the cutest little puppy I ever did see.

'Oh my goodness, how adorable,' I say, before pulling myself together. 'Sorry, I – I beg your pardon. These are for you.'

The man does his best to juggle the small dog under one arm and the flowers in the other hand, while I do my best to focus on the job at hand.

'For me?' he asks. 'Are you sure?'

'I'm sure,' I reply. 'You *are* Danny Sullivan? Gosh, sorry, I was so distracted by the dog I didn't even think to check your name first. Beth's husband? Danny?'

For the record I couldn't see anything wrong with his dress sense – a suit which was a little formal, but then again, he was probably still in his work attire. Maybe he'd some weird fashion preferences on weekends.

'I have a card to read out to you,' I said, clearing my throat for my big moment.

'Is this normal?' he asks.

'No, no, it's not normal at all,' I reply. 'It's not usually part of the service, but Beth and I agreed you deserved something a little bit extra, so here goes. *I love the way you . . .*'

He looks genuinely confused.

'This *is* from Beth, right? Not you?'

'Yes, yes, of course it's from Beth,' I reply. This isn't going as well as I'd imagined. 'It's just a few words we put together to go along with the roses. It won't take long.'

Remembering this telegram style of delivery was all my idea isn't something I care to admit to him considering his reaction so far.

'Great! It's just I'm kind of letting all the heat out,' he says, glancing around him. 'Do you mind reading it in the hallway if I shut the front door?'

I look behind me, though I don't know why. I make a

guess that it's about twenty-five minutes past five, so I should be safe enough to step inside knowing Beth can't be far away, unless this is a plot to kidnap me.

'Of course, thank you,' I tell him. 'OK, I'll start again. Ahem.'

He is all ears at last, so I read out my and Beth's attempt of salvaging their weekend ahead, and maybe their first Christmas too.

'*I love the way you share your food, even when I said I didn't want any in the first place,*' I read aloud. He softens immediately. '*I love the way you dance at weddings like no one's watching, not that you'd care if they were because you are lost in your own carefree world. I love the way you always make others feel like they're seen and heard, even strangers in your workplace or the little people that you teach in school. You make everyone feel special and unique. I love your generosity, your big heart and yes, even your big feet. Danny, let's never mention that silly game again. I love how you love red roses and aren't afraid to admit it, so I'll keep sending them to you every birthday and Christmas we share. I'm sending them on this, our first Christmas, and I will do so on every single Christmas in future. I love you more than I love anyone else in the world, even Justin Timberlake and that's saying something because he came first. I love you and Crumb, our little family. Now, what's your Vinted password so I can take that lovely shirt off the market? Only joking. Keep being you. I don't want to change a thing. Not even your ancient jeans that need to go in the bin. True love is forever, not just for Christmas. Beth.*'

I'm very proud of that last line, which was all mine, and

when I look up, Danny has his eyes closed. Maybe this hasn't been a disaster after all? It seems he has been taking in every word as he holds their gorgeous puppy close to his face.

'Are you OK?' I ask.

'Yes,' he says quietly. 'That was – that was a lot better than I expected. Thank you.'

I hear a car in the driveway, so I carefully set the card down on the hall table and go to walk towards the front door.

'Don't thank me, thank your wife,' I say.

He calls me back. 'Do you often do this type of thing?' he asks me.

'Sorry?'

'What I mean to say is,' he continues, 'if I called your shop tomorrow to go over it, could you send Beth something similar in return to her workplace on Monday? I'd like to do that.'

I feel a tingle of excitement. This could be the start of something.

'Yes, I can do that,' I reply. My whole insides glow. 'But you're going to have to give me some steer on the content, because I know don't know nearly enough about your lovely wife.'

'I've lots of nice things to say about her.'

'That's a great start, then.'

Beth comes through the door in that very moment, just as I've slipped my business card his way.

'They arrived on time, thank you, Lou!' she exclaims. 'Thank goodness! Babe, are you OK?'

Danny puts the dog down on the hallway floor, then

hands me the bouquet of roses. His wife falls into his arms, and with mumbles of 'I'm sorry' and 'I love you' from both of them, I tiptoe out and leave them to it. I set the flowers by the card first on the hall table and lean down for a sneaky pat of Crumb's velvety brown head, making a mental note to ask Danny when he calls me tomorrow what type of dog she is. I'm guessing a dachshund. Oh, I've never seen anything as cute in my whole life. I can't wait to tell Gracie, but there's no way I'm mentioning it to my mother, or she'll be ringing round to hook me up with the dog's baby mama in the blink of an eye.

By the time I get to the car, I feel full of romance and hope for humanity, having witnessed the power that having the courage to say sorry or 'I love you' can bring. I turn on the ignition, in wonder of love, and then remember that Ben Heaney is back in town.

My stomach sinks. Argh, why does he still have such a hold on me?

I need distraction and fast, so I pick up my phone, hoping for something, anything, to get me through what's looking like a very long weekend ahead. There's only so much reading I can try to do, or box sets I can try to watch, when I know he isn't far away. Gracie is right. I need to find some new hobbies to occupy my free time now that my business is well on its feet. I need to reconnect with some old friends to see what they're up to after all these years. I need to start *living* again, instead of existing to work, eat and sleep.

What I also need to do is charge my phone, but as I plug

it in, the last thing I expect is to see Ben Heaney's name at the end of a very sweet text message with an invitation that truly takes my breath away.

I grip the steering wheel, leaning forward in the front seat of the car while doing my best to concentrate on the short journey back to the village. The windscreen wipers swipe off the slush, and an oncoming driver flashes his lights to remind me to dip my headlights, but I'm doing my best under the circumstances.

I can't stop shaking.

I glance at the clock on the dashboard. What time is it in New York? I do a quick calculation in my head. It's just after twelve-thirty in the afternoon.

There's no way I'm going to ask Gracie for advice of a personal nature, but I'd love to chat it through with my friend and former neighbour Michelle, who would certainly listen as I thrash out how I should reply.

Or I could ask Pete, my old running partner, who cried as I was leaving. Oh, but no, he cried because he finally admitted having a long-term crush on me, so he's out of the question. You snooze, you lose, Pete. I'd been waiting for far too long, but he'd caught none of the hints I'd been dropping for months and months beforehand. Or I could chat to Dermot, an Irish friend I first met through my ex. He is the most kind and considerate soul and steps in to help me whenever I'm short-staffed or need an extra pair of hands at interior showcases.

Or maybe I'm overthinking it. Why do I need to discuss

it with anyone at all? I can make up my own mind, thank you very much.

I'm sure Ben didn't need to think for long about each word and syllable before he sent the message which came through only a few minutes before I knocked on the Sullivans' door. Thank goodness I didn't check my phone before I delivered the extra-special card and flowers to Beth's husband, or I'd really have made a mess of it. If I'd been any earlier, I probably would have, so thank goodness I was running right down to the wire.

'That's the butterfly effect,' I remember my mum explaining to me not so long ago. 'A small single action or occurrence can set off a chain of actions that have a bigger consequence.'

'A bit like sliding doors,' I'd replied.

'Exactly.'

Like my mother, I've always found it fascinating too, and on this occasion the butterfly effect was on my side it seems, because now I've to make up my mind and quickly.

Do I meet Ben Heaney for a drink later this evening like he's asked me to, or do I protect my foolish heart from shattering all over again?

My heart tells me to go, but my head says I need to keep moving on.

Chapter Ten

Lou

THEN

Christmas Eve, 22 Years Ago

Olivia Major first came to Ballyheaney House in the summer while I was away working as a barista in Wildwood, New Jersey, with my friends from school, before we parted ways for university.

She was a leggy, super-confident twenty-year-old socialite type, with flame-red waist-length hair, an award-winning background in showjumping and a modelling contract on the horizon around her performing arts studies in Dublin.

My first thought when I saw her mucking out the stable was one of pure awe of her beauty, but then relief when her true colours emerged from the second she uttered her first hello.

'So, you're the hired help,' she sneered. 'You don't look like someone associated with the Heaneys, do you?'

I just laughed in her face. She had no idea.

While I only had to pop home from Belfast once the holidays came in, Ben had a bit further to travel from Paris and it seemed he'd left it later this year. But we'd already made lots of plans. Long mornings on the boardwalk down by Lough Beg, cosy evenings by the fire in the local pub, and all the fun of the Christmas Eve party, which by then was more than special to both of us.

I looked up at Uncle Eric as he stretched the string of lights along the wood panelling, his mouth tight and his eyes steely with concentration.

'Are you sure you don't want to swap roles?' I asked him for the third or fourth time. He was sprightly and fit, but I'd noticed that he couldn't stop talking for long enough to fully concentrate on the job at hand. 'I can reach higher than you think, you know. I've grown since you last saw me. Look. No, don't look for real or you might fall!'

We'd spent the best part of two days lighting up evergreen firs on the lawns, we'd scrubbed and polished windows until they glistened in the midday winter sun, and every room on the ground level of Ballyheaney House was a feast for the senses, with glowing hearths, polished floors and the smell of turf mixed with cinnamon and citrus filling the air.

In just a few hours, this place would be full of friendly chit-chat, song, and hustle and bustle; Christmas Eve was something I looked forward to all year round.

And in just a few minutes, Ben would be home to join in on this year's celebrations.

'Nobody brings cosy comfort and festive cheer to this place like you two do. The ultimate dream team,' Cordelia told us as she made her way to the kitchen. She and I had bonded recently over boyfriend trouble – hers – and I'd so enjoyed getting to know her much more over recent days.

'Put our names on at least two cookies and three ginger-bread men,' Uncle Eric told his niece. 'Each, that is. We'll call you for the big pre-party Ballyheaney Christmas Eve toast very soon.'

'No, wait until Ben comes,' a high-pitched and rather out-of-place voice piped up from behind me. 'Tilda said his flight was in at three, so she should be home with him any minute.' Olivia Major clasped her hands with unashamed glee, which made me feel far too competitive for my own good.

She was a vision in her cream jodhpurs, fitted black jacket and riding boots, framed by cascades of tumbling red hair. Worst of all, she was returning from spending the afternoon riding on Little Eve around the village. Now that was a step too far in my book. Not only did she have her manicured scarlet nails set on clawing into Ben, she had also taken over the care of our precious Little Eve. And she did it so well too.

'Perhaps, Olivia, you could offer some assistance in the kitchen? Cordelia is slaving away in there on her own, so I'm sure she'd welcome a bit of help,' Uncle Eric said to her.

I could hear the sting in his voice. Uncle Eric was right on my level when it came to Olivia. He knew that to do such a thing would be very far removed from her grand inner notions. She was much too precious to bake or cook, even though she didn't mind traipsing in there with horse manure on the boots she was on her way to discarding in the boot room. Being hidden away in the kitchen was not her style.

'Oh, Eric, I would love to,' she said on her return, 'but I need to change into something a little more suitable before Tilda gets back with Ben. I can't be around hot ovens in smelly jodhpurs ahead of meeting him for the first time. Mind you don't fall, Eric. Maybe you should listen to Lou and let her do the donkey work instead? That's what she's here for, after all.'

She walked upstairs with her nose in the air. I closed my eyes and counted to ten.

'Have you ever heard of the saying "familiarity breeds contempt"?' Uncle Eric muttered as he slowly clambered down the steps of the ladder. 'That one thinks she was born and bred here. She was only meant to come for a bit of work experience in the summer, but she's hanging in like a dung fly hoping that Ben will arrive home today like a knight in shining armour and fall madly in love with her. I know my nephew. There's no chance of that happening.'

Uncle Eric patted himself down. I suspected he was a lot gladder to be back on solid ground than he was letting on.

My tummy flipped at the thought of seeing Ben again, even though we'd spent more time together that year than ever before.

He'd flown home to be with me for my father's funeral in early spring, when an accident on the factory floor claimed my precious daddy's life in a cruel heartbeat. Right before he died, Dad had taught me to drive, and taken me to a rock concert: he was helping me to bridge the gap as I became a young adult and there was so much more we had planned for that summer and the future. The raw pain of grief made me want to run away, so I did exactly that in the summer with my mother's blessing. I ran away from it all.

Ben came to see me there, in New Jersey, for a few days, and held me tight as he mopped up my tears, but no matter how much we talked or no matter how much we grew closer and closer, spending those summer nights between the sheets where the passion was inescapable, neither Ben nor I made the move to commit further.

'I know you have girlfriends in Paris,' I stuttered out one morning when we were having coffee before my shift at work in Wildwood.

'I'm not as popular as you might think,' he laughed. 'Though I've no doubt you've many admirers too.'

I couldn't deny it. I never took things seriously, but now that my A levels were over a whole new social scene had opened up where I partied and dated occasionally.

'So why do we keep drifting back to each other, letting our paths cross or deliberately making them do so?' I asked him.

He shrugged.

'Because we want to,' he said. 'It will stop when we don't want to any more, though I can't see that happening.'

'Fair enough,' I said, stirring my coffee, even if I secretly wished for more.

Distance was a huge obstacle, but why didn't one of us suggest we give it a proper try? Why did everything that happened in my life, good or bad, make me want to run and tell him first? And he was the same. Apart from his love life and mine, we knew everything there was to know about each other.

Physically, we knew every inch of each other too. We were lovers as well as friends, with a passion we both agreed was incomparable with anything we could have hoped for.

'That's him,' I said when I heard Tilda's car pull up outside. I was doing my best not to let the joy I felt be so palpable, but my glistening eyes gave me away.

'That's him,' said Uncle Eric, as Cordelia bounced into the hallway, followed by a very sultry Olivia, who pouted and preened herself as she waited.

We all watched the huge front door until it clicked open.

'Welcome home!' we clapped and cheered in unison when Ben and his mother came inside, their shoulders already damp from the afternoon sleet outside.

Ben dropped his bags, looking right at me almost with disbelief, even though he knew I'd be here.

'Ben, this is Olivia, who I've told you all about,' said Tilda, extending her arm in Olivia's direction, but Ben only glanced at her quickly without saying a word.

He didn't need to say a thing. He could see no one else in the room, not even his sister, who had been so looking forward to welcoming him home as much as I was.

After the toughest months of my life, full of grief and despair for my daddy, I felt a glimmer of happiness at last.

Ben was back home. My favourite person in the whole world was here at last.

'Penny for your thoughts,' I said when we sat in our usual corner of the local pub that evening after the party had subsided. 'You're quiet this year. Is everything OK in France?

Or are you planning something with that new girl, Olivia? You can tell me. I can see your mother is trying to play matchmaker.'

He fidgeted with a beer mat, his eyes darting round the room everywhere except in my direction.

'You can read me like no one else can, Lou,' he said, laughing at first but then turning serious. 'But no, I've hardly noticed Olivia, despite her insane efforts to throw herself my way. And my mother will see through her eventually, I've no doubt about that.'

'Phew,' I replied, trying to keep things lighter than it really felt. 'I was sure she was going to swoop in and snog your face in front of us all earlier.'

Ben put the beer mat down, took a deep breath and finally looked me in the eye.

His voice cracked as he spoke.

'Lou, this has been such a tough year for you, and I'm so glad I was there to see you through some of it,' he told me. 'But now we need to talk. Wouldn't you agree?'

'Go on,' I said, as a lump the size of a small planet formed in my throat.

'I love you, Lou,' he said, his eyes so full of pain, his hand holding mine tightly now.

Oh God.

'And I'm not saying that just because it's Christmas, or because I'm so sad you lost your dad,' he continued. 'I love you and I want you to know how much you matter to me. You matter more than anyone else in the whole world, you know that?'

My tummy swirled and my eyes widened as I sensed a 'but' coming. How ironic for me to hear the words I'd been longing to for so long, only for them to be laced with conditions?

'But I can't do a long-distance relationship when I'm at uni in a different country,' he continued, swallowing hard as he spoke, 'and I don't think it's fair to expect you to settle for that either. We deserve more. We both deserve it all when the time is right.'

I did my best to stay calm and cool, but the truth was, I'd been thinking of this too, tossing and turning at night, giving up nights out with my friends in Belfast to stay in waiting for a call or a text from Ben. It wasn't healthy. It wasn't good enough. He was right. We deserved so much more.

'I understand,' I whispered, staring at the table.

'You do?'

'Ben, I don't want to half-love you over texts and phone calls either,' I told him. He reached across and pushed my hair so tenderly off my face. 'I want you for real. All of you. And that can't happen now.'

I was agreeing with him, but inside I was screaming at the unfairness of it all.

'My love for you will never change,' he told me, kissing my forehead long and slowly. 'Please always know that, but maybe for now we leave space. Real space. And when we find our way back . . . which I know we will one day soon, then it'll be when we're both ready to make it work for real.'

I looked away. I knew he was right, but that didn't make it any easier to hear.

'Say something, Lou,' he whispered. 'Say anything.'

I took my time, doing my best to find the right words. I could hear him breathing beside me despite the noise in the busy pub, with revellers toasting Christmas Eve to the sounds of Shane MacGowan and Kirsty MacColl.

'It's hard, but yes, I guess it's where we are for now,' I replied. My voice was shaking. My hands were shaking too. 'I love you too, Ben. Just so you know that. I love you too and I always will.'

'Same,' he replied.

I put my head on his shoulder, staring at the Christmas tree lights across from us, and sat with his hand in mine for what felt like forever, knowing we had made a very difficult decision but one that was long overdue.

We were choosing love, and we were letting go, all at the same time.

It was a conversation and a Christmas Eve that would change both our paths for the rest of our lives.

Chapter Eleven

Ben

NOW

She doesn't respond to my text message.

It was a bit of a shot in the dark, I guess, so I do my best to shake her off my mind as the evening draws in by doing what I came to Ballyheaney House for. With notebook in hand, I take one room at a time, jotting down information not only on what we need to fix up a little but also on what improvements we can make overall. I scout around the attic, finding rather groovy decorations we still have from yesteryear to bring some festive magic and warmth back, but with every step I take around the house I'm haunted by memories of happier times.

Voices from the past echo through my mind and fill my senses as I stand in the blue ballroom. I see the string quartet in the corner on my dad's makeshift stage, which was made from wooden pallets we'd stained a deep mahogany colour, topping it up annually for the big occasion. He was always so pleased with the result and would spend hours in the outhouses sanding and painting by himself before revealing his work of art. Then he'd stand back and admire it all in place, before lighting up like a child when he saw the stage in use on Christmas Eve.

I look up to the high ceiling, where I can see in my mind's eye the long, heavy strings of lights draped from each corner to the grand chandelier centrepiece, carrying large yellow bulbs to give the room a warm glow, while in the fireplace a turf fire burned 'for smell and a cosy atmosphere', according to Cordelia, even though year after year we'd let it smoulder away before the room became too hot.

And as I move from room to room, I repeatedly check my phone for a reply from Lou, but there's nothing.

I repeat to myself that at least I tried.

Uncle Eric throws together a feast of home-made pepperoni and mushroom pizza decorated with rocket and olives for dinner, pouring red wine like there's no tomorrow, while Ava laps up all the maternal love and attention my mother gives her in bucket loads.

'A tasty margherita pizza just for you, Your Majesty,' my uncle jokes as he sets a bubbling cheese version down in front of my daughter, who is already licking her lips. Uncle Eric has discovered cooking in his later years. I sometimes believe it's been his saviour as he tends to his small but prosperous vegetable patch in the garden and a greenhouse that bursts with colour in summer. He's taken great pride in sending me photos since Cordelia gave him a crash course on the iPhone last year.

While we eat, I break all our usual dining rules by having

my phone within reach, which gives me both comfort and waves of anxiety as I watch and wait for some sort of message from Lou.

It was a very humble invitation, nothing suggestive or presumptuous on my part, but perhaps I should have worded it differently. Or should I have made a phone call instead of a cop-out text? It dawns on me once more that I know absolutely nothing about her life now. I don't know where she lives, or who she lives with. I don't know if she's single or if she's still with John after all this time. I don't know how her daughter Gracie is. She must be twenty years old now. My God, there's been a lot of water under the bridge since then.

'This is the best pizza ever,' Ava announces, which makes Uncle Eric sit up in his chair across from me. 'Even better than the ones from The Sphinx, and they're our favourites, aren't they, Dad?'

I hear her, but I'm barely listening.

'Sorry, darling?' I curse myself for drifting off instead of enjoying this special moment with my family.

'This is better than The Sphinx at home?'

'Yes, you're absolutely right,' I reply, determined to stay in the present from now on. 'Far better. So where are you taking us next weekend, Uncle Eric? China? India? This is going to be great fun now that you're a super-chef. I'd never have thought it in a million years, but credit where credit's due. This is top-drawer pizza.'

Uncle Eric thinks for a moment as he chews his food.

'India sounds like a good shout,' he says, his eyes dancing

with excitement. 'I never did make it there in real life, despite my intentions, but now you say it, I quite fancy dabbling in a chicken tikka masala. Maybe you could help me download a recipe before you go home, Ava?'

And as they chat, I drift off once again to a place in my heart I'd hoped I'd closed the door on long ago.

'I'm going to pop out for a while if you don't mind, Mum,' I say after washing up. 'Are you OK here with Ava? I'll be home well before her bedtime.'

If I'm not mistaken, I can see my mother fight off a smile as she dries the last few plates with a tea towel. We have an industrial-size dishwasher in the utility room at Ballyheaney House, but Mum still prefers us to wash the dishes by hand when it's just ourselves for dinner.

'Where are you off to?'

I do my best to sound nonchalant about my plans for the next hour. When I was thinking of coming here I'd imagined a workhorse-style trip where I'd tackle as much as possible in a very short space of time, no doubt exhausting myself and dreading the drive back to Dublin where I'd plunge myself into work once more and juggle all the plates in the air with Ava's homework, music lessons and sporting commitments through the week.

But now my mouth is watering for a cold, creamy pint of stout down at a bar where I know I'll always be greeted like an old friend, no matter who is there and no matter how much time passes between visits.

'I'll see where my thoughts take me,' I reply. 'I quite fancy the walk to clear my head. Are you sure you don't mind?'

Mum raises her eyebrows and puts her hand on my upper arm.

'Ben, of course I don't mind. You take no time for yourself these days,' she whispers. 'Let me take over for as long as you're here. Ava and I have a movie lined up and a chocolate feast to discover in the pantry, so go and chill out for as long as you need to. We won't wait up. I only wish you could do this more often.'

I go to the sitting room where Roly is keeping company right by the fire, but that changes as soon as he senses his lead in my hands.

'See you soon, Uncle Eric,' I say, wondering when his days of a pint in a local bar at Christmas ended, how we never knew it would be the last, and how I didn't savour it more. 'We'll have a chat about the horse racing when I get back.'

'Go and see who you can see,' he says without taking his eyes off the 24-hour news channel. 'You're still a young man, you know, Ben. This Christmas is going to be a good one for us all. And the whole world is your oyster.'

The sound of low conversations and the smell of old ale meets me the moment I step inside Doc's Bar in my home village. It's a tiny, one-roomed pub with TV screens on the wall, but with its square brown tables, chequered upholstery and a crackling fire in the corner, it oozes old-worldly charm. A modest Christmas tree lit up in blue sits by the end of the bar, and long icicle-style lights hang from the roof, and while I could never claim to be a regular, the atmosphere greets me like an old friend.

145

Doc's Bar is full of memories of days gone by, no matter which way I look.

It reminds me of my dad sneaking in for a bet on the horses while sitting me down on a bar stool with a bag of Tayto crisps and a bottle of Coça-Cola with a straw.

It reminds me of my first proper pint of beer, still feeling like an impostor at the legal age of eighteen, a place where Lou and I downed tools from the manic party preparations and toasted our success.

It reminds me of long, fun-filled evenings with her playing cards by the fire, feeling very grown up as we shared a bottle of wine and our traditional bag of peanuts, when in reality we were only students trying to save a few bob to get us through the next semester.

'Mr Heaney, welcome home,' the barman says when I order a pint of Guinness. I glance at the clock on the wall behind the bar. It's already gone five minutes after eight o'clock. She isn't here.

Even though she didn't reply to my text message earlier, a tiny part of me still hoped that she might show up. I'd pictured her sitting by the fire here, a glass of red for old time's sake on the table and that wondrous smile of hers that lights me up every time.

But no. She isn't here. And I know by now that she isn't coming.

I make some small talk with the barman, who admires my dog then asks how I've been coping. He recounts where he was and what he was doing when he heard of Stephanie's passing.

'The whole village was in shock for you,' he tells me, a genuine sadness in his eyes. 'My brother lost his wife when she was far too young too, so I've a bit of an idea what you've been going through.'

He asks how expensive it is to live so close to Dublin, and if I'd ever dream of moving back up north where the cost of living is still quite high in parts but nowhere near what it is down there. Then he grabs my attention on a whole new level when he tells of how the whole village is full of craic about us bringing the big party back to Ballyheaney House.

'My own mother has her outfit picked out already,' says a younger man by my side. 'She's bought tickets for herself and her sister.'

'We're going as a family for the first time this year,' his buddy tells me. 'Our twins turned sixteen this year, so they're of an age to join us. It's hard to believe it's been twenty years since the last one.'

I watch the dark ruby liquid cascade from the tap, foaming up in a creamy, rich layer. I lick my lips in anticipation.

'I think you've just made it feel very real,' I tell him, doing my best to ignore the lurch in my stomach at the thought of it all.

'I'm telling ye. There's a real buzz, Mr Heaney,' he says while the punters propping up the bar nod in agreement. 'And what a great charity cause too. Fair play to you all. Will you get it ready in time, do you think? That's what some are wondering. Ye know, short notice and all that?'

I shiver at the thought of the task that lies ahead.

We used to have a perfect team in place to get the house

ready for the party, but now it's just me, my twelve-year-old daughter and my sister who lives in a different country. There's not much point relying on Mum and Uncle Eric, though I know they'll do their best. Now that I've stepped out of our bubble, the enormity of what we've taken on almost overwhelms me when I hear this from the horse's mouth.

People are excited. People are buying tickets. But people are worried we're doing it all at very short notice.

So am I.

'I do love a challenge,' I reply to the barman, who nods in agreement. 'And it's a good excuse to get out of my own head for a while, I suppose. I'll take my pint down by the fire if that's OK?'

'Best spot in the house,' he tells me, though that I already know. 'I'll bring it down to you once it settles.'

He does exactly that, allowing me to zone out from the banter at the bar while Roly cosies up on the floor. My to-do list runs like a freight train through my mind, causing a tight pain across my chest. I breathe steadily, then I lift the glass to my lips, allowing the cold taste of home to soothe my busy mind.

I'm hypnotised by the smooth, familiar taste as well as the heat of the fire. Everything begins to slow down at last. My shoulders drop. Roly is already snoring by my feet.

'I did my best to ignore your invitation, but I never could ignore you, Ben Heaney,' an all-too-familiar voice says from my right. My heart leaps. 'Now move over and let me in by the fire where I always sat. We've got a party to plan, and fast.'

I look up to see her standing there, her cheeks pink from the cold and her eyes fixed on mine with that wondrous smile that shows off her dimples. The sight of her has never failed to melt my heart.

'I'll get you a glass of red,' I say, doing my best to keep my cool. 'And a few packs of peanuts for old times' sake?'

'I'm looking forward to it already.'

Chapter Twelve

Lou

We clink glasses.

'*Slàinte*,' he says to me, his voice a lot more casual than his demeanour suggests. I play along, both of us hesitant to cross the bridge of time that sits between us.

'It's good to see you again,' I croak, hoping we get round the inevitable small talk, and fast. 'I sometimes wondered if it would ever happen.'

'It's been what? Four hours or so?' he says, glancing at the clock on the wall. 'I always said you'd got it bad.'

I'm glad to see he hasn't lost his sense of humour.

'Very funny,' I reply, doing my best not to stare now that it's just the two of us. 'I wrote a reply to your text at least ten times but couldn't find the right words. Then it was time to be here, so I thought I'd take a chance and just show up instead, hoping you would too. I'm sorry for leaving you . . . what is it they say these days?'

'You left me "on read",' he laughs. 'In modern times that's deemed the ultimate insult. I won't take it personally.'

'Phew,' I reply. 'Gosh, I'd hate to be a young person on the dating scene these days. Such pressure.'

He wears a navy sweater that looks soft to touch, but it's not my place to do so after all this time. He's aged of course. Lines are etched on his face, while his hair is greying at the temples. Time is a thief. It has robbed us both of so much, yet enriched us with a lot more than we will ever catch up on. Two very different paths taken, and two very different lives built.

'I hope my message wasn't pushy.'

I chuckle at his suggestion. It was far from pushy. It was perfect.

'No, it wasn't pushy at all, but it did take me very much by surprise,' I admit, feeling the doors of honesty slide open already. I'd coached myself for the past hour on how to play this cool should I go ahead and accept his invitation under the guise of picking my brain on how best to organise the party. 'I hope you know how much this means to the community.'

'What, me coming back into the village on my white horse?' he laughs. 'Didn't you hear the fanfares and see the parades?'

'It was the talk of the village. Your big return in all your crowning glory,' I reply. His face is like an old favourite book, but now it has its own very different story. 'I got a huge welcome myself when I arrived back from New York. It's not all about you, Ben Heaney. You may have had fanfares and parades, but I have been given the freedom of the village. And an elephant to carry me through the town on request.'

'I'm sure you have,' he says, his eyes crinkling at the sides. I hold on to the stem of my wine glass like it's a lifesaver, and in many ways it's the crutch I needed earlier. At least it gives me something to do with my hands. 'But seriously, Lou. Why did you come back here? I never thought I'd see the day.'

'By accident,' I admit to him swiftly. 'Gracie spotted an opportunity, then the rest fell into place like it was almost meant to be. I think village life in Ireland might suit me much better than a big city like New York after all, though I do have moments of unwavering doubt that I've taken a giant leap backwards. I suppose time will tell.'

We skirt over the small stuff and the big stuff too, our daughters being the perfect icebreakers as we both do our best to settle into the moment while avoiding the urge to skip to the highlights of days gone by.

'Work is busy, thank goodness,' he tells me. 'I've an amazing partner in Matt, who also happens to be my best friend, so that helps. Who'd have thought when we were delivering that baby foal, I'd end up making a career out of it.'

'Well, if you ever need a hand, you know I'm not too far away,' I joke. 'You've been through a very hard time, Ben. I'm sorry.'

He lifts his pint and thinks for a moment.

'As have you,' he says, as graceful and humble as he ever was. 'You've made a big move coming home after creating a life for you and Gracie out there.'

I get the feeling he doesn't want to get too maudlin about Stephanie, so I leave it at that.

153

'In the beginning, I was like a square peg in a round hole in New York,' I explain, 'but in time I found my own feet. I'd no choice but to when my darling husband ran off with the kindergarten teacher. They are now living happily ever after with their two young children.'

He looks genuinely surprised. I thought he may have heard on the grapevine, but it seems not.

'I should be asking why you stayed in New York for so long then, if that's the case, rather than why you came back,' he says, looking right at me for the first time since I got here. I order another drink. He barely catches his breath. 'You deserved so much better than that, Lou. You should have told me what you were going through out there.'

I rewind the years, calculating almost to the day when it was that John packed his bags and left our New York apartment. I physically shiver.

'I should have told you, but my life was very different from yours by then,' I say. 'Plus, I'd no idea where in the world you were, or who you were with.'

He shrugs. I have a feeling he doesn't agree, but to be honest, telling Ben Heaney my life had gone tits up was the furthest thing from my mind at the time. I was instead determined to face up to a future of single-parenting in a city where my only daily conversations had finally moved on from small talk with the postman or the lady in the grocery store. I had been settling in at last, but then the rug was swept from beneath my feet.

'I put my shoulder to the wheel, knowing I could turn it around with sheer grit and determination,' I continue. 'I carved out a career in interiors, I bought an apartment and learned to love the challenge of it all. It was mostly fun. It was character building, that's for sure.'

He stares at his pint before he speaks.

I would have run to you if you'd told me.

He doesn't say so, but I can read his mind.

'And now, here we are, full circle,' he says quietly. 'I'm a widower and single parent, you're a single lady with your daughter raised and the world at your feet. It's weird, isn't it? Very strange.'

'That's one way of putting it,' I laugh, knowing we need a subject change before we're both crying into our drinks with regret. 'So anyhow, how's Uncle Eric? And your mum?'

Despite my efforts to lighten things up, I almost choke when I mention their names.

My first thought when I got back here was to rock up to Ballyheaney House to say hello to Ben's family, but nerves and pride wouldn't allow it. Instead, I hoped I'd bump into them organically, maybe in the park or the post office, or maybe they'd come and see me if they heard I was back in town.

No matter how or when I saw them again, I've always hoped that we could pick up where we left off without any animosity or hard feelings.

Ben may have broken my heart, but I shattered his too.

'Uncle Eric is vying for a place on *Masterchef*, while Mum is craving friendship and company but will never admit it,' he tells me. 'They're both rattling about the big house, determined they're fine on their own. The finances are a strain again. It's a bit like history repeating itself, so Cordelia and I are going to have to make some big decisions very soon.'

'I totally understand.'

'It's tough, isn't it?' he replies. 'I've only been here a couple of hours and I'm seeing cracks in more than the paintwork, if you get me. It's like watching something slowly erode that was once indestructible. I need to be here more, and that's a fact.'

'Which brings us to the Christmas Eve party.'

'Which brings us to the Christmas Eve party,' he echoes. 'Ava and I will come back here again for the holidays next weekend when school finishes up. Do you think we're crazy bringing it back?'

That's a loaded question, but with Ben I've always found it easy to be honest and tell him the truth.

'I did when I first heard about it, I won't lie,' I tell him. 'Well, not crazy perhaps, but I was shocked. On a deeply personal level I felt every emotion under the sun. I was a bit stunned. It was like ripping open an old wound, but then I felt tinges of jealousy too. I imagined all the preparations I used to be a part of, and I wondered who would do it all this time round.'

He tilts his head to the side.

'You were the leader in so many ways, even though you might not have realised it,' he tells me.

My heart fills up with a rush of adrenaline as I remember the thrill of helping to organise something so beautiful.

'That's not the only reason I wanted to see you this evening, by the way,' he says. 'I need to make that clear. Yes, I'd love to have you on board for the party, even if I think you agreeing to is a long shot, but I also knew I couldn't leave here tomorrow without seeing you one more time.'

I nod in agreement. I was desperate to see him again too, even if fear got in the way of any rational thinking on my part.

'It's exciting,' I say, the words tumbling off my tongue before my brain cared to register. 'I've missed the buzz of the party. Those really were the best days.'

'I agree,' he says. The walls are softening between us ever so slightly.

'Even if you did "friend-zone" me the last time we sat here,' I reply.

Ben almost chokes on his pint laughing.

'You really are up to speed with the lingo,' he tells me. 'And by the way, that was the hardest thing ever at the time. I was so in love with you.'

Well, that shuts me up for at least ten seconds, but soon we are chatting again.

We reminisce and reflect, we laugh and we almost cry, we talk about Little Eve and the joy she brought to so many, we roll our eyes when we remember the summer of Olivia Major.

'She was so determined to make my life a misery, and so keen to get her hands on you,' I say, doing my best not to sound bitter, but boy, I was so mad at her. 'Then she turned up here to the pub on that tricky Christmas Eve evening, uninvited, not long after our big decision to give each other some space. Talk about pushy!'

'She had spaghetti arms, that's for sure,' Ben replies, laughing heartily. 'I'll never forget your face, Lou. She got so drunk and told you to go home so she could have me all to herself.'

We're on a roll now down memory lane, and it feels good.

'She was on a real bunny-boiler mission, no doubt about it,' I tell him, recalling the look on his face when the three of us sat in this very spot by the fire all those years ago.

'I was secretly terrified of her,' he says with a shudder. 'Thank goodness you were graceful enough to take her home in a taxi, even if you had to listen to her attempt to sing "Last Christmas" on repeat all the way to her parents' house.'

'Graceful is one word, I suppose,' I say. 'I think you and I both needed rescuing from her antics that evening, but I wouldn't have let her travel home alone when she'd had so much to drink. I walked her to the door and made an excuse to her worried parents that she'd had an allergic reaction to something. They called me the "Ballyheaney House hand".'

How flattering! Did you ever hear from her since?'

He looks horrified at the very idea.

'No – well, not in person, but she sent me scathing texts for days saying how you and I deserved each other,' he says. 'She claimed she was far too good for me anyhow and how you were – well, we don't need to go there. Teenage crushes, eh . . . mad how they come and go.'

A weighted silence hangs in the air between us at the idea that we too were a teenage crush that simply lasted longer than average.

'Loving someone when you're university age isn't exactly a teenage crush, is it?' I suggest, feeling the words scratch my throat. 'But maybe that's what we were.'

He bites his lip and rubs his forehead before replying.

'I've tried for a very long time to understand what we had, Lou,' he tells me. 'I don't for a second believe it was a teenage crush. It was way more than that, and it lasted way longer than that. For me, anyhow.'

'For me too,' I whisper, as the anxious feeling in my tummy starts to settle.

We skip past the ending of our story, choosing without saying so to move on to business since time was of the essence. We discuss the party in as much detail as possible, as we have a very short time frame to make the party happen without a glitch, not to mention meeting the guests' very high expectations. We don't need to mention the last party in any shape or form, but we both know we don't want any last-minute setbacks. This one is going to take all eyes on the ball. And this time, those eyes belong to me, Ben and Cordelia.

'Fancy sharing a taxi home?' I suggest when last orders are called at the bar. 'My house is on the way to yours.'

'Perfect,' he tells me. 'It's been so good, hasn't it? This. You and me making our to-do lists and planning together.'

'It has,' I agree with a smile.

We swap some final ideas and then we get into the taxi, which takes me to Katie's Cottage first. My heart sings when I see him gasp at the sight of my new abode.

'Lou Doherty, you dark horse! You bought Katie's Cottage?' he says in awe. 'Wow. That was your childhood dream, Lou. I can't – I can't even tell you how happy I am for you.'

We sit on either side of the back seat of the car, but he

reaches across and touches me for the first time, taking my hand into his for only a few seconds.

'Dreams do come true, Ben,' I tell him. 'But I always did believe so.'

It was a productive evening, it was promising, and it made me feel more alive than I have done in a very long time.

'Never mind raining cats and dogs, it's raining monkeys and giraffes out there.' Nana Molly shuffles into Buds and Beans the next morning sporting a new and very flashy red raincoat which clashes with her burgundy hair. 'Oh my goodness, it's busy, Lou. You should have called me earlier. I've spent the last twenty minutes browsing in the library.'

'That sounds like heaven to me,' I reply as I steam up another frothy coffee.

'Oh, it was, but I can do that any time,' she says. 'I told you from the start I'm here when you need me.'

She hangs up her coat on the hooks by the front door and makes her way behind the coffee bar, where I'm setting up three cappuccinos and a chai tea for a brand-new set of customers who are in the area for a carol service in St Mary's Church.

'I've served Master Campbell his third cinnamon latte today – and he's been in here every day this week, not that I'm complaining,' I tell her. 'He's very welcome and a very easy customer. His face lights up when he sees you or Mum, Nana. Maybe you're the reason he's here.'

She tuts at my suggestion.

'I'm sure it's not because of me in particular. Loneliness

is an epidemic, Lou,' she tells me. 'It's so tough for anyone on their own at this time of year, but especially for Master Campbell as he does have a family but they're so far away.'

I watch him from across the room, wondering how he's really feeling as he learns to manage without Agnes and with his only son on the far side of the world. I consider it a privilege that he likes to spend so much time here, even if I'd love to have a magic wand so I could zap that loneliness away for him.

So far this morning we've talked about the whereabouts of some of my more memorable classmates, the rise in fuel prices and, on a lighter note, the Christmas Eve party, which I haven't told anyone that I'm involved in yet.

But Nana already smells a rat.

'You look different,' she says, staring at me as I busy myself with the coffee bar. She tilts her head from side to side, doing her best to read my face, which she's always been so good at. 'What is it, Lou? You haven't had your hair done, have you? No, you still have that dreadful grown-out fringe. You haven't changed your outfit. Still the uniform denim dungarees and green apron.'

I can't help but giggle as she analyses me from head to toe.

'Thank goodness I was born with a thick skin,' I reply.

'Your cheeks are rosy in a way they haven't been in a long time, and you're wearing a smile that would brighten a nation,' she says to me. 'Now, call me old-fashioned but to me that's normally a sign of . . . Lou, have you met someone new?'

'No,' I tell her, confident in my truth.

'Oh my goodness, that's it, isn't it!' she says, clapping

her hands. 'You've been on one of those dating sites and you swiped left!'

'It's swipe right actually, but no, Detective Inspector Molly, I haven't been on a dating site,' I correct her. 'Mum has been at me all morning wondering the same, so I've tasked her with a delivery to get her out of my hair.'

'My Liz is a chip off the old block when it comes to intuition,' says Nana proudly.

'You two should work for the FBI,' I say, raising an eyebrow. 'Now, when you're done dissecting every move I make, can you take these coffees across to table three, please? I really need five minutes to myself. Thanks, Nana. You're the best.'

I can feel Nana's eyes still on me as I make my way to the tiny kitchen area at the back of my workplace for a very short breather. It's only just gone eleven but I feel like I've run a marathon already, even though I most definitely woke up this morning with a new spring in my step after an enjoyable evening catching up with Ben.

I lay awake for ages last night though, mulling over our conversations that evening, digesting and analysing all we had to say and all we must do going forward to get the party ready in less than two weeks.

'Everything OK out there?' I call out.

I hear a rattle from the coffee bar which shakes me back to the present, so I jump to get to Nana's rescue. As fresh and astute as she very much still is, I don't like to leave her on her own for too long, especially on a busy Saturday morning.

However, I don't get far before my own mother meets me on the way.

'I knew it, Lou!' she says, putting her hand to her chest with a beaming smile. 'I knew there was something you weren't telling us this morning.'

'What have you heard now?' I ask, feeling my legs tremble and my face flush. I was going to tell my family later today about my new affiliation with Ben and Ballyheaney House, but I feared word would get out beforehand, as it often does in the village.

'There's a very, very handsome man asking for you at the coffee bar,' Mum whispers, stopping me in my tracks. 'Is this why you're looking so upbeat and fresh this morning? I knew it! I'd just got in through the door from my delivery – very emotional moment, I have to say. Poor woman is so sick. Anyhow, I offered to help the man, but he insisted on speaking to you personally.'

My heart races. Has Ben popped in to say one last goodbye before he heads back to Dublin this evening, even though he'll be back again Friday? No . . . and anyhow, Nana would recognise him instantly, having only chatted with him a day ago. My mother has the memory of an elephant, so she'd cop on too.

But still, just in case, I grab my lipstick, pat down my apron and take a deep breath before I walk out front, doing my best to disguise my inner glee at the thought of how Ben might have wanted to call by.

'Oh, hello,' he says with an air of confidence I didn't notice so much on our first meeting yesterday. 'I hope it isn't too late to make my special order?'

Mum does her best not to bleat with excitement while I

do my best not to show my disappointment at the sight of the young man at the counter. He is indeed very handsome. He is indeed looking for me personally.

But he is not Ben Heaney.

'You're right on time,' I reply, seeing my grandmother staring at us from the corner of my eye. 'Let's go this way, Danny. We'll get some beautiful flowers and a very special message written for your beautiful wife, all in time for delivery on Monday.'

Chapter Thirteen

Ben

Five Days to Christmas Eve

The week stretches on and on as I count the days until it's Friday at last, the day when Ava and I are back on the road north to Ballyheaney House. We'll be there over Christmas, so I've packed up our presents for all the family and my ridiculously expensive decorations, much to both of our excitement.

Never in a million years did I think I'd ever be like this, but I feel a thrill and a rush every time I think of the upcoming party. The buzz of seeing our plans come together is already brightening my whole being.

'The primary school was absolutely delighted to be invited to sing in the welcoming reception,' Lou told me during the week, when we caught up before bedtime on the phone. 'So I've asked Mr Lowe, the principal, to prepare a selection of favourites as well as some upbeat singalongs we all know like "Jingle Bells". That will be a sweet and festive way to open the party. And the lady from the cancer charity is going to set up an information stall in the drawing room, where we'll also have some goody bags sponsored by a few local businesses. She'll drop those off the day before.'

'Gosh, you have been busy,' I said, sitting at the island in my kitchen. 'Well done on sorting all of that at such short notice, Lou. If you can let me know how many kids there'll be, I'll put down a reminder on my notes here to get them some chocolate treats for their contribution. I'm sure I can pull in a few favours close to me here too.'

I clicked my pen as I scrolled down my to-do list, wondering not only how I'd ever have managed without Lou, but also how unbelievably uplifting it was to be around her energy again. She always had filled me up with so much joy, no matter what was going on in each of our lives, but as much as we're progressing professionally, our personal connection is staying very cool and collected.

'I'm also waiting on confirmation from a jazz quartet as the main entertainment.'

'Jazz?'

'Yes, a four-piece jazz band, what do you think?' she asked. 'A piano, double bass, percussion and sax? I thought it would raise the roof and bring a totally different vibe from before, but in the best possible way.'

'Wow.'

'Wow exactly,' she said. 'We want this party to blow everyone's socks off, Ben. No half measures. Cordelia agrees that it's a good idea, but I told her I'd run it past you first of course.'

'You rock,' I said, knowing already this could be the best

Christmas Eve party ever. 'Or should I say, you jazz. Sorry, that was a horrible dad joke. But honestly, Lou. You've no idea how much of a difference you're making already.'

'My pleasure,' she replied. I could hear the delight in her voice. She was enjoying the party planning as much as she used to.

'Cordelia's canapé menu is outstanding,' I said, starting on my own list of updates. 'I've pulled in a sponsor for the ingredients, and a friend of a friend has agreed to donate a crate of sparkling wine. Mum says the local committee are sending some extra hands on the day to help with serving food and drinks, so we're covered in that department too, which is a relief.'

'Serving food and drinks just like we used to do when we were young and fresh-faced,' said Lou. I had an instant flashback to how in those early days we couldn't walk past each other in the ballroom without a cheeky touch or a playful word.

And now, with only five days until Christmas Eve, it's time to get planning in person again.

'Freya was so jealous when I told her I'm allowed to choose a playlist for the drawing room, Dad, but she has no idea of the work I'm putting into it all,' she says in the car as we travel up north at last. 'Lou told me to try and cater for all age groups and all tastes, and to keep it festive. Not to mention helping Grandma bake more gingerbread men this weekend after our first trial run was such a success. And I haven't even thought of what I'm going to wear yet.'

We drive along in silence at that, knowing that once again

Ava isn't like the other girls at school who get to go clothes shopping with someone who'll fuss over them and help them choose the right colour and style with perhaps a few arguments along the way.

It's not a sexist thing on my part. Some dads have a superb flair for fashion, but while I adore the idea of helping Ava with her wardrobe selection, I also know that no matter how cool I try to be, it's simply not my thing, especially as she approaches her teenage years. I'm out of touch. I know I'll only make her roll her eyes and get frustrated. Still, I can't help trying.

'Don't you have a really nice red sparkly—'

'Dad, please,' she giggles. 'I had that dress when I was ten. Aunty Vic gave it to her niece once I'd outgrown it.'

'I'm sure Vic would have helped you choose something. She has excellent taste.'

But my suggestion for Matt's wife to help is met with a deep sigh and more silence.

'I'd like to kind of dress differently when I'm older,' she says. 'You know, like Nana Molly, who works in Buds and Beans? She doesn't follow fashion, she told me. She creates her own.'

I can't help but raise my eyebrows. If I'm correct, Lou always questioned both her mother's and her grandmother's somewhat eclectic taste in clothing.

'There's nothing wrong with wanting to be unique,' I tell her, being as diplomatic as I can, but sure, what would I know?

'She told me last time I could hang out with her again in

the florist's,' Ava tells me. 'Maybe I could call in again this weekend?'

'Of course you can,' I say, feeling my insides glow. 'You can pick her brain on where she gets her clothes too, perhaps?'

Once again, I seem to have said something totally ridiculous.

'Nana Molly is like eighty or something, so even though I like her style, I don't think it's for me just yet,' she says eventually. 'I messaged Cordelia to ask her for ideas and she suggested she could paint my face with snowflakes and tiny Christmas trees. Dad, seriously. She still thinks I'm a baby when I'm practically a teenager now.'

'Practically,' I reply as I drive along to Chris Rea on the radio with a million plans in my head. As this is the last weekend before Christmas Eve, we need to keep everything rolling if we're going to be ready on time.

The heat is on, but I've a feeling that with Lou on board and Cordelia on catering, it's all under control.

For the first time in a long time, everything in my life feels in very safe hands.

'You're jittery, son,' Mum says as I walk around the rooms of Ballyheaney House with my clipboard in hand and a frown on my face. 'Is it because Lou is on her way?'

'Of course not,' I reply. 'Why would I be jittery over Lou? She's one of those friends where it feels like we've picked up where we left off. It's easy.'

'Gosh, it really is going to be like old times, isn't it?' she says, touching the walls as if they could talk back to us. 'Uncle Eric has spent all afternoon in his dressing room, deciding what to wear for her grand arrival, even though I've told him to stop fussing. As if Lou will even notice!'

'Ha, Lou always did love Uncle Eric's style.'

'Well, he's not one bit impressed with how he didn't know she'd been back in the village for the last six months working on Castle Street,' Mum tells me. 'You've no idea what I've had to listen to all day before you arrived. He was like a child, huffing and puffing at every opportunity.'

Roly follows me around at the same pace as my mother, sniffing into corners and whining at Uncle Eric's absence. I don't know what it is about my elderly uncle, but our dog adores him even more than he does me or Ava. And that's a lot.

'I'm with Uncle Eric on this one,' I say, stopping in my tracks. 'Are you honestly saying you didn't know she had opened a place on Castle Street? Or that she'd bought Katie's Cottage? Come on, Mum. I didn't come up the river in a bubble. Why didn't you tell me?'

Ava's dramatic interruption is timely.

'Quick, Grandma! Quickly! Dad! Help!'

Round two of the gingerbread men trial isn't going as well as last time, it seems, and the smoke alarm lets us know there's a disaster in the oven.

'The feet are burnt, Grandma,' cries Ava as my mother follows her back to the kitchen. 'All of them. We can save the heads and bodies but they're totally footless gingerbread men now, which is so embarrassing.'

As the smoke alarm sings and Roly howls like a wolf in its direction, Uncle Eric comes out of his dressing room in only his boxers and stands at the top of the stairs, scratching his head. I go to help Ava, only to see that Lou has arrived – but instead of receiving a warm welcome in the traditional sense, she is opening windows at the speed of light to let out the smoke.

'I rang the doorbell but there was no answer,' she calls out, waving a tea towel through the air. 'Then I heard the chaos, so I hope you don't mind me taking the initiative to try and help?'

The smoke alarm stops at last.

'Thank you!' I reply in relief.

'You're very welcome. All in a day's work.'

I make my way towards her, full of apologies for the commotion. She looks so young in her denim dungarees under a heavy khaki coat, with her dark hair falling over her face as usual and a red hat covering her ears.

'Your timing, as always, is impeccable. Thanks for saving us from the madness,' I say, greeting her with a friendly kiss on the cheek. 'Let's go say hello to Mum and Ava in the kitchen. Don't suppose you know how to rescue gingerbread men with burnt feet?'

But before we have taken another step, my mother and daughter arrive in the hallway to meet us, still flustered from the great gingerbread man rescue.

'How about some brightly coloured icing to give them winter boots?' Lou suggests to Ava, who looks truly heart-broken. 'Or you could always give each one a nice pair of Christmas socks to wear? Reds and greens and golds?'

Ava's eyes light up as she almost dances on the spot.

'That's the best idea ever!' she says. 'How did you think of that so quickly?'

Lou shrugs and gives Ava a high five.

'The best thing is,' whispers Lou. 'You can give them extra-long socks if their gingerbread *legs* are a bit burnt too. And have them mismatch just for fun.'

Ava raises her eyebrows and purses her lips tightly in thought.

'Sounds like you still have all the best ideas, Lou,' says my mother, extending her arms for a hug. 'Ah, you always were our secret weapon here at Ballyheaney House, not only at party time but in summer too. It's so good to have you back again. And it's so good that you'll be reunited with your old friend at long last.'

Lou and I exchange a shy glance.

'I agree,' I tell them. 'Uncle Eric is—'

'Uncle Eric is what?' I hear him interrupt as he scuffles down the stairs. 'Uncle Eric is very, very glad to see Lou Doherty again at long, long last, that's what Uncle Eric is. Hello, duck!'

Lou meets him at the bottom of the stairs and throws her arms around him in a huge embrace, making all the time between them instantly disappear.

'Hello, my old goose,' she replies. 'It's been far too long.'

'Our girl,' he mumbles into her shoulder. 'That's our sweet, sweet girl.'

I see Mum bite her lip and bow her head at the sight of their emotional reunion, so she takes Ava back to the kitchen to try out their new approach to festive gingerbread men, while I watch on with glee.

'How about we make ourselves useful?' asks Lou. 'No time like the present to get stuck in.'

Uncle Eric and I both roll our eyes.

'Some things never change,' I say to Lou. 'You have us marching to your tune already.'

'Well, I'm off to the kitchen, so, to count plates and glasses, is that OK, chief?' asks Uncle Eric, still licking his lips and clapping his hands.

We laugh as neither of us have appointed a chief, but I have a strong feeling he's talking to Lou.

'And Ben and I are going to take on our old job of stringing the fairy lights around the walls in the hallway,' she tells him. 'Then we'll switch them all on and toast this year's party, just like we always used to.'

Uncle Eric's fluffy white eyebrows bounce up and down. He sings 'O Come, All Ye Faithful' in a deep baritone as he walks away from us, which makes my heart sing too.

Moments later, I'm standing by a stepladder, handing a string of lights up to Lou.

'I can reach, don't worry,' she tells me. 'I know exactly where they used to be hung. It's like time has stood still, it really is. Uncle Eric and I used to do this in record time.'

I can hear laughter coming from the kitchen now that the

gingerbread men are back on track, Uncle Eric is clattering his way through the dishes and glasses, and out here it's just the two of us, like it used to be in the very early days all those years ago, when Lou and I were captains of this ship.

Until I left for university in Paris, that is. Then Uncle Eric and Lou became the dream team around here.

'Imagine after all this we plugged these lights in and they didn't work,' Lou says as she stretches as high as she can to tape them on to the walls. 'I hope you tested them out this evening like I asked you to, Ben. Your poor father spent far too long at the eleventh hour one year looking for replacement bulbs when someone bought the wrong ones.'

I think she is enjoying being in charge just a little bit too much, but I like it.

'Ah, I knew I'd forgotten something. Sorry, boss,' I reply, only to hear her gasp in response. 'I'm kidding! I haven't forgotten a thing. I'll have you know that I've been very efficient since I got here.'

'You could tell me anything,' she says. 'But the proof will be in the pudding. We'll soon find out.'

'I beg your pardon,' I say. 'I've dusted more cobwebs than I ever knew existed, I've cleaned down chandeliers and I've marked the walls with masking tape where they need a touch-up of paint, though that's Uncle Eric's next job. He just doesn't know it yet. And as I'm sure you noticed, I've draped the fir trees outside with what felt like a million lights, but we've waited for you for the switch-on as usual.'

She isn't going to let me get away with any bragging though.

'You're the best boy, Ben Heaney. The very best boy. Now, does that look OK?' she asks when she's fixed the last few inches of lights on to the walls. 'I've tried to keep each loop between as even as I can, but it's hard to tell from up here.'

I step back into the wide hallway, watching her every move as she examines her work with pride, but the pride I'm feeling is for her. The way she pushes her hair from her eyes, the way she squints when she's thinking. The way she asks for my approval even though we both know she'll do it her own way anyhow. The familiarity of every move she makes stirs up old feelings inside of me.

'It looks . . . it looks absolutely perfect to me, Lou,' I tell her. 'Great job. You'd almost think you'd done this before.'

She shoots me a friendly smile, then dusts off her hands and grips on to the top of the ladder to make her descent.

I instinctively rush to hold it at the bottom as she climbs down, which creates an intimate space between us, one charged with electricity and unspoken yearning.

'Take your time, I've got you,' I say, doing my best not to stare.

I feel my heart thump in my chest as her hands graze past mine on the way down. She reaches the final step, still within the circle of my arms, which makes every nerve ending in my body tingle.

She is taking her time. I am too. I close my eyes for a second, as the scent of her fills my senses. Her hair, her back, every part of her body is so close to me now. I can barely breathe.

She stops when she reaches the bottom step, but I don't

want to move a muscle. I get the impression that she doesn't either. I want to savour this brief interaction for all it's worth, for as long as we can possibly hold it.

'So, I've counted forty-five side plates and there's only twenty flute glasses, but we can get more of those from – oh, am I interrupting something?'

'Uncle Eric!' we both sing in unison, springing backwards.

'Not at all,' I say, as if I've been electrocuted on the spot. 'So, yes, that's so good to know. I'll write that down before either of us forgets.'

My hands are shaking as I grab my pen and clipboard from a table on the other side of the hallway. Lou looks like she might explode with giddy schoolgirl laughter, while I do my best to hold it together. We are both in our early forties, yet we reacted just now like we were teenagers again.

And it felt so good.

'I think we should get Cordelia on FaceTime now for our grand switch-on,' Lou suggests. This is the perfect distraction for Uncle Eric, even though I'm not sure exactly how much he saw just now.

'Great idea! I'll fetch Ava and Tilda from the kitchen,' he says with a wry smile. 'You two continue what you're doing in the meantime.'

'We're all done, honestly,' says Lou.

Uncle Eric waves back as he hobbles away. 'There's no hurry, is there?' he says, turning in our direction once more with a wink and a nod. 'It's been a long time since Ballyheaney House was lit up for Christmas like this, so we can wait another few minutes if we need to.'

'Seriously, we're all good,' I call out to him.

'We don't need to worry about a power cut, that's for sure,' laughs Uncle Eric, continuing on his way. 'There's enough electricity in this hallway alone to light the feckin' Eiffel Tower.'

I take a deep breath. My heart is thumping, so I excuse myself and go outside for some fresh air.

Lou doesn't follow. Maybe that's a good thing.

Chapter Fourteen

Lou

THEN

Christmas Eve, 21 Years Ago

Ben wasn't coming home for Christmas, which was probably a good thing after our conversation about creating space between us the year before. It had been hard not hearing from him as much as I used to, but we'd stuck to our plans, checking in only now and then with a quick catch-up rather than knowing each other's every move.

I missed him terribly though, and I know he missed me too. He'd tell me in the odd drunken text message, particularly on days that had meant something to us.

His staying away for Christmas meant I hadn't planned on being involved at Ballyheaney that year, but his sister wasn't letting me off that lightly.

'Oh come on, please, Lou,' Cordelia said when she turned up on my doorstep, begging me to jump on board at the last minute. 'Uncle Eric is like misery's mother without you.

Mum's bloody prize peacock Cleopatra was poached, so she's going round like a zombie, and my father is having a hissy fit because the front window got smashed by an errant tennis ball. I haven't admitted it was me and probably never will as I couldn't bear the incessant moaning. With Ben swanning around some Christmas market in Berlin this year with some girl, please come to Ballyheaney House and help me stay sane. I need you.'

I pictured Uncle Eric, forlorn with no one to bounce ideas off, and Tilda without her precious peacock, who she'd talked to like it was human. With Ben out of the picture, maybe I *could* have some festive fun with a family I'd grown to love almost as much as my own?

So I got dressed, we went foraging down by the lough for some greenery and bare twigs to dress the tables with, and I immersed myself in all things Ballyheaney House, safe in the knowledge that Ben was far, far away.

He'd dropped the bombshell of his German visit at Hallowe'en in a very hurried early-evening call when he'd rung to 'say a quick hello' as he waited on the Metro. He was rushing to a punk gig in the Pigalle area of Paris with some German classmates. In much less glamorous surroundings, I was dressed as Marge Simpson and was on my way to a fancy-dress party in the Students' Union, where I would drown my sorrows with a rather convincing Captain Jack Sparrow in the form of an American student called John Taylor.

'Tell me all about him,' Cordelia said when we took a breather from our duties on the day of the party. 'Is he lush? I can only hope he's as wonderful as you are.'

So I spilled the beans to her – not all of them, but enough to give her a good idea of my latest romance, which was turning into so much more.

Quiet, unassuming, charismatic John Taylor, with his long, flowing chocolate-brown hair, dimpled smile and electrifyingly smooth guitar licks, had caught my attention long ago, but I'd been doing my best to play it all very cool. Even his lecturers were bowled over by his gift of the gab and engineering expertise, both inherited from his Tipperary-born father who had raised him and his four brothers in Yonkers, New York.

We'd fallen into each other's company back in May at a drunken student party in the infamous Holylands area, the epitome of university life in Belfast, and when he'd kissed me against a staircase with a bottle of Buckfast tonic wine in one hand and a cigarette in the other, I'd got on with my life without dwelling on it.

It was nothing more than two students sharing a drunken snog at the end of a long night.

Until it happened again, and again, and again.

'I'm thinking of spending the summer in Ireland instead of going back home,' he told me a month later as we sat on a tartan rug in the Botanic Gardens, the sun bouncing off our skin and the smell of coconut tanning lotion mixed with the cheap beers we'd taken to share over my home-made sandwiches.

'You're not going home at all?' I asked him, sensing a pledge of commitment on the horizon.

'My landlord says he'd halve the rent cos I'd be doing him

a favour,' he explained. 'And aside from that I can gig in the bars in Belfast to earn some money.'

'Cool,' I replied. He leaned across and kissed my cheek, then rested his head on my shoulder. I gulped back some fizzy wine.

'I'd love to hang out with you more,' he said to me. 'We could go road-tripping? Visit my long-lost relatives down in Tipp.'

'It's a long way to Tipperary,' I said, thinking I was hilarious by referencing the famous song, but also wanting to buy myself some time with his suggestion. I knew what he was hinting at. He wanted us to be more exclusive, like a proper couple, rather than a week-by-week arrangement where we'd meet for a pint over lunch, or go to the cinema to break up the monotony of the Queen's University Library where most of us spent our evenings.

I changed the subject, my head filling with notions that if I did make plans with John, and Ben was home in summer, what would I do then? Could I make a commitment to someone else knowing that if Ben arrived back in Bellaghy, I'd find it impossible to stay away, despite our conversation the Christmas Eve before?

'This is no way to live your life, Lou,' said Catherine, one of my closest uni friends, when I tried to explain it to her. Catherine was a no-nonsense cello player from Newry who would often vocalise her frustrations with how I'd put everything on hold – holiday plans, seasonal adventures and now romance – in case Ben Heaney came riding into my life on his white horse, declaring his undying love and commitment to me once and for all. 'You make the call and never mind what Ben's doing for summer. What do *you* want to do?'

'I was hoping to see Ben, but I'm happy to keep up my lease on my digs here too and get a part-time job in the city,' I said. 'I'm teaching music two evenings a week already.'

Catherine seemed happy with that.

'Well, John is here in Belfast, Ben isn't. You'll be here in Belfast, Ben isn't. John is up for a proper relationship, Ben isn't,' she told me. 'You can't keep putting your life on standby for someone who is calling all the shots without giving you anything in return. It's hardly rocket science, is it?'

At nineteen years old, with my first full university year in Belfast closing in, I knew I'd a decision to make for my own sanity. But when I tried to broach the subject, Ben didn't seem to have the same urgency to see me as I did him.

Though my questioning was far from direct.

'Any plans yet for the rest of summer?' I texted him as I made my way to our weekly pub quiz. John would be there with all his mates, saving a space at the table for my later-than-usual arrival. 'I'm wondering if we'll get to see each other.'

'We'll see each other, for sure,' he messaged me straight back. 'I've a job lined up in Amsterdam on a building site with some lads from Berlin. Did I tell you about that?'

I'll never forget how my stomach lurched as the stretch of another summer so far apart loomed.

'No, you didn't tell me that,' I replied with a sigh. 'Sounds like fun.'

'You could come visit?' he wrote back within seconds,

probably because he was on his way to class or studying in a café or library somewhere. If he'd been with his friends, I'd have been waiting until the next day for a reply. 'Stay a while. I'd love to introduce you to the gang, Lou. Check out some flights and we can see what would work for us both.'

I sat down on a wall as I digested the ongoing casual nature of it all, watching the sun slowly glide behind tall grey buildings of Belfast city in the near distance. Something shifted within me.

Introduce me to the gang? Did that include this mysterious German girlfriend? He hadn't told me about her, but I was reading between the lines.

It was all so vague, so Ben, so I took it as the wake-up call I badly needed, even if it cut so deeply.

I felt empty. I felt further away from him than I'd ever felt before, but it was what we'd agreed, so I just had to run with it.

I smoked a cigarette while sitting on the wall, the tears rolling down my cheeks, then I took my time before I made my way to The Botanic Inn. John's eyes lit up as soon as he saw me, as if he'd been watching the door the whole time. He patted a seat beside him while his friends handed out pens and paper.

'Just in time, Lou,' John said, putting his arm around my shoulder. 'It's the music round first, so we'll be off to a flying start. We're calling our team "The Dejected".'

I faked a smile. They couldn't have been more accurate if they'd tried.

As the weight of Ben's studies became heavier, and my

own circle of friends in Belfast's music scene grew wider, our phone calls became even less frequent. John and I toured Ireland in a camper van during the whole of July, playing music around campfires and busking on the streets for extra cash to fund our next pit stop. It was wild, it was carefree, it was exactly what I needed at the time.

And from what I'd heard from Ben in his sporadic messages from Amsterdam, he was having the time of his life too.

Soon, I found that when something super exciting came my way, like when I was chosen out of hundreds to perform solo at a winter recital in the prestigious Waterfront Hall on Belfast's River Lagan, Ben wasn't around to take my call. And if he was, it was short, sweet and to the point.

'I'm so proud of you,' he said when I got to tell him eventually. 'Let's catch up soon. I suppose a few days in Paris is out of the question?'

Of course it was out of the question. His veterinary degree was a huge commitment, but my music was equally as important and time-consuming to me, not to mention how John and I were growing closer. Days rolled into weeks, and one weekend passed after another. Soon Ben and I could go without speaking properly for longer than I could once have ever imagined.

Yet, when I played at the winter recital in front of more than two thousand people at the Waterfront, including the Lord Mayor, I looked out at the audience still wishing I could see his face in the crowd.

'Focus on the people who are here, not on those who could be but aren't,' Catherine told me at the interval, so I did my best to focus on John, who was there with my mum and grandmother, clapping me on with enthusiastic pride.

'He's an angel!' Mum exclaimed when we finished our evening with a delicious Chinese meal at my favourite Asian restaurant after the concert. 'You two seem to have so much in common and I am obsessed with his accent. And his long hair! I like how he makes you laugh, Lou. That's very important.'

Ben made me laugh more, I thought, cursing myself for allowing such thoughts to enter my mind. Ben made me cry more too, I remembered. Well, the distance and silence between us made me cry, but John was there as a constant companion, always lifting me up when I needed it most.

Soon, we were spending more time together than we were apart, and by Christmas we were well and truly official.

Very official.

We said a tearful if temporary goodbye at Dublin Airport once our studies finished in December, and I made my way home to Bellaghy, wondering if the lure of Ballyheaney House would catch me in its net again as the party season drew closer.

Though as much as I had going on with John in Belfast, nothing could have prepared me for the pain of winter nights back home without having Ben close by to comfort me.

Now that I had John, maybe it was a blessing in disguise.

Yes, here I was, telling Cordelia all about my love story with John as the snow fell down outside, while secretly thinking it had always meant to be with her brother instead.

'I'm so happy for you, honey,' she said, but there was a sadness behind her smile. I had no clue how much she knew about Ben and me. Cordelia and her brother were close, but I wasn't sure how much they confided in each other when it came to matters of the heart.

Maybe that was a good thing for me. I left her to her kitchen preparations and went into the ballroom to finish setting tables, glad of the peace and quiet to gather my thoughts as ghosts of Christmas past danced around me.

I could see him in every corner. I could hear his laughter. I could feel his hand in mine as we slipped off to find a quiet space alone, year after year.

And just before I finished setting the table, I heard a commotion in the hallway.

I heard Ben's voice.

I heard raised voices, angry voices. Not the type of sound associated with Christmas Eve at Ballyheaney House.

My heart stopped as I went towards the ballroom door for a closer look. Why the hell was Ben home after all?

And on top of that, why were they arguing so openly in the hallway?

They must have forgotten I was here.

Chapter Fifteen

Lou

NOW

Four Days to Christmas Eve

'You guys are the best! The party is a sell-out!'

Cordelia is home, and it's like someone has switched on the big light above us when she bounds in to see me on Saturday morning not long after I've pulled up the shutters at Buds and Beans. Her bobbed, bleached hair is shaggy and still damp from the shower, despite the frost outside, and her glasses fall down her nose as she speaks. She is a breath of fresh air, just like she always was before.

'It's so good to see you!' I tell her, squeezing her tight then standing back to look at her like a proud big sister. 'Ben wasn't expecting you home until Monday!'

'Ah, what can I say, I had FOMO,' she says, pulling out a stool by the coffee bar.

'That's fear of missing out,' I explain to Mum, who is

pretending she isn't listening but is all ears as usual. 'Well, I'm so glad you're here. I'm sure your family are too.'

Cordelia has been keeping a close eye on ticket sales via the QR code link, as well as chatting daily with the post office staff, and with four days to go to the party it's a great result.

'I think my entire organs just did a somersault at the thought of it being just around the corner,' I tell her as I serve her a coffee. 'One hundred and fifty people, wow. And we've already covered all our costs with sponsorship, so hopefully we'll raise lots of money on the day to top up our total.'

Cordelia fills me in on the plans at her end. Ava, who has proven a dab hand on a design app, has created menus which have already gone to print, while Ben is on a wild goose chase this morning for their mother's Christmas present, according to his sister.

'He won't tell any of us what it is,' she says. 'I've guessed a thousand things, but he says I'm not even close. Did he tell you?'

'Why would he tell me?' I ask her.

'Because he used to tell you everything,' she says, her voice animated. 'I imagine that's the case again, no matter how much water has gone under the bridge between you two. Are you getting on well? Not that it's any of my business ... but when I mentioned your name to Ben, he seemed a bit coy.'

'Coy?' I repeat.

'Yes, coy,' she says, laughing. 'My big brother is a pretty

cool, strong and confident guy, but I swear he went a little bit quiet.'

'He has a lot on his mind,' I remind Cordelia. She gathers her coffee, keys and hat from the counter, pays for her coffee and bids us farewell for now.

'I've a lot to be getting on with too,' she says excitedly. 'I'll see you later, yeah?'

'Absolutely,' I tell her with a smile as I watch her skip out of the shop into Uncle Eric's car, leaving me to daydream about the evening before, when we'd switched on the festive lights.

It was breathtaking. It was the perfect distraction after our fumble by the stepladder when I thought Ben was going to make a move. Thank goodness Uncle Eric came in when he did.

'It's like a castle,' young Ava said when Uncle Eric had flicked all of the switches, lighting up the gardens and the front of the house. 'It's like a real winter wonderland. This is already the best Christmas ever, Dad.'

I watched as she cuddled into her father's side, his arm around her shoulder. He leaned down and kissed the top of her woolly hat, then we all clapped and cheered before Ben declared a movie night, where everyone would snuggle down to watch *Home Alone* in front of a blazing fire.

'Please stay, Lou,' Ava begged when I said I'd leave them to it. 'We have salt *and* sweet popcorn, and Uncle Eric is going to make nachos. You should try them. They're so good.'

I felt all eyes on me as I contemplated her kind offer, but I didn't want to overstay my welcome.

'I've a big day tomorrow,' I said, much to her disappointment. 'And I believe there's a very special young lady coming to help us in Buds and Beans in the afternoon?'

Ava brightened up immediately. 'Yes! Nana Molly said she never breaks a promise, so I'll be there by lunchtime if that's OK?' she replied. 'She expects it will be busy with everyone wanting flowers at the last minute for their Christmas celebrations. She said I could help with the hot chocolates too.'

Ben nodded along with Ava's plans, smiling.

'You do know that Buds and Beans is Lou's place, not her Nana Molly's,' he joked to her. 'Are you sure Ava won't get in the way?' he said to me. 'Tomorrow will be crazy for you, I'd imagine.'

'I think an extra pair of hands will come in very handy,' I replied.

'That's very kind of you all. It will be good for Ava too,' Tilda said. 'It will be nice for her to be around that strong female energy. I'm sure that you, Liz and Molly will look after her very well.'

Ben walked me to the door while the rest of his family prepared their snacks in the kitchen. Well, apart from Uncle Eric, who was already snoring in his armchair with the dog at his feet. I don't think the poor man had seen such activity around Ballyheaney House in a very long time.

'I honestly can't thank you enough for everything you've done for us already, Lou,' Ben said as we stood on the doorstep. 'Even Mum is like a different person. Uncle Eric too.'

I was hoping he wouldn't mention the moment at the stepladder. My heart raced at the thought of it.

'I'm enjoying it all,' I replied. 'It's given me a new lease of life too. Hopefully I'll hear good news from Gracie tomorrow and that will be the icing on the cake.'

Ben tilted his head.

'And if it isn't the news you're hoping for, we'll all get you through it,' he said. 'Every step of the way. I know it won't be the same, but I'll have your back. Whatever I can do to make it easier, I will.'

It had been a happy evening, a productive evening, and despite that heart-stopping moment in the hallway by the stepladder, I smiled all the way home, then after a long, hot shower I fell into the most satisfying sleep I've had in a very long time.

'Liz, can you help with some coffees while I tackle a few dishes? They're piling high.' Nana says to my mum during a much-predicted mid-morning rush in Buds and Beans. 'Where is everyone coming from this morning? A lot of strangers too, taking photos of their coffee and the chalkboards. As long as they don't photograph me this morning! We don't close until Tuesday, yet it's like the apocalypse is on its way.'

'I'm sure our Lou isn't complaining,' says Mum, who is stocking up our festive traybake selection. 'A bit of social media won't do this place any harm.'

'And did you see how many bags of shopping that blonde lady had?' Nana cries. 'The one who wanted a chai latte? I thought a chai latte was a place in the Far East, for crying out loud.'

'Nana, can you at least try to be a little bit more discreet?'

193

I say, laughing, on my way past. 'Ah, I think I'm going to run out of greenery for the big Ballyheaney House garland, but not to panic. I'll go foraging for more in the next day or so. And we're totally out of poinsettias too. This Christmas rush is very welcome, even if we're finding it hard to catch our breath.'

My feet are aching already, but it's not bothering me as much as it usually did as I watch the clock tick down to lunchtime. As soon as Ben gets back, he'll drop Ava off for an hour and hopefully I can show him how my floral centrepiece displays are coming on ahead of Christmas Eve on Wednesday.

'Lou, I know you're incredibly busy, but could I have a quick word?' Master Campbell asks me from his usual table when I rush past to carry on with my floral preparations. 'I can follow you so as not to disturb you too much. We can talk as you work.'

'Of course,' I reply, hoping he isn't sick or worried about something too serious. 'Come this way. Is all OK, Edward?'

It feels strange calling him by his first name, as he'll always be the schoolmaster to me, but after he's told me to at least three times, I feel it's only polite to oblige.

I walk towards my long workstation table at the back of the florist's, where a selection of elegant white roses, pine cones, greenery, gold ribbon and church candles are waiting for me to bring them together for the tables on Christmas Eve.

While the smell of fresh coffee from the far end of the store can be overpowering, I'm delighted that today the entire place smells of floral aromas and Christmas trees. All I need now is for Gracie to call with her final decision on where she plans to spend the holidays, and with luck, everything will fall into place in the way I am hoping.

Talk about leaving it to the last minute.

'So, it's nothing serious. Don't be worrying, but I've bought two tickets for the Christmas Eve bash at Bally-heaney House,' Master Campbell tells me in hushed tones, even though there's no chance anyone could hear him over the festive music, the coffee machine and the chatter from across the room.

'Oh yes?' I say.

'But that's the problem, you see,' he says. 'I bought *two*.'

The penny drops.

'Ah.'

'I think I did it out of sheer habit, Lou,' he says, his friendly face forlorn. 'I mean, I've never bought one ticket to anything in my life, so I automatically bought two as if I'd someone to go with. What a silly fool I am.'

I can barely look him in the eye, as his words resonate with me so much. When John and I parted ways in New York, I'd been so used to buying tickets for the two of us to see theatre shows and concerts, or even reserving a table for two in a restaurant, that it was hard to adjust. After a break-up or a bereavement, it's another slap in the face when you're reminded of how even the simplest things are so very, very different now.

'I don't think you're a silly fool at all,' I say. Suddenly, my nimble fingers feel thick and clumsy as I try to keep working as we're talking, like he suggested. 'I think a lot more people than you realise would understand your thinking totally. It's a long, difficult journey you're on, but you're doing so well.'

'Yes, yes, I suppose so,' he replies. 'I hope I am.'

'The event has completely sold out,' I tell him. 'So, if you want to leave your extra ticket with me, I can easily sell it on and give you your money back.'

He doesn't reply as quickly as I thought he might. Instead, he is looking over towards the coffee bar, where my mother and grandmother are in a heated debate over something or other as usual.

'Unless?' he suggests.

I wait for him to continue, but he doesn't.

'Aha!' I say, my eyes widening like saucers. 'Unless you ask someone to accompany you to the party?'

'Yes,' he says, brightening up already. 'That's what I was thinking.'

'Now, that would be a perfect solution,' I tell him. 'I imagine you might want to leave it until we're a little less busy, then pop the question. Everyone loves going to Ballyheaney House at Christmas – well, almost everyone – and I don't think anyone wants to make a grand entrance alone.'

'Not in a romantic way, of course,' he declares. 'That might be too soon, but then, time waits for none of us, does it?'

'Time waits for none of us,' I repeat after him. 'I say go for it.'

He shuffles from foot to foot, staring at my handiwork.

My hands have finally found their mojo again now that I know I've helped him find his way.

'I've been thinking about this all morning, Lou,' he says, 'so I hope you don't mind me running it by you for some clarity?'

'Of course not.'

'That's another thing I miss,' he says, his eyes following my hands as I arrange tiny white roses around a thick church candle. 'I don't have anyone to run things by, you know. We all need a second opinion now and then, but my son is so far away, and I always struggle with the time difference if I do need to ask him something.'

I stop what I'm doing and look him in the eye.

'You can always get a second opinion from me, Edward,' I tell him. 'Always. Any time. Please know that.'

He stands up straight and puffs out his chest, looking much more like the old schoolmaster I've admired for so long.

'I was hoping you'd say that, actually. Thank you, kindly. I'll hurry along now,' he says, his mouth quivering as he speaks. He clasps his hands together and gives a light bow in my direction. 'The world is a better place for people like you, Lou Doherty. I'll go for a walk by the lough and prepare my speech for later. Thank you.'

I watch as he makes his way through the shop and towards the coffee bar, where he says his goodbyes before fetching his coat and hat from the hooks by the door.

I can't help but wonder what his plans are for Christmas Day. Surely he isn't going to have dinner for one? Maybe his son and his family will surprise him by coming back here since it's his first without Agnes, but then New Zealand isn't exactly around the corner, and I'm told they spent at least a month in Ireland last year around the time of her passing and the subsequent funeral.

I get on with my work for the next hour or so, glancing at my phone every few minutes and hoping I'll hear of my own offspring's plans for Christmas, even if my gut tells me to prepare for the inevitable. It's Saturday, which means flights will be almost impossible to find, if not extortionately priced for Christmas, so as much as I'm holding on to the tiniest glimmer of hope, I've come to realise that Gracie's final decision had probably been made a long time ago.

'Penny for your thoughts?' I hear. 'That was a very deep sigh.'

Ben's arrival with Ava, who is already at the coffee bar making up a drink for a customer and being very generous with the marshmallows on top, has gone completely unnoticed while I was lost in thoughts of Gracie on the other side of the Atlantic.

'Sorry, I was miles away in my head,' I tell him. 'Literally. How are you? Is your mission impossible complete? You do look like the cat that got the cream.'

I do my best to ignore his sexy stubble, his woollen green jumper that shows off the definition of his arms, and his jeans that sit comfortably on his strong thighs.

'All organised, signed and sealed,' he says, his eyes dancing with excitement. 'It's a good one. Probably the best present I've bought this year by far, but she's my mother and she deserves it.'

I am deeply intrigued as well as impressed.

'Cordelia was here earlier,' I tell him. 'What a surprise to see her home early!'

'Yes, she nearly gave my mother a heart attack this morning when she called needing a lift from the airport. Of course, I had to go get her,' he says. 'But yes, it's so good to have her home earlier than expected. We're cruising along nicely with only four days to go.'

'And the whole thing's a complete sell-out, so now of course I'm wondering if my centrepiece displays are up to scratch,' I say. 'What do you think? I've gone for a church candle with white roses, pine cones and gold ribbon as well as a touch of greenery. And here's one I made earlier.'

I hold up one of my finished pieces, watching as he breaks into a smile and nods his head.

'Classy,' he says, unexpectedly taking my breath away with a glance in my direction. 'Last night was fun, even if you didn't take us up on our movie night offer. I can easily recite every word of every *Home Alone* movie by now, yet I still want to watch one every Christmas.'

'I remember how much you loved those movies,' I tell him. 'You're a sucker for a classic.'

'I suppose I am,' he says, looking round to make sure he's out of earshot. 'Look, I'd love to treat you for all your hard work, Lou. And please say no if you feel any pressure.'

'Don't tell me, you've chartered a plane to jet me off to the Maldives?'

'Not quite that, I'm afraid,' he says, 'but if you don't have any plans this evening, I'd like to take you for dinner. As a business meeting too, of course. No such thing as a free lunch, as the saying goes. We can go over everything one more time.'

I'm distracted by some commotion up by the coffee dock, so I down tools to see what's going on.

'That would be lovely,' I say to him with a hearty smile as I make my way to see what's going on. 'Let me just see if everything's OK up here.'

Ben follows me towards the front door, where Ava, my mother, my grandmother and a few customers have made a circle around someone, totally blocking the entrance to Buds and Beans.

'Crumb!' I exclaim, recognising Beth Sullivan's puppy before I even acknowledge the woman herself. 'Sorry, Beth. How are you? Come in if you can get past your fan club.'

They disperse, some covering their mouths with their hands at the puppy's cuteness.

'I think it's Crumb's fan club rather than mine, but I completely understand,' she coos. 'I don't blame anyone for marvelling at her cuteness. She's the best girl in the whole world.'

She lifts the puppy up to her face and closes her eyes as she snuggles in.

'I know if I ever need a crowd in here, I'll invite you and Crumb to be the special guests,' I tell her. I look behind me to see Ben watching on with a look of love in his eyes, which I imagine is for the puppy, or at least Ava's reaction as she circles us.

'Ava, darling, why don't you give your special customers

some space,' he says, coming closer. 'I apologise. My daughter is helping here today and is perhaps a little too keen.'

'She's fine,' Beth says quickly. 'Honestly. And besides, I'm not hanging around, as much as I'd love to. I only wanted to drop by to say thank you, Lou, for all you've done for Danny and me over the past week or so with your exceptional writing talent, not to mention the stunning flowers. I think you might have started a craze.'

'There's just no end to your talents, is there, Lou?' says Ben with a smile.

'She's like a marriage mender,' says Beth. 'I ordered flowers for my husband after we'd had a row about what gives me the ick, and Lou thought of telling him all the things I loved about him in a letter, which she read out. It worked a treat.'

I decide to take the compliment wholly, rather than brush it off like I usually do.

'I always did say she was magic! Lou, we'll catch up later when I come back for Ava,' says Ben. 'I'll text you the plan for dinner before then, OK?'

'Great, see you soon,' I call after him, before getting back to Beth and Crumb. 'Sorry, this place is crazy today. Can I get you a coffee or anything?'

Beth is barely listening though as her eyes follow Ben through the window until he gets into the car and drives off.

'I know I shouldn't be passing remarks as a happily married woman, but *hubba hubba*,' she says with a cheeky smile. 'There'd be no ick with him, I bet.'

I'm suddenly aware of Ava, but she's being kept busy by Mum and Nana, thank goodness, lifting empty cups from tables with a very important air about her. I notice she's wearing a little mascara and lip gloss and how she sings while she works. She's a sociable little thing, much more so than her sometimes quiet and reflective father. My throat stings when I think of how strange it is that here we all are, watching and admiring her, praising her efforts, yet the one person who should be cheering her on, isn't.

'Ben and I are very good friends,' I say to Beth. I don't know her very well yet, so I don't need to tell her any of my business, as much as she seems a very affable young woman. 'He's only human, so I'm sure he has icks aplenty like the rest of us.'

'True,' she says. 'Well, I'll be off then. I posted on Insta about your service like I said I would. I hope you don't mind?'

'Well, that explains a few things,' I tell her, patting the little dog before they leave. 'I'm sorry I'm distracted right now. I've so much on my mind. But it means a lot that you called in today. Thank you, Beth. And thank you for bringing Crumb in to brighten our day too. She's a very cute puppy, and so well behaved as well.'

Beth smiles, her red hair bouncing as she walks towards the door, before Ava stops her one more time.

'Is she a sausage dog?' she asks Beth, who seems more than glad to take questions about her precious pooch. 'I have a very old Labrador called Roly who is my best buddy.'

Beth leans forward to let Ava rub the puppy's head again.

'Yes, a ten-week-old dachshund, so she's still very brand new to me,' she says. 'Her brother was meant to go to a neighbour of ours, but they changed their mind, so I'm tempted to take him too if no one else does.'

My eyebrows raise and my ears prick up. My mother's do too, even though it looked like she was in a deep conversation with another customer by the counter.

'Would you mind giving me the owner's details, please?' Mum asks. 'I might know someone who would be interested, once they've thought it through properly.'

I take a deep breath, knowing I'm going to have to dig deep for self-control over this one.

'Are you going to get the boy puppy, Liz?' Ava asks my mum, clasping her hands while balancing on her tiptoes. Beth is scribbling down details on a napkin.

'Not me,' Mum replies. 'Just someone else I know who might need a friend. I've done enough research to know that these dogs are very adaptable, and they adore one-to-one company, so it's certainly worth an enquiry. Thank you, Beth.'

'You're most welcome,' she says. 'But remember, a dog is for life, not just for Christmas.'

'I couldn't have put it better myself,' I call after her, wondering who she reminds me of with her confident stance and natural beauty. 'Right, kids, let's get back to work. Are you having fun, Ava? Don't let them boss you around too much while I'm busy down the back.'

Ava giggles, already wiping down tables. She is loving this, I can tell.

'When I'm older, maybe I can work here for real?' she asks me. 'Dogs and hot chocolate and Christmas treats. I love this job.'

I feel like giving her a hug, but I know I don't know her quite well enough just yet. Nana Molly is busy cleaning cups in the back room, unaware of the party proposal that's coming her way, Mum is gaga over a puppy, and little Ava is singing as she works.

With Cordelia home early, and Ben's dinner invitation, so far today has been full of surprises.

Chapter Sixteen

Ben

In the evening, I drive on to the lane at Katie's Cottage, around the back by the row of whitewashed outhouses, and I leave the car engine running while I wait for Lou. Our table is booked for 7.30 p.m., so I'm a little early, but our plan is to take our time over a drink first before we make the short walk from Doc's Bar to The Taphouse, another local place that's full of memories for both of us.

Katie's Cottage is a treat for the eyes, no matter from what angle you look at it. I imagine it's like a Tardis inside, with all the nooks and crannies from days gone by, as well as a modern-day renovation that has still managed to keep all the old-world charm of the place.

It was once a milking farm according to my late father, with crops of potatoes and vegetables in the adjoining fields, but now the thick white stone walls frame a perfectly mani-cured garden.

My mind drifts back to the day Lou and I spent a rare day in summer together, before everything went terribly wrong between us. I'd come back from my studies in Paris for my father's sixtieth birthday and, as chance would have it, Lou was back at home after touring around America.

'Since it's usually either lashing with rain or snow is thick on the ground when we're together, how about we do something totally different when we can?' she suggested to me. 'Any ideas?'

She was eighteen then, I was just a year older, and we thought we'd all the time in the world to be together when it suited, both believing that a future together was inevitable.

'I could borrow my dad's car and we could hit the coast for a beach day?' I said, but I knew there was something else on her mind by the way she scrunched up her face. 'Too obvious? I love how you ask me for suggestions when you've already a very firm plan in that clever head of yours.'

She led me to the bike shed at Ballyheaney House, where we found Cordelia's old Raleigh as well as my Cannondale, which was barely used. Then we raided the fridge and packed a picnic of home-made sandwiches, fruit and a bottle of fizzy wine before we hit the roads of Bellaghy, stopping off right here at Katie's Cottage along the way.

'There she is,' she marvelled, waving at an elderly lady who was washing the windows. 'That's Katie, or Kathleen, who owns the place. Isn't it the most precious place you've ever laid eyes on?'

'It's special,' I said, already calculating how much it would take to renovate and modernise the cottage from what I could see from afar.

'My dream is to live here one day,' she told me, her eyes

like saucers as she drank in its beauty. 'But I know it will probably never, ever come up for sale. Not in my lifetime, anyhow.'

Yet here she is.

I spot her through the white net curtains that hang on the sash windows, just like Katie had back in the day, but when I look closer I can see that she's on the phone, so I sit back and turn up some music while I wait.

Seconds later though, I look again to see how she's wiping away tears while trying not to ruin her make-up. Should I go inside to see if she's OK? Or should I mind my own business and give her space to come out to me in her own time?

I decide to wait, but I can't help glancing in every few seconds in case she needs me.

'Are you and Lou going on a date?' Ava had asked me before I left Ballyheaney House only a few minutes ago. She, Mum and Uncle Eric had big plans for an evening of board games and gnocchi, as his Italian theme in the kitchen continued. 'Or is it only a dinner meeting about the party?'

I looked towards my mother, who just shrugged her shoulders while Uncle Eric waved his hands, which told me I was getting no input or advice from them on how to answer.

Not so long ago, Ava had been very keen for me to date, and for a time she was as bad as my friends Matt and Vic as she threw names around like confetti.

The lady who worked in the corner shop. The one off the telly who presented the weather. Everyone, it seemed, was fair game.

Until I tried out dating, that is. Then she couldn't

decide if she wanted a person she hadn't even met to be her stepmother instantly, or if she wanted to keep me all to herself.

So, even though she's on the verge of becoming a teenager now, I'm reminded to tread carefully.

'Lou is a very dear friend to me,' I tell my daughter. 'She is very kind and very funny too, but we have a lot of planning still to do for the party. And I promise you that if I ever go dating with anyone, you'll be first to know.'

Mum nodded her head and kept quiet, as did Uncle Eric. Ava too seemed pleased with my response, but she wasn't letting it go that easily.

'I bet she'll look very pretty,' she said. 'I really like her style.'

'And if you do decide it's a date and not a business meeting,' my mother said to me, 'you can let yourself in quietly. We won't wait up either way.'

From what I can see from the car, Ava was bang on with her prediction. Lou is wearing red, which was always her colour with her dark hair. I wish I knew what has upset her though.

What could it be? Has she had bad news?

And then it dawns on me. Gracie has decided to stay in New York for Christmas. That will be it, for sure.

I get out of the car and make a dash through the rain for the back door of the cottage, then I quietly make my way into the living area where Lou now rocks back and forward on an old-fashioned floral armchair, still talking to her daughter.

'I'm not crying. I think I've got a bit of a head cold, that's all,' she sniffles, even though I can see the tears in her eyes. 'And you've no need to cry either, Gracie, my love. I'm happy for you. I said from the beginning that whatever you chose, I'd be right behind you every step of the way.'

She signals to me to have a seat, so I do so on the armchair across from her, already wishing I could do something to ease her pain. She used to love a cup of hot tea with sugar when she was feeling low, but she might not take sugar in her tea any more. She might not even take tea any more. Plus, I've never set foot in her new home before now, so I don't want to be presumptuous by rooting around her kitchen.

'Yes, of course I'm disappointed, but I'll be fine,' she tells her daughter. 'No, no, you don't need to make any plans yet for your next visit. You're a busy girl and this is a big year for you with your studies. Let's take everything one step at a time. I'll see you very soon, baby, I promise. We'll make it happen. We have lots more happy times to look forward to, you'll see.'

She hangs up and puts her head in her hands, letting her true feelings show.

'I'm so sorry, Lou.'

'Can I get you anything?' I ask her. 'Tea? Or wine? Water, even?'

She looks up at me, her beautiful eyes smudged with black mascara.

'No, I'm fine, but thank you. I'll go and fix up my face and we'll get going,' she tells me. 'If we hang about here for much longer, I'll be a bigger mess and I won't be in a fit state to go out. I've been looking forward to our dinner all day, so I don't want to sit here and stew or it will make matters worse.'

I stand up at the same time as she does.

'You don't have to go if you don't want to.'

'I do want to,' she says, then she breaks down and properly sobs her heart out. I can't just watch her cry like this, so I sit beside her and I smooth down her hair and hush her like I used to do in the old days.

'I held on and held on, but deep down I knew it would come to this,' she says through her tears. 'I saw it coming as time ticked on, yet I still held on to hope, even with only a few days to go.'

'That's totally understandable,' I say.

'I mean, how naïve of me to think I'd have her all to myself when I moved here?' she asks. 'Gracie can't split herself in two when it comes to special occasions. I've created this horrible, heartbreaking situation where we're oceans apart at Christmas. I put us in this mess by moving away.'

I put my hand on her cheek and wipe away her tears.

'Please don't blame yourself for starting a new chapter,' I say to her. 'You've made a very big dream come true by coming here, Lou. Gracie wouldn't want that, and you don't deserve it either.'

'It really hurts, Ben.'

'Yes, and it's OK to be sad,' I say to her softly. 'Distance is hard, but it doesn't in any way take away the love and emotional connection you have with your girl. This is part of growing up, isn't it? You give them wings and then they fly. And you love it but you hate it too. You and Gracie have so much still to look forward to.'

She looks up at me, her lips still trembling as she does her best to pull herself together.

'I left here at twenty-one for New York, almost the same age as she is now, and I only ever came back home twice for Christmas,' she reminds me. 'I never for one second thought of how my mother felt being so far apart, but now I know what she was hiding. I'm hurting, but I only ever want what's best for Gracie. If she's happy, then I'm happy too, even if the rejection stings like a bitch.'

I can't help but laugh just a little.

'She isn't rejecting you, Lou, I promise,' I tell her. 'She probably tossed a coin or something similar to help her make a very tricky decision. And no matter which way the coin fell, someone was going to be hurt. This time it's you, next time it will be her dad.'

'She put both our names in a hat,' she says.

'I thought as much,' I tell her. 'Now, as pretty as your home is from what I've seen so far, I think you're looking way too good to be kept indoors, so how about you go get sorted and I'll wait for you in the car?'

'OK.'

'Let's go and have a wonderful evening together, best we can.'

She stands up and blows out a deep breath.

'I'll be right there,' she says, making her way out of the sitting room through a latched door while I go back outside and warm up the car for her.

The restaurant is thronged with couples, family get-togethers and the odd staff party when we get there, all adding to the bustling, festive atmosphere and the perfect place to lift the spirits.

With our later-than-expected arrival, we've decided to forgo our pre-drinks and go straight to our table, which is ready and waiting. It's just as warm and friendly there as I remember, even if the decor has changed to a tasteful brown and gold, made all the cosier with lit-up garlands along the walls and a vintage Santa Claus as a quirky centrepiece by the modern bar.

'I'm tempted to go all out and have the Christmas dinner,' Lou says as she scours the options on offer once we've ordered drinks and heard the special dishes of this evening. 'Everything looks so good, I can't decide.'

'That's a good sign. Take your time,' I say to her. 'I've never seen you wearing glasses before. You suit them.'

She catches my eye above the menu, flashing a very sultry smile. I already know I'm in trouble. I knew this might be the case in such an intimate setting. It's one thing going for a drink together, but sharing a table for two over dinner puts us in an entirely different realm.

'This is surreal, isn't it?' she says.

'Surreal? Yes, I suppose it is,' I reply. 'Did you ever think this would happen again?'

She lays the menu down and takes her reading glasses off.

'It depends on what *this* is,' she says, firing the loaded statement at me.

I know exactly where she is coming from, but it's a bit early in the evening for old wounds to seep through.

'This. Us.'

'If you mean us spending time together,' she says, 'then yes, I thought coming back here upped the odds of our paths crossing at some point.'

'It's nice,' I tell her, doing my best to keep things as light-hearted as possible, even though she's had a tough start to the evening.

'Yes, it's very nice,' she says, unable to hide her smile. She takes a sip of her wine. 'I never thought we'd share dinner alone again, Ben. No. I didn't ever allow my mind to go there. It was too much to handle, but I did imagine seeing you again. I enjoyed that fantasy a lot. The rest I couldn't cope with.'

I can only agree.

'So, what's it going to be then?' I ask, swiftly refreshing the conversation before we find ourselves on murky roads. 'Turkey, ham and all the trimmings? I'm tempted by the fillet steak.'

'Now, there's a surprise,' she jokes.

'Some things never change,' I reply. 'Do you remember when we came here one year on the night before the party?'

She lights up at the memory.

'How could I forget?' she says. 'We sped through the final preparations like Tasmanian devils to get here before they closed.'

'You gave me a Pink Floyd vinyl.'

'Wasn't that the year before?'

213

No, it was that year because I remember I'd bought you a fine gold chain I'd picked up in a market in Bali.'

'With a turquoise stone,' she recalls.

'That's the one.'

'I still have it, you know.'

'The necklace?'

'Yes, the necklace,' she tells me. 'I never wore it since, but I kept it tucked away and when I moved back here six months ago, I found it in Mum's house right where I'd left it, at the back of the drawer in my bedside locker.'

I feel my heart soar, even if we are picking at scabs in a way I'm uncomfortable with. I can't believe she kept it.

'We have so much old ground we could go over,' I say, hoping to nip this conversation in the bud. 'But like you say, we are where we are now, so let's try and enjoy the present.'

'Yes, and since we've twenty-plus years of life experience behind us, we should hopefully be a lot more mature than we were back then,' she says.

We both hold up our hands in agreement, then make a 'peace out' sign which makes us laugh. It used to be a regular signal between us when we wanted to be friends again after a petty argument.

'Thanks, Ben,' she says to me after a few moments of silence.

'Thanks? What for?'

'This,' she says. 'Tonight. Everything. For asking me to help out with the party. For being you in the way I always loved and remembered. I know I'm being a bit of a nettle over

Gracie, but I can't tell you how much I enjoy being around you again.'

'Ditto,' I tell her.

'You always seemed to have this way of helping me find the right track, or at least you made me feel like my world wasn't *actually* falling apart when I thought it was. Thanks for what you said earlier about Gracie too. It helped me a lot.'

I raise a glass and we clink together, in a quiet nod to whatever comes next for Lou and me. She orders monkfish with a total change of heart, which is so Lou Doherty, while I stick to my fillet steak, and as we eat together, we fill in the many gaps of what we'd learned and loved about the twenty years before.

'It's the morose stares that get to me,' I tell her, making a very sad face to illustrate my point. 'And they're still everywhere. The school gates were the worst, and don't even start me on parents' night. Or the Christmas concert when in junior school. Ava always seemed to have a lead role, making it even more of a pity party, but people forget you've got functioning ears when you're a single parent. The kindness, don't get me wrong, that was immense too, but the whispers of pity have become a little bit tiring, especially in front of the child.'

Lou covers her mouth as she tries to chew and laugh at the same time.

'I know my situation was different, but sometimes it was no easier in New York, believe me,' she says, much to my surprise. 'I sent Gracie to the smallest school I could find in

Brooklyn, where I even made it on to the PTA. There were all sorts of families at that school, yet when it came to the crunch, the kids with anything other than a standard mum and dad and a white picket fence were looked upon ever so slightly differently.'

'In Brooklyn?'

She pauses, fork in mid-air.

'Actually, no,' she says with a giggle. 'But I felt it was like that. Only because it was common knowledge among parents that John had made off with Gracie's kindergarten teacher. Yes, *that's* what made me a prime case for morose stares.'

We both make a pitiful face at the same time, which makes us burst out laughing again when we stop.

'What is it about us?' she asks me when we finish our main course. 'Even after all this time, there's no one and I mean no one in this whole world that makes me feel like you do, Ben Heaney?'

I smile at how she uses my full name.

'Ditto,' I tell her. 'I feel like that when I'm around you too. Maybe it's because we fit.'

'We fit? You always used to tell me that. You still think so?'

'Yes,' I say, doing my best to think of how to explain it further. 'We understand each other in a way that can feel intuitive. Everything feels effortless and right, like we can communicate without having to say the words. You get me, and I get you. I suppose that's it in the simplest terms. We're not perfect, but we fit.'

She reaches across and grabs my hand.

'How about we buy some ice cream in the supermarket,

grab a bottle of something nice and take it back to my place?'
she asks me with a twinkle in her eye. 'I'd love to show you
around some more.'

I shift in my seat, my eyes searching for the waiter to grab
our bill.

My voice croaks when I try to speak.

'I think – I think that's an excellent idea,' I tell her.

'If you're in no hurry to get back to Ballyheaney House
tonight.'

I raise an eyebrow. 'I'm – I'm in no hurry to get back to
Ballyheaney House tonight,' I reply.

'I was hoping you'd say that,' she says. 'After a very delicious dinner, I'm feeling in the mood for dessert.'

I wasn't expecting this at all. My hands shake. I can barely
pay the bill quick enough, especially when I look at her glowing so happy by my side.

The cold barely touches me when we make our way out
on to the street, and with every step we take, the distance
feels unbearable.

I stop on the footpath. She does too. And then, without
saying a word, she comes into my arms and we kiss.

It isn't gentle, not at first.

Instead, it's everything we haven't said for over two decades. All the longing, the ache, the what-ifs, crash into this
single, breathless moment.

My hands cup her face, my cold fingers warming against
her skin with her mouth on mine like it has been so many
times before. And like before, when we are together it feels
like there's no past or future, only now. Only us.

'My God, I've missed you, Lou,' I tell her, looking into her eyes as the snow falls down. 'I've thought of kissing you again so many times, never knowing if it would happen.'

'I've missed you too, Ben,' she tells me, her eyes smiling. 'Can we do it again?'

'I was hoping you'd say that,' I reply, before our lips meet again, more slowly this time, though as sensational as ever.

But there's something I need to tell her. Something I hope she'll understand. Something from the past that might hurt her enough for this kiss to be our first and last in so long.

'Let's go back to the cottage and get warmed up,' she says to me, her enthusiastic smile making my insides swirl. 'Now you've started that, you've left me wanting more and more.'

We walk towards a waiting taxi, hand in hand, and it's like I'm walking on air.

I only hope she can forgive me for what I'm going to tell her next.

Chapter Seventeen

Lou

THEN

Christmas Eve, 21 Years Ago

Ben was home after all.

He hadn't told me. He hadn't told anyone, from what I could hear coming from the hallway.

I held my breath behind the huge ballroom door, praying I didn't cough or sneeze or make any other sound to suggest I was within earshot. It's not that I wanted to pry. I simply didn't have anywhere else to go.

'You had no need to cancel your plans in Germany, Ben,' Tilda cried. 'We have it all under control, don't we, Jack?'

Uncle Eric was talking so fast I couldn't make him out entirely, but when Jack Heaney shut him down it became loud and clear.

'Eric, with all due respect there's nothing you can do to help the situation. There's more at play here than you know, so keep your opinions to yourself,' said Jack. I'd never heard him talk so much in all the years I'd known him. His voice was gruff but laced with emotion. Whatever was going on, it wasn't for the faint-hearted.

'I'm a Heaney too!' said Uncle Eric, who was more than capable of holding his own, it seemed. 'If you've made a balls-up on the stock market and our family home is at stake, I deserve to know the detail!'

'For God's sake, tell us the truth, Dad!' Cordelia shouted over them all. 'There's no point beating around the bush when there's over a hundred people due to come here in two hours. The musicians have just arrived outside, my waiting team from the catering college are on their way, and the charity is expecting this to be a big hit, so we're not pulling the party no matter how bad it is. For crying out loud, just tell us.'

My hands are clammy and my breath quickens from my hiding place on the other side of the wall. Have they really forgotten I'm in here? Surely Cordelia can't have when not so long ago I was spilling my heart out to her about how I'd met John.

Oh my God, John.

I closed my eyes, willing my mind to picture his face instead of only seeing Ben's. John's presence always calmed me down when I needed him the most. He made me laugh too, and I'd come to miss his sincerity and his one-liners since we'd said goodbye for Christmas. I'd no business being caught up in this family drama with the Heaneys. Ben Heaney was in my past; John Taylor and all our plans were my future.

So why, more than anything in the world, did I long to hold Ben closely and tell him that whatever was going on with his family, it was going to be all right?

'There's no way I can stand here and pretend this isn't happening while the whole village takes over our home,' bellowed Jack. 'It's a farce at this stage. The whole thing is a farce, keeping up the pretence that we're some sort of heartbeat of the village when the reality couldn't be further from the truth. Never mind raising funds for charity, we can barely afford to keep the lights on!'

'It's hardly that bad, don't exaggerate, Jack,' said Tilda almost under her breath, but still loudly enough for me to hear. 'You're frightening the children.'

'We're not children, Mum,' Ben chimed in. 'I'm twenty-one years old. I deserve to know if my family's finances are about to put us out on the street! This is our home, Dad. What are you saying? Are you really in so much trouble that we can't afford to keep the house going?'

'I said I can help!' shouted Uncle Eric.

'I don't want your help!' shouted Jack in return. 'I will sort this mess out myself. I created it, so I will sort it!'

Jack's mouth was tight and his face reddened like I'd never seen before.

'Don't shout at your brother when he's offering to get us out of a mess that, like you say, you created, Jack Heaney,' said Tilda in a tone I'd never heard her use before. 'If you're selfish enough to risk it all to feed your habits behind my back, then be man enough to accept help when we need it.'

I had to get out of there. I looked across the room,

wondering whether, if I opened the window, I could slip out on to the lawn without falling and causing myself an injury. It was absolutely freezing outside, so the thought of lying in the frost without as much as my coat on was a risk but perhaps one I'd have to take. I didn't want to hear any more.

But would they really cancel the party? Whatever Jack Heaney had done with the family finances, it had caused him so much shame he seemed to think that was the best idea. I felt sorry for them all already. The Heaneys were revered in this village, deeply admired and respected for their philanthropy and dedication to making it a better place, with their regular donations to local schools and churches.

'I'm begging you, Dad,' said Ben. I could tell he was doing his best to stay calm. 'Let us go ahead with the party as planned. We've gone too far to call it off, and if we do, it will spark off more rumours and gossip than we need right now. Let's all stay cool, get this afternoon over with and we'll have a family meeting afterwards where we'll decide whether or not to accept Uncle Eric's help on this occasion.'

'I'm not accepting a handout from my younger brother!' said Jack. 'I'll get another job if I have to.'

Boy, he was more stubborn than I'd thought.

'Well, it's not only up to you, is it, Jack?' said Tilda a lot more calmly. 'We'll deal with this absolute fiasco later. Ben's right. We can't call off the party. It's too late. Let's paint on our happiest faces and never breathe this to another. No one and I mean *no one* outside of this family needs to know a single thing about what we've discussed or the trouble we are in.'

I heard them mumble in agreement.

'Even if I win the lotto, this will be the last party here at Ballyheaney,' said Jack. 'I'm on the verge of a bloody heart attack and I'm going to have to pretend I'm on top of the world.'

'With all due respect, Dad,' Ben suggested, 'why don't you sit this one out, yeah? Go upstairs and close the door until it's all over. To be honest, I think after the mess you've made it would make it easier on all of us.'

There was a period of silence that felt like forever.

'Lou!' I heard Cordelia say as if she'd just remembered I was there.

Oh no.

I scurried across to the centre of the room where the long banquet table was already looking immaculate and started polishing cutlery like my life depended on it.

The ballroom door burst open. I wished I had headphones or something so that it looked as though I hadn't heard a thing, but the expression on Jack Heaney's face said it all.

He knew I'd heard every single word.

'You can go now, Louise,' he told me. He wasn't rude, he wasn't cross. He was just very much to the point. 'This is a family matter, and you aren't family.'

I nodded in his direction and walked past him as he stood in the doorway.

'Dad! Lou needs to stay for the party!' cried Cordelia.

I couldn't look her in the eye.

'I said this is a family matter,' said Jack, and turned to go upstairs. Tilda walked away with her head down, while Uncle Eric followed Jack. In many ways, I was glad to be making an escape. The party was destined to be a disaster with such an atmosphere in the house.

'Wait a minute! Lou!' Ben called after me as I got my coat in the hallway and made my way outside as quickly as I could. 'Lou, I need to talk to you. Lou, please don't go.'

'Don't listen to my father,' Cordelia cried out to me. 'Lou, come back. We need you. I don't care what you heard! I know you won't say a thing! Lou, the party?'

My heart was thumping. Never in a million years did I think I'd exit the Heaney household like that on Christmas Eve, when it had always been the most special day of the year.

Never in a million years did I think I'd have Ben running after me while I made my way to the car, declaring his feelings once and for all.

'Please, Lou, I love you,' he said, following me through the sleet towards my car. 'I came home to see *you*. Not for that shitshow, but to see you. Please, Lou!'

I could barely catch my breath, so I waited for him by the car, ignoring the cold that cut through me.

I decided to hear him out, but there was something I had to tell him too. Something that would change everything.

'I love you, Lou,' he said. 'Forget what I'd planned for Christmas in Germany. I couldn't do it. I couldn't do Christmas without you. Please tell me you feel the same.'

I loved him so much too.

If only I could find the words to tell him this was far too little, far too late.

Chapter Eighteen

Lou

NOW

Three Days to Christmas Eve

When Cordelia Heaney unexpectedly knocks on my yellow door at Katie's Cottage late Sunday morning, it's almost like history repeating itself. Only this time, she has no idea how exhausted, confused and ever so slightly hungover I am from the night before when Ben and I had dinner.

'Seriously, Lou, how bloody gorgeous is this cottage?' she cries after almost squeezing me to death on the doorstep. 'I'm jealous, I can't lie. Every time I come back home, I'm more and more convinced of how I want to find my proper place in the world back here on Irish soil. I'm thirty-nine years old, so it's really time I knew what I was doing with my life.'

I think she's selling herself short. Cordelia has long been admired for living the kind of carefree, nomadic life that many others yearn for.

'Don't be so hard on yourself,' I tell her. 'You're a highly sought-after freelance chef, you've lived and worked in some of the most beautiful cities in the world, and you've a family who are immensely proud of you. Not to mention a niece who idolises you too. She's been counting the days until you get here.'

Cordelia doesn't seem convinced.

'I get all that and I appreciate every bit of it, but you know when something isn't filling your soul any more, no matter who you meet or what you do?' she says.

'I know exactly what you mean.'

'Anyhow, I'll figure it out,' she tells me. 'Christmas always makes me nostalgic, so I'll soon snap out of it or finally give myself the kick in the ass I need to do something about it.'

I go to make a pot of coffee, then set it down on the table with some shortbread from Buds and Beans and a small selection of chocolate brownies. Two empty wine glasses sit on the draining board. Grey ashes from last night's turf fire lie in the grate. If Cordelia hadn't unexpectedly called in when she did, I'd probably have given in and curled up on the sofa, licking my wounds.

'Hopefully you'll get to relax over the holidays, once the embers of the party die down,' I say to her. 'Sometimes, stepping out of your own world and letting your brain switch off can spark the best ideas.'

She nods in agreement as she indulges in one of my American-influenced brownies.

'I've been *longing* for a walk by Lough Beg to clear my head for weeks now,' she tells me. Then she stops mid-chew, as if she's studying my face properly for the first time since she got here. 'Oh my goodness, Lou, I don't mean to be rude, but you look exhausted.'

I was hoping she wouldn't notice my red eyes. As much as I was thrilled to see her, I was partly hoping she wouldn't stay very long so I could crawl under a duvet and flick through Netflix, even though I was already showered and dressed, doing my best to plod on and face the day ahead.

But the conversation from the night before has been replaying again and again in my mind like an old movie. As I struggle with how I'm feeling about what he told me, I can still hear every syllable he said as clearly as if he were sitting here now. I was lost for words at first.

After our heart-stopping kiss on the street outside the restaurant, we'd cuddled in the back seat of the taxi all the way home while I sang along in cosy bliss to Shakin' Stevens on the radio, wondering what my younger self would have made of the evening we'd just had.

'Say something, Lou,' Ben had pleaded with me when he broke the news not long after we'd got to the cottage.

I thought it was a joke at first. I think I may have even laughed, but the way he held both my hands and looked into my eyes brought me up sharp. He was very serious. It was true.

Everything had been heading in the direction we'd both dreamed of until he'd started to confess to something that I know I've no right to be upset about deep down.

But he'd lied to me. And about her, of all people.

'Olivia Major,' I repeated. I let go of his hands and stared

227

into the dancing orange and yellow flames from where we were sitting on a rug by the fire. 'You and Olivia? Together? You spent years saying you couldn't have a long-distance relationship with me, yet you went the distance with her as soon as I was off the scene? Ben! How could you?'

'I'm sorry!'

'But I asked you last week if you'd ever seen her since and you said no,' I reminded him. 'You looked horrified at the very idea, yet now you're telling me that only days after we said goodbye you were with her – not once but lots of times. That you were a *couple*. You were in a proper relationship. How? Why?'

He closed his eyes.

'Revenge, maybe?' he said, his voice dropping to not much more than a whisper. 'That, mixed with a spurge of hot-blooded hurt and a young, busted ego after that last horrible scene at the party, I guess.'

I was puzzled.

Olivia was a beauty, there was no doubt about that, but Ben couldn't stand her. He couldn't bear to be around her for more than about five minutes, and most of all he knew every detail of how she'd done her best to bully and belittle me that Christmas at Ballyheaney House, humiliating me at every turnaround.

'You were a couple,' I said, my brain unable to process it. 'We never were a couple. It was all I ever wanted, but for years you said you couldn't do it. Not while you were in a different country. Yet you instantly made it work with her.'

'It's like I'm being stabbed every time you say that,' he told me. 'Look, I swear it was meant to be nothing, but time went on and it turned into something before it became nothing again. It was nothing!'

'Please don't say it just happened,' I said, laughing even though it was far from funny. 'All I ever wanted was for you to make that commitment to me, but you left it until it was too late. Then you hooked up with Olivia long-distance style in the blink of an eye.'

'I'm doing my best to explain here, Lou,' he told me. 'And I'm not blaming you or Olivia. I was a mess.'

The few drinks I'd had and the way Olivia had behaved towards me heightened my emotions as I remembered things I'd buried deep down in my mind. The time she'd mocked my music plans as a 'Mickey Mouse career' or how she would talk to me in front of others while deliberately staring at my clothes or hair with a sarcastic grin in an attempt to intimidate me.

'Her family came to Ballyheaney House to help clear up after the party that disastrous Christmas and ended up staying a while,' Ben recounts. 'As the days rolled on, I was missing you so much, so I played along with her games, thinking I'd nothing to lose as I'd already lost you.'

A million thoughts ran through my head. It wasn't really my place to be offended or angry with him for being with Olivia, or anyone else for that matter, especially given the bombshell I'd dropped on him that last Christmas Eve.

'Of all people, though,' I said. 'She knew what we had, and she didn't care one bit.'

'She didn't,' he said. 'She told me as much. In fact, knowing we had something deeply special seemed to drive her on more.'

The wine I'd chosen so carefully for our romantic late night was tasting sour in my mouth.

'I'm a bit taken aback, mostly because you said you hadn't heard from her since, yet you did,' I told him. 'So, how long were you a couple?'

The very word 'couple' when it came to Ben and Olivia made me sick to my stomach.

'A few months,' he told me. 'Lou, I don't want any secrets between us, so you can ask me anything and I'll tell you.'

'How many months?' I asked, knowing no matter what the answer was, it was only going to sting me more.

'Five, maybe?' he said. My mouth dropped open. 'Six? She came to Paris to see me a few times before it very naturally ran its course. It was her call in the end.'

I covered my mouth, then got up from the floor from where we were sitting and went over to the armchair by the fire. He looked different already. He wasn't the person I'd missed for so long after all. He had lied to me.

'She made the call to end it?' I asked. 'Why?'

'Ironically, she said she couldn't do long distance,' he told me. 'She couldn't connect with me because I was a mess over you. A broken, drunken, horrible mess and not the dashing, eligible bachelor she thought I was. I'm so sorry I lied to you, Lou. I really am.'

I gathered up our drinks and saw him to the door, then I watched him leave in a taxi. This wasn't how I'd predicted our evening would end. Instead of the making-up-for-lost-time making-love buzz we'd both been on as we left the restaurant, I was left alone in my cottage feeling empty inside.

Where do we go from here? He said it was up to me. I didn't know whether to laugh or cry.

'I'd a later night than I should have, that's all,' I tell Cordelia. 'Ben and I had a little bit too much vino.'

'Good! I was afraid you were upset over something. He told me you'd had dinner,' she says to me from my kitchen table. 'I think he's off getting Mum a new car, though she'll definitely need some refresher driving lessons if that's the case. Whatever it is, my brother is on some sort of secret mission and isn't telling a soul what this secret present is.'

I'm only half listening as Cordelia contemplates her brother's Sunday-morning whereabouts.

'Turns out he's good at keepings secrets,' I say, unable to conceal the bitterness that lies inside me still.

Cordelia raises her eyebrows as I sit down to join her, doing my best to shake myself into the present and stay there rather than keep going over old ground that can't be fixed any more, but still I do.

'Just so you know, I felt so bad about abandoning you all that last Christmas Eve,' I tell her, hoping to put a lid on the past once and for all. 'But your father made it clear I was getting in the way of family business.'

Cordelia, as always, has a way of setting things back on the straight and narrow.

'Lou, you had enough on your plate back then to be

worrying about how the party ended up,' she reminds me. 'My family's financial mess on Christmas Eve was out of everyone's control, including yours. But Uncle Eric came to the rescue. My father was a stubborn so-and-so, but I did feel sorry for him getting into such trouble. It was an investment gone wrong. If it hadn't been for my uncle, we'd have had to sell up. And it looks like one of us is going to have to step in again very soon.'

'That bad?' I ask, slightly taken aback.

'Not as bad as before, but the clock is ticking,' she says. 'Not as bad as my father's mistake when he turned our whole lives upside down. It took years to get back on our feet after that.'

'How sad,' I reply. 'And the famous Ballyheaney House Charity Afternoon Tea Party was never to see the light of day again.'

'Until now, baby!' says Cordelia, standing up with her arms outstretched to shift the energy. 'We're back and we're even better, bitches. Even the weather is on our side. There'll be no rain this year, that's for sure, 'cos it's all in feckin' Spain where I left it.'

Her enthusiasm lifts my mood a little.

'The dream team,' I chuckle. 'Isn't that what we used to call ourselves?'

'The absolute best around,' she says, reaching for a high five. 'Ben sent me pictures of your centrepieces for the tables, Lou. They're amazing, and such a nice touch to remember Dad with the white roses. Thank you. You really do think of everything.'

I can't help but smile, knowing my efforts haven't gone unnoticed.

'I chose New Dawn white roses in memory of your dad and his walled garden, fir branches from the shores of Lough Beg for everlasting connection, and gold ribbon to represent the prestige and pride in Ballyheaney House,' I explain further. 'The pine cones I threw in purely for aesthetics, but yes, I'm glad you think it all works.'

She sits back down again and takes in her surroundings, looking in wonder at the old-fashioned grandfather clock as it chimes midday, the dinky net curtains that belonged to the previous owner and that I simply couldn't replace, and the framed black-and-white photos on the walls depicting scenes from our village, including one of the bronze statue of a turf digger outside the historic house Bellaghy Bawn.

'We need this as a family more than anyone could ever know,' she says quietly. 'I'm still pinching myself that Ben agreed to being part of it after all he's been through with losing Stephanie.'

Her eyes skirt around the room some more.

'That was hard for you all,' I say. 'So heartbreaking. I can only imagine how hopeless you all felt watching Ben and Ava wrestle with grief for all these years. It's a cruel old world.'

'She was something special,' she tells me. 'So positive, so graceful and so damn realistic, even when facing up to her own mortality.'

'I'd love to know more about her,' I say, genuinely touched at how Cordelia is opening up to me.

Cordelia smiles as she remembers her late sister-in-law.

'She adored Ava of course,' she tells me. 'Children were high up on her priority list. She used to joke how she'd love to fill the house with them. She loved this time of year too, with all the hustle and bustle, but her favourite season was summer. She'd never miss a glimmer of sunshine. I think of her every time I'm basking in the sun in Spain, knowing she's really not that far away as long as the sun is out.'

'She sounds like an angel,' I say, shifting in my chair. 'I'm so sorry you lost her.'

Cordelia lets out a deep sigh.

'My brother has made some silly mistakes in his love life, but Stephanie made up for them all,' she said. 'She reminded me a lot of you. The same tenacity, the same creative energy and an endearing loyalty to those she loved. I'd easily class losing you as Ben's biggest mistake, though I'm sure he'd come right back at me with a list of some of the mistakes I've made too.'

I'm very touched at Cordelia's honesty. It's good to hear a little more about Ben's late wife, who sounds like a darling.

'Stephanie was adamant that Ben and Ava should make the best life together as soon as they felt strong enough to,' she says. 'She told us all how she'd cheer them on from the clouds above. She joked that if they didn't learn to be happy without her, she would haunt them both.'

We sit in silence, both lost in thoughts of our own, though mine quickly drift back to the night before and how any glimmer of happiness that might have been coming our way had been quickly squashed by Ben's big revelation.

'He told me about his five-month relationship with Olivia Major,' I blurt out, addressing the elephant in the room at last. 'Or was it six months?'

'Oh shit,' she laughs. 'What a joke that was!'

'That's one way of putting it,' I say, doing my best not to scowl. 'I had no idea they were a thing, Cor. And I'm kicking myself for reacting this way, as I've no right to feel anything about what happened after me.'

Cordelia frowns before taking a deep breath.

'So that's why he was so quiet over breakfast this morning,' she tells me. 'I kept asking how you two were getting along, meaning the party planning with a hint of whatever else may have happened by now, but he was so vague and kept changing the subject to Ava and her newly found baking skills, or how she can now whip Uncle Eric in a game of chess.'

I shrug.

'Five or six *months*,' I say to her. 'How did he tolerate her for six days, never mind six whole months?'

'Five or six whole months with the safety of the English Channel and the Irish Sea between them,' she explains.

I bite my lip.

'He doesn't owe me an explanation and neither do you,' I say to her. 'My only disappointment is that I asked him directly last week if he ever heard from her again and he said no. She tried to make my life hell, Cordelia. And she took such pleasure out of it too.'

Cordelia looks out through the window. I follow her gaze to see a tiny robin help itself to the bird feed I've hung from a tree in the field across the way.

'He doesn't tell me everything, so I can't claim to have any big insight into what he saw in her back then,' she says. 'Don't get me wrong. We're very close as far as siblings go, but Ben can be a closed book when he wants to be. We all can. What he did tell me was that the last Christmas party conversation broke his heart, that he'd never get over you, nor did he want to. He enjoyed the pain, which took me years to understand until I had my own heart broken, and then I knew exactly what he meant. Feeling pain for someone you love is better than feeling nothing at all.'

I feel fresh tears prick my eyes as a hard relate comes to mind. I took myself off to New York in denial of the turmoil Ben was in back home, but just like him I didn't want to completely ease the pain. Part of me needed it to still feel that connection with him, even if silently and from afar.

Feeling nothing would have been worse.

'We were so worried about him, Lou,' she continues, hugging her coffee cup with both hands. 'Mum and Dad were afraid to take their eyes off him for ages. He wouldn't tell us why at first, but all over Christmas he said he wasn't going to go back to Paris, then he launched into the drinks cabinet and spilled his guts out to me when our parents were asleep. He'd lost heart in his degree course, in his friends, in everything, so Olivia was a timely distraction who made her move without knowing what he was going through, or how he felt about you at the time. I can only imagine that Ben acted on it out of sheer grief, Lou. I know he beat himself up over it for a very long time.'

I pour some fresh coffee into both of our cups, wondering how much more of our broken romance Ben had told his family about.

'It's not my place to be angry or to blame Olivia or Ben,' I reply, doing my best to create some space. 'There's been a lot of water under the bridge between us, over twenty whole years to be precise. It was a shock when he told me and it still is, yes, but I'm a big girl. I'll shake it off eventually. After all, I'd rather we keep moving forward and let bygones be bygones.'

Cordelia reaches across and lightly touches my hand. When she smiles, I see the years have been kind to her with her sparkling eyes and sun-kissed skin. She has lived and loved too, I'm sure, yet I can see in her a longing to put down some roots and get her teeth into something. Perhaps a bit like I felt when I knew I wanted to come back here.

She has changed. I have changed. We've all changed so much since we were last together.

'I was always rooting for you two,' she says, her face so relaxed and open now. 'From the very start, when you both came into the millennium party with flushed faces and the joy of delivering the new baby foal, I saw something between you that could never be matched or denied. I was only a kid, but I was cheering you both on from day one.'

I sit back and fold my arms, mirroring her cheeky smile.

'You knew we had something going on even then?' I ask her, shaking my head in disbelief. 'And all this time we thought we were the best-kept secret of Ballyheaney House.'

Cordelia clasps her hands on the table and leans towards me.

'Even the dogs on the street knew you two were love's young dream,' she says with a wink and a smile. 'Uncle Eric was almost as devastated as Ben was when you left. I think it reminded him of losing his own one true love, though he still won't tell us who she is or was. What is it with my family and secrets?'

I furrow my brow and tilt my head.

'He nearly told me her name once, you know,' I divulge as Cordelia's eyes widen. 'He was *so* close to telling me until your father, bless him, totally burst our bubble by coming into the drawing room looking for his reading glasses. That was it, subject closed. I'll never forget it.'

Cordelia looks wistful at the mention of her father.

'You've no idea how good it is to have you back in our lives,' she tells me, her voice now soft. 'Even if you and Ben never get it together, we all love you, Lou. I hope you'll never forget that. No matter what comes next.'

Her words soothe my bruised and battered heart a little.

'We're getting far too serious and heavy for a crisp Sunday in December,' I say, gently squeezing her hand. 'Now, how about we take a day off from reminiscing and party planning and instead we go let our hair down somewhere for a few hours?'

I don't need to ask Cordelia twice, that's for sure. She is

already on her feet, looking around for where she left her red woollen coat and thick cream scarf.

'That sounds like a plan,' she says, dancing on the spot. 'You and I have so much to catch up on, so let's go somewhere nice for a big fat Sunday lunch. My treat?'

'Only if it's a Ben-and-Olivia-free zone?'

'You'd better believe it,' she agrees. 'Remind me to tell you about the illicit festive romance I had in Edinburgh last year with a fine Scot called Angus. You're not the only one to have jingle bells ringing at this time of year, you know.'

We slip and slide, arm in arm, across my yard, already in wrinkles from laughing on our way to the car.

'I want to hear every single spicy detail of your Scottish fling, Cordelia Heaney,' I tell her. 'You've made me feel so much better already.'

We drive out of town with the radio blaring, leaving my thoughts of Olivia back in the past, where I know they belong.

The only question lingering in my mind is whether I can let go of the fact that Ben lied to me, so that I can focus instead on the wonderful time we'd had at the restaurant last night and what might happen between us next.

Ben still has my heart. There's no question of that. He believes we still 'fit'.

I so want to believe him.

With only three days until the party, I really hope I can.

Chapter Nineteen

Ben

'Five, four, three, two, one – ta-da!'

Ava and I are on our way back to Ballyheaney House, practising how we're going to give the extra-special early Christmas present to my mum. Our two-hour round trip has been the perfect medicine to take my mind off the events of the night before.

I'm towing an enclosed trailer on the back of the car, the light fall of sleet is giving my windscreen wipers a run for their money, and we've the heat blasting as we face the last leg of our journey.

To fill the time, Ava is having great fun gauging her grandmother's reaction to our very creative idea for her Christmas present.

We both know it could go either way. She's going to either love it, or she's going to chase us right back to County Antrim where we got it from, with an order to return it immediately.

'Your turn, Dad,' Ava tells me. 'I've done the countdown, so I'm us and you're Grandma. You've seen the present, so what do you say?'

I do my best to imitate my mother's soft, serene voice, which rarely changes tone.

'Oh, how did you think of something so unique, darling son and granddaughter?' I purr as Ava goes into fits of giggles. 'I might even shed a wee tear. It's a work of art! I'd go so far as to say it's the best Christmas present I've ever had in my whole life. Even better than the red collared dress I got when I was ten years old. Have I told you about that dress, Ava? I still have it in the attic, you know. Good as new. It might fit you, you know?'

Ava throws her head back laughing. She has heard about the red collared dress every single Christmas since she was born, as have Cordelia and I. My father once joked how our mother would have got married in that dress if it had still fitted her.

I'm silently preparing myself for the worst when I reveal our Christmas surprise, if truth be told. Last night's conversation with Lou has knocked me off my axis, but I had to tell her about Olivia. It's as much about respect for her as it was to get it off my chest.

But that was then, this is now, and while Lou and I have the memories of Christmas Eves at Ballyheaney House and a sizzling chemistry to cling on to, a lot of our time together from now on will be like starting from scratch.

'On an equally important note, do you have any more Christmas shopping to do?' I ask my daughter. 'Now that Cordelia is home, you should nab her for a quick trip into Belfast to find a few bits for your wardrobe.'

Ava drums her fingers on the car door in thought.

'I could always wear Grandma's red collared dress,' she says to me, then, imitating my mother's voice, 'Do you have all your shopping done, Benjamin?'

'OK, OK, drop it before we get any closer or she'll hear you,' I tell her with a smile. 'Yes, I've all my shopping done. Well, I think so. I might like to get Lou something to thank her for all her help with the party. Any ideas?'

I know I'm being slightly optimistic when it comes to Lou wanting any sort of gift from me, but I'd rather try to show some sort of appreciation than not.

'Flowers?' says Ava, still in giddy mode.

'That's very helpful,' I nod. 'Now, why didn't I think of buying flowers for someone who runs a florist's?'

Ava hums along to the Christmas songs we've been playing as we arrive at Ballyheaney at last.

'OK, run me through it all again, quickly,' she says, glancing over to the big house across the lawns.

'You distract Grandma in the library or the kitchen,' I remind her. 'I'll pretend I've to show Uncle Eric a last-minute minor repair out here, and when the time is right and our gift is on full display, we'll call her outside. Then we'll soon see if we still have a Christmas to celebrate here or if it's cancelled.'

Ava nods, drinking in my every word. Her love of a challenge reminds me of her sweet mother so much sometimes, especially if we can make it fun.

'Loud and clear, boss,' she says with a fist pump in my direction. 'Loud and clear.'

Moments later, after Ava has gone inside the house, Uncle Eric is making his way towards me dressed for an Arctic expedition even though the winter sun has decided to make a late-afternoon appearance. I can barely see any of his face, he's so covered up in the collar of his puffy navy coat and his grey woolly hat.

'I told her not to make a fuss, but she wouldn't listen,' he says as he walks towards me. 'Cordelia has gone out for the day, you two were off on your travels, so I told her in no uncertain terms to be cooking such a big meal, but would she listen? She's roasting a duck as we speak, watching the clock for your return.'

I open the trailer as I listen.

'Not to worry, we'll be ready for some food once we make our big presentation.'

'Don't you want to wait for your sister, if it's such a big deal?' asks Uncle Eric.

The thought had crossed my mind more than once, but Cordelia seems to be on her own mission today. She isn't answering her phone, for starters.

'This isn't the type of thing that can wait,' I tell my uncle. 'And Cordelia will be just as surprised when she sees it later as she would be if she were here now. Where is she, anyhow?'

Uncle Eric scratches his head as he tries to find a peephole in the trailer.

'Out to lunch with Lou, last I heard,' he says. 'Ben, if this is a pony, you know we don't have the manpower to look after it round here. Not to mention the finances. We're struggling enough without another mouth to feed.'

I take a moment to let what he is telling me sink in. I've

had my head buried in the sand for too long, yet somewhere along the way I knew this was coming. I've had a suspicion that something was afoot, but now isn't the time to go into the family finances. Cordelia and I will discuss it with them after Christmas.

'We'll sort it, Uncle, I promise. Now, it isn't a pony,' I reply, my brain working overtime as I think of Lou and Cordelia off somewhere together. 'Right, let's get this trailer opened up. Stand back, Erico! Are you ready? Ta-da!'

He stops dead and puts both hands to his face when he sees what we have in store for my mother.

'Oh my goodness!'

He swallows. He scratches his head again. He leans in for a closer look.

'Is that a *good* "oh my goodness" or a *holy shit, Ben, what have you done* "oh my goodness"?' I ask him. He rubs his chin and stares into the trailer where a large cardboard box with peepholes for air sits in its centre. A trumpet-like honk makes his eyes widen. 'Quickly, Uncle. Have I made a giant mistake?'

'I've always said your biggest mistake was letting Lou Doherty go,' Uncle Eric says. 'But if you can't get her back, and if this is what I think it is, then this might be the closest thing to nostalgia I've seen round here in a very long time.'

We are both too busy staring inside the trailer to notice Ava behind us.

'Where did you let Lou go to, Dad?' she asks.

I look at Uncle Eric in surprise. He can only stammer and stutter in response.

'Ah, we're reminiscing about old girlfriends,' he says. 'It's nothing important.'

'And old *friend*, you mean,' I correct him quickly. 'Lou was a great friend to us all when she worked here, especially at Christmas. That's what he means. We were talking about parties of days gone by and Uncle Eric said—'

'Never mind, here comes Grandma now,' says Ava, but I know I'm in for a lot more questioning later. 'She wants to know if you'd like duck for lunch. I said I'd ask you. Obviously, she wants to ask you herself, so here goes nothing. Will she like our present or loathe it? We're about to find out.'

Beads of sweat form along my forehead, even though it's still freezing cold outside, despite the brief glimmers of sunshine through the clouds. I want to shake Uncle Eric, but then he didn't know Ava was within earshot. I must also remember that at his age he's not quite as sharp as he once was.

I look across to the house to see Mum waving and smiling as she makes her way to the courtyard where we're standing, guarding the back of a trailer like it contains the Crown jewels.

'Wait!' I call to her, realising that it's now or never. I'd planned this so differently in my head. 'Take your time, I mean. I've something very special to show you.'

She slows down, which gives me time to get everything ready a lot more quickly than I'd expected to. I open the box, careful not to make any sudden movements, just as I'd been instructed.

I hear Uncle Eric gasp. Then Ava gives me a thumbs up with a reassuring smile.

'We've got your Christmas present, Grandma,' she says gently, now my mother is closer.

'Already?' asks Mum. 'But it isn't even . . .'

Her words trail off while we all stand back to take in the breathtaking display as the peacock finds its feet beside us. Its striking train opens like a fan, showcasing an array of rich, shimmering hues in turquoise blue, emerald green and hints of gold and purple. Each feather is adorned with an eye-like pattern, the vibrant colours swirling into delicate, mesmerising designs.

'Meet Alexander the Great,' I whisper to my mother, who seems lost for words.

'Alexander the Great,' she repeats. 'Oh, wow! He is beautiful!'

'We didn't do our countdown, Dad,' whispers Ava. 'Five, four, three, two, one.'

'Ta-daaa!' we both say sheepishly.

I feel my heart beating in my chest as I await Mum's further reaction. Five, four, three, two, one. I count it down in my head once more.

She visibly takes a deep breath, dabs away her tears and then breaks into a smile I don't think I've seen the like of in many, many years.

'Do you like him?' I ask her.

'We got you a peacock because we know how much you missed Cleopatra, Grandma,' Ava tells my mother, whose look of disbelief is crowned by tears running down her face.

'I - I absolutely love it,' she says. 'He's stunning. He's like a work of art.'

Ava clasps her hands, then gives me a high five. I see Uncle Eric puff out his chest from the corner of my eye.

'Well now, that's a gift to remember,' he says, then coughs into a tissue like he always does when choked by emotion. 'Good thinking, Ben. Good job, Ava.'

As Alexander walks on to the lawn, his glorious patterns come to life, shifting and glistening in the December sunlight.

'You've got me so much more this Christmas than you'll ever know, my darlings,' Mum tells us. 'I've been so incredibly lonely. But you've got me a new friend.'

I walk towards my mother and hold her close. Ava joins in too, as does Uncle Eric, and I don't know whether I want to laugh or cry.

As we huddle on the courtyard in our blissful bubble, the first person I want to tell about all this is Lou.

I would love to share my happiness with her. I want to share every precious moment with her from now on.

I can only hope she feels the same.

'You're playing a blinder this Christmas,' Uncle Eric tells me when we're touching up the paintwork in the blue ballroom later that day. 'This house hasn't witnessed so much joy and, dare I say it, so much noise in far too long.'

'Ah, come on, Uncle,' I reply, hoping to get back to our usual banter before we fall into mutual praise. 'I've heard you snoring. I've no idea how these walls are still standing after all the rattling they've had since you came to live here.'

He chuckles and shakes his head.

'Stairs creaking and my snoring are a given,' he tells me. 'It's the laughter I've missed, Ben. And I never thought I'd see the day when Cordelia's rendition of "Rudolph the Red-Nosed Reindeer" would be the sound I was waiting for, but now that she's home, it's like we're complete again.'

I steal a glance over to where he stands, a few metres from me. His frail hand is trembling as he lifts the paint pot to pour a little more into his tray, and the look of concentration on his face is more intense than it used to be. I've deliberately given him patches to fill in at his own eye level so he doesn't have to bend or stretch too far.

'I'm pottering,' he tells me as he goes at a snail's pace. 'Thank you for letting me potter, Ben. I know you'd be much quicker yourself.'

We've covered the floor in dust sheets, and the long, tall windows are bare as we wait for the return of the curtains from the cleaner's, but there's already a feeling of excitement in the air.

'Promise I'll do some of the dirty work tomorrow,' Cordelia told me in a text message when we'd finished our meal. 'Having a super catch-up with Lou.'

I think I may have read the last line at least ten times.

'I would be quicker, yes,' I reply to my uncle. 'But then I'd have to find something else for you to do. At least I can supervise you when you're right under my nose.'

Ava has set us up with some classical music in the background, at Uncle Eric's request. His taste has changed immensely as the years have rolled by. Once a rocker in his day, with a lifelong passion for loud Led Zeppelin, he prefers now to be able to chat over his music choices, so we've settled on the Royal Philharmonic Orchestra's *Christmas Classics*. It sets the tone of our relaxing task as we drift between conversation and long silences, both deep in thought.

Soon, the inevitable subject of my evening with Lou the night before comes up. I'm not sure I really want to talk about it, so I skirt around it before turning the conversation back to my uncle's love life – or lack of it, after he came here on a permanent basis following my father's death ten years ago. I wonder if he will tell me at long last about his one true love.

'Was she someone you knew when you lived in Wicklow?' I ask him. 'Give me the first letter of her name at least. I have a good memory of your farm and some of your friends back then. Was it Gertrude the singer? I have a vague recollection of you dancing with her at a summer barbecue. Was it her?'

He pretends to zip his lips with his fingers, unable to hide the cheeky smile that peeks through.

'Good guess, but Gertrude was a fleeting fling which suited both of us at the time,' he tells me. 'I'd two failed marriages, don't forget, and no children, so I was very much footloose and fancy-free.'

'You were a kind man, though,' I remind him. 'I learned a lot from hanging out with you when I was a wide-eyed student. Everyone told me you were a gentleman, which made me very proud.'

He pauses, frowns and tilts his head in thought.

'Are you complimenting me, Ben?' he asks. 'Was that a compliment, because I think it may have been?'

'Maybe it was,' I confess. 'Gosh, we're all going soft around here. OK, back to default mode. Two divorces aren't anything to brag about, are they?'

He guffaws at this so much that he puts his paintbrush on the tray to stop him dripping blue paint all over the place.

'A broken heart leads to very bad judgement,' he says, more wistfully now. 'It's like trying to drive a car with no oil or expecting a clock to chime when you haven't taken the time to wind it up properly. The term "fools rush in" could have been my motto in my thirties, though I know now that I was running on empty and expecting to cross a finishing line that was so far out of reach.'

'You're right,' I say, his words resonating with me so much that I don't even have a proper comeback. 'She is real, then? Your one true love who got away?'

He raises his eyebrows and lets out a deep sigh.

'Oh, she's real all right,' he replies, staring at the wall. 'I know where she is, but I don't know *her* any more. I've no doubt the tides of time have changed her like they do us all. However, I hold the version of her I do know very close to my heart.'

Then he smiles as if he's remembered something new.

I can hear that Ava and Mum have come back from their self-titled 'winter wildlife walk' with Roly. Mum is still on a high about her new friend Alexander, and while she'd usually prefer to curl up with a book after lunch on a winter's day like today, instead she put on some layers and invited Ava to join her on a walk round the estate, where she undoubtedly told Ava stories of every nook and cranny they came across.

'Do you think Lou and I have changed too much to really know each other like we used to?' I ask Uncle Eric.

It's a pretty loaded question which he doesn't rush to answer. Instead, he picks up his paintbrush again and dips it into the blue paint, scraping the excess against the tray with his shaking hand.

'Not necessarily, Ben,' he tells me. 'But you'll need patience. Enjoy getting to know each other again, learn from before but don't take anything for granted. And make a goddam effort, Ben. Don't leave anything to assumption. If you want her, tell her so.'

Ava bursts into the room with Roly still on the lead. My mother is following close behind.

'We saw deer footprints in the mud, Dad, and some Whooper Swans,' she tells us. 'We even found a cool hut that looks like it's been there for years and years.'

'And Roly chased a rabbit down a hole so far we didn't think he'd make it out again,' chirps Mum. Her mood has lifted immensely over the past few days, especially since Cordelia arrived.

But my mind is going into overdrive as I think of how I'm going to make things better between Lou and me before Christmas Eve.

Should I say something with a gift? The best Ava could suggest was flowers . . . which has given me an idea.

I know exactly what I'll do. In fact, I'll go and sort it out right now.

Uncle Eric hands Ava his paintbrush. He looks tired, though he still has one more piece of advice for me before he hands over the reins to my daughter.

'Take it from an old fool like me,' he says. 'Second chances with your one true love don't come along very often. I only wish I'd had such an opportunity when I was your age. Don't let her go again. Fight for her.'

He shuffles out of the room, leaving me deep in thought. So much so, it takes me a few seconds to realise that Ava's little face has dropped.

'Your one true love?' she says, her eyes already overflowing with tears. 'Is that Lou?'

'Ava, wait,' I say quickly, but it's much too late.

'I'm sick of this!' she says. 'I thought your one true love was Mummy.'

'Let me explain, darling.'

She puts the paintbrush down and runs upstairs before I can say anything more.

Chapter Twenty

Lou

THEN

Christmas Eve, 21 Years Ago

I closed my eyes, feeling the longing in my veins rush to the surface as it only ever did in his company, but my stomach was sick at the reality of it all.

This was not meant to happen.

'I tried,' he said before I even turned around to face him. 'I did my best to make other plans, to try and sever whatever this is, Lou, but no matter how I tried to convince myself we could leave it and move on in other directions, when I think of Christmas all I can think of is you.'

'Ben . . .'

'And when I think of my future,' he continued, 'all I can think of is you.'

I swallowed hard, knowing I was going to have to find more self-control than I'd ever done in my entire lifetime.

Everything had changed. I had to tell him so.

I pictured John, who'd already called me twice that morning to see how I was, even though it was the middle of the night in New York. I hoped that imagining his face and hearing his sweet voice in my head would snap me out of this dreamy world where all my plans could be changed by the right words from Ben Heaney, the one person I believed was truly right for me.

'You should have told me you were on your way,' I said, coaching my brain not to give in to emotion as I turned to face him in the rain. 'I'd have made a place name for you. Or at least made sure there was an extra sausage roll or two.'

I didn't want to look at his face. I needed to stay in control. This time was so different from the Christmas Eves before, and it was nothing to do with the fact that he wasn't supposed to be here.

'Don't I get a hug at least?' he asked, his arms outstretched. 'Lou?'

I didn't budge. He was still wearing his coat and scarf, having been stopped by the big family row the second he came back to Ballyheaney House.

I shook my head.

'You don't look very happy to see me,' he said, his handsome face crumpling.

'I'm always happy to see you, Ben.'

'Well, tell your face that?' he joked. 'I know this year we've been busy, and we couldn't see any plans through, but we're here now, yeah? We can have a lovely Christmas together like we always do?'

I took a deep breath.

'Like I said, I'm always glad to see you,' I said, doing my best not to raise my voice. 'But Cordelia told me you were in Berlin with some girl.'

'Ah.'

'Yes, Ben,' I told him. 'Ah!! Not that it's any of my damn business who you spend your Christmas with.'

He shook his head.

'I was going to meet a girlfriend, yes, but I couldn't do it, so I called it off yesterday and booked a flight home instead,' he told me. He looked over his shoulder before dropping his voice. 'Lou, you and I had made an agreement to keep our distance until the time was right, but when Astrid invited me—'

'Astrid?'

'Yes, she's the one I've been seeing lately, he mumbled. 'It was getting serious and don't get me wrong, she's a beautiful person inside and out, but I panicked because I knew I wasn't being honest with her. I also knew I wasn't being honest with myself.'

I laughed, but it was only coming from a place of nerves. I wasn't finding what he was telling me in the slightest bit funny.

'Astrid. A beautiful person with a beautiful name,' I spat, knowing I was being childish, especially when I'd spent the past few months getting to know John on a much, much deeper level. I'd even cried when he left to go home over a week ago, but I'd a very clear explanation for why I was so emotional. 'Don't say you ended it with her to come home to me? Don't you dare say that.'

'But I did!' he exclaimed. 'That's exactly what I did.'

'You can't keep doing that, Ben!' I tell him, not caring if Cordelia and the hired chef who were now getting stuff from a van, or anyone else for that matter, could hear me. 'You can't fall in love with other women, then get cold feet just because it's Christmas and you know exactly where I'll be as your safety net! Life isn't as easy as that. It doesn't work that way. I don't work that way!'

'Can we sit in the car? You're soaked through.'

I agreed, but when he took his coat off and then his scarf, draping it on the back seat, I shut my eyes tightly.

I didn't want to see the shape of his shoulders, the way his waist tapered in, how the belt hung around his hips or how his jeans fitted like a glove.

'You're right, it doesn't work that way, but we could make it easier if we wanted to,' he said, sitting far too close to me in the passenger seat. 'I know we both want to, Lou. We haven't addressed it before.'

'You weren't available.'

'Lou, neither were you, but can we talk about how we can make it easier?' he pleaded. 'I only have one more year to do in Paris after this one, you'll be finished in Belfast then too and we can make a proper effort to be together at last. I promise I'll do everything I can to see you at least once a month between now and then.'

How I wished I could have said yes. He was finally saying what I'd always dreamed he would say.

I focused on breathing.

Outside, sleeting snow was landing on the manicured lawns of Ballyheaney House. The clatter from the kitchen and some tasty expletives from the hired-in chef brought me back to our days of laughter and fun there, as well as my overwhelming love for the place. A few feet away, Cordelia was running back inside to the kitchen with the chef. They'd soon be filling the air with savoury, fragrant aromas.

Not long after, the musicians would be doing their soundchecks, which would usually ramp up the excitement and add a beat to all of our steps, and when the first guests arrived the rush and adrenaline would be turned up to eleven.

Everything sounded the same as before, everything looked the same as before, yet everything had changed.

I sat like a statue in the front seat of my car, my hands clenched tight by my side while Ben leaned across and wrapped his arms around me, pulling me to his chest. I couldn't hold back any more. My arms folded around his waist and I leaned into him, inhaling every bit of him while knowing it was for the last time. Nothing and no one else could compare. He was my safe place, so comforting and familiar.

So Ben Heaney.

'I tried to talk to you so many times this year, but you were never there,' I whispered, allowing the tears to flow.

'I was trying to stick to our agreement,' he told me.

'Your suggestion, not mine,' I reminded him. 'I missed you, but then I couldn't do it to myself any more. I should have been more straight up with my feelings, maybe. I should have asked you straight out if you were ever going to say to me what you're saying now.'

I sat back, peeling myself from the warmth of his arms. I didn't want to move away, but I knew I had to.

'So we're here now. Better late than never, right?' he suggested. He cupped my face in his hands, wiping away tears with his thumbs like he'd done so many times before. 'We're still so young, with the world at our feet, so why do we always come full circle? Why punish each other when the only place we ever want to be is together? That has to mean something.'

I bit my lip. I shook my head.

'I'm sorry, but it's too late,' I told him. 'I should have said more. You should have said more, but now it's too late.'

He jolted. I'd never seen Ben cry before, yet he looked like he was going to break down.

'No, Lou. How can you say that?' he asked, his eyes creasing. 'Lou, it's me! We can make this work if we both want it badly enough. I know I do. Please tell me you do too? It's never too late.'

I stared at the lane in front of me, where in only a few hours, a hundred and fifty people would make their way here without a care in the world, but for Ben and me it was the end of an era, the closing of a chapter of a story we thought might go on forever.

I couldn't answer.

'If it's someone else,' he said, his words catching in his throat. 'I know you told me about the American guy, John. Is it him?'

I stared out the window as he focused on the footwell of the car.

'I'm not saying I expect you to change anything if you're happy, Lou,' he continued. 'Are you happy? I'll wait for you for as long as it takes, but if you're happy with him – well, some day I'll learn to be happy for you. Do we walk away, Lou?'

'What's changed, Ben? Why now?'

He searched for answers. 'Because I was meant to go and meet a girl in Germany and I realised I couldn't do it,' he told me. 'It felt wrong. All I wanted to do was get back here to you as quickly as I could, so that's what I did. My future is with you, not her. Not anyone else. Is it John?'

'Yes, it's John,' I told him as gently and quickly as I could. 'I can't be with you because I'm with John.'

He went pale. It was like he stopped breathing. His jaw clenched and his hands trembled as he wiped a tear quickly with the back of his hand, nodding as he did so.

'Is he a nice guy?' he asked me. 'Is he good to you, Lou? I only hope he's good to you and that you're happy.'

'He's good to me,' I replied as the lump in my throat grew bigger. 'Ben, it's not as simple as me choosing him over you.'

'Well, it sounds like that to me.'

'No,' I cried. 'No, I don't want us to leave it like this. I don't want you to think I'm making a flippant choice or throwing my rattle out of the pram just because we've drifted apart! It's bigger than that. Much bigger!'

He put his hand to his chest like I'd shot him.

'How?' he asked. 'Are you in love with him?'

I almost choked on my reply, because the truth was, I didn't even know the answer to that question.

'Ben, I need you to understand that no matter how long it is between our visits or our conversations, nothing about how you make me feel will ever change, even though I wish it would. Even if I don't see you for ten years or twenty years from now, it will never change how I feel inside, or how much I will always love you.'

His eyes lit up in a last glimmer of hope, so I knew I had to cut to the chase, and fast.

'I swear, Lou,' he told me, moving closer to me again. 'I know we should have said so much more so much sooner, but—'

'Ben, wait,' I said, stopping him in his tracks for a final time. 'I haven't told you everything.'

I tried to say it. I tried to speak, but my breath kept catching every time I opened my mouth.

'Are you OK?'

My mouth was dry.

'I'll be all right,' I told him at last, panting out short breaths as the words spilled off my tongue like hot lava. I was far from all right, if truth be told. I'd never been so terrified in my whole life.

'Well, that's good.'

The irony hung in the air for what I was about to say.

'I haven't even had the guts to tell Mum yet,' I told him. 'I've no idea what my nana is going to say or what I'm going to do about university. I'm so scared, Ben.'

'What is it?' he asked, but I'd a hunch he knew what was coming.

'I'm pregnant,' I whispered, my hand finding its way on to my very slightly bulging tummy. 'I can't be with you because John and I are having a baby.'

Chapter Twenty-one

Lou

NOW

Two Days to Christmas Eve

'So, that's five bouquets, three holly centrepieces and the last of the wreaths all packed into the van for today's deliveries,' Mum says, dabbing her forehead with her apron. 'Then, tomorrow, the Ballyheaney House flowers need to be delivered by noon, ahead of the big day on Wednesday, but aside from all of that I think we've everything under control before we close for Christmas. Well done, Lou!'

Nana Molly is chatting to a customer at a table; Declan the delivery guy is milling around, telling anyone who will listen about his mother's untimely hospital visit; and as the Christmas buzz builds around the village, I only wish I could shake myself into feeling it as much as I should be.

'You're amazing, Mum. Well done to you too,' I say to her. 'Sorry, I'm not myself at the moment, but everything you and Nana do for me here is very much appreciated.'

'We already know that, honey,' she says. 'Any more word from Gracie?'

I shake my head.

'She's gone quiet, bless her,' I reply. 'We've arranged a video call on Christmas Day to open presents together. Thank goodness for technology is all I can say.'

I stifle a yawn, which makes my eyes glisten. As a headache brews, I'm reminded of how the events of the weekend have taken their toll in more ways than one. As well as the head-spinning reconnection with Ben, our heated row over that silly Olivia Major, Gracie's decision to stay with her dad for Christmas, and yesterday's boozy lunch with Cordelia, I've been unable to think straight.

'You're exhausted, Lou,' Mum tells me while folding a stack of fresh tea towels. She's had her hair done again in time for the festivities and looks as fresh and radiant as ever. 'It's not like you to be so quiet or defeated, even if Gracie's Christmas plans are a disappointment. Is there anything else I can do to help ease the pressure?'

I let out a long sigh, the type reserved for only someone who I can be fully honest with.

'I'll be fine, I'm just licking my wounds,' I tell her. 'Ah, I was so looking forward to having her here with us all on Christmas Day. On top of that, I was so glad of the rush and excitement of helping organise the big Ballyheaney House party, but now I'm feeling like it's not my place to be there after all.'

'Now that's very hard to believe,' says Mum. 'You were once part of the furniture up there, especially at this time of year. What's happened? Is it anything to do with Ben Heaney?'

I turn my back to her, pretending to be busy at the sink while I do my best to stay in control. My nose tingles, my throat tightens, and a loud involuntary sniffle gives the game away.

'It's everything, Mum. It's Ben, it's me, it's the fear of being hurt again, it's love and regret and a whole lot of other things,' I say, feeling her gentle arm around my waist. She leans her head on my right shoulder. 'I broke his heart once before – badly, Mum. Worse than I thought I did, but I was an absolute wreck too. I know I ran away from it all and I didn't tell you about Ben, but you were already struggling with me packing up and leaving for New York. I'm so sorry.'

Mum sits me down on a little stool out of sight of customers, tells Nana Molly that she is in charge out front, and gets me a strong cup of sweet tea as I tell her about my afternoon with Cordelia and then, more importantly, the truth about Ben.

'So, I dropped out of uni in April, Gracie was born in August and we moved to New York in October,' I remind her. 'Ben and I had been messaging a little. He'd heard I'd had my baby and wanted to see how I was feeling. Then he booked a flight from Paris and landed literally at our doorstep out of the blue.'

'Jeez, that was a big gesture,' she says, all ears.

'A very big gesture,' I agree with her. 'It almost put me and him over the edge. I think it made everything harder, which was not his intention. But it did.'

267

Mum does her best to be a neutral, understanding ear, but I know this is a huge bolt out of the blue. As I tell her more about Ben's eleventh-hour visit when my bags were packed for New York in the hallway, I see tears fill her eyes.

'What did he suggest to you?' she asks me. 'Does anyone else know about this?'

'No one else has ever known,' I tell her. 'You had taken the baby out for a walk, John was saying his goodbyes in Belfast to all his mates, and I was having a quiet moment to myself before I left Bellaghy for a place I'd only ever holidayed in. I was terrified, Mum, but I was excited too. John's job offer was a huge opportunity. They'd lined us up with an apartment and a car as part of his deal, so it was an offer we couldn't refuse. Then there was a knock at the door, and it was Ben.'

Mum stares into space for a moment while I gather my thoughts.

'He asked you to stay, didn't he?' she says, her voice cracking. 'And you said no.'

I bite my lip. I look her in the eye.

'He said he'd look after me and Gracie if I'd stay,' I whisper.

Mum sits back on the stool and leans against the wall as it all sinks in. Then, as if it were a magic potion, she sits up straight and comes slightly towards me with new vigour.

'I suspect you two still adore each other,' she tells me.

'I do too,' I say, briefly closing my eyes. 'That will never change.'

'So please don't hurt each other again,' she says. 'I think both of you have been through enough heartache already.'

I take a deep breath.

'Which is why I've made a very difficult decision,' I say to her. 'Ben has lost his wife, he deserves only the very best for himself and Ava from now on, so I'm stepping back for both of our sakes. I've really enjoyed helping out this far, but I'm not going to the party on Christmas Eve after all.'

'Oh, I didn't mean it that way,' she tells me. 'I was trying to say you should both learn from the past, that's all.'

But I've already made up my mind. There's too much hurt. Too much water under the bridge. Too many skeletons in the cupboard, cobwebbed and dusty after so many years.

'I think it's best for all if I stay away to save any more old wounds from opening. I've done as much as I can to help, and I loved every minute of it.'

Mum's face is a mixture of confusion and pity, though I know we can't chat for much longer. Things are heating up out front, and it won't be long before Nana Molly needs help.

Now that I've stopped talking, I realise Mum has been holding my hand the whole time.

'And when he begged you to stay, did you even contemplate saying yes to him?' she asks me.

I nod as tears flow down my face.

'Of course I did, Mum, but I was so torn. I wanted to say yes, but I couldn't so I told him again and again that although I'd always love him I couldn't do it to John,' I explain.

'I can only imagine how difficult that was for both of you,' she says. 'No matter what way you turned, someone was going to be badly hurt.'

'I did love John, and we had Gracie, Mum,' I explain. 'She was only a few months old and she deserved to be with her mum and dad. John and I had a life planned. Ben had his final year to complete, so how could he give up all that to look after me and someone else's baby? It would never have worked out.'

'But it might now,' she says. 'Don't you think so?'

I shake my head.

'He has Ava to focus on,' I remind her. 'His little girl has to come first. There are too many factors, too much potential for another mess, so I'm calling it quits from now on.'

Mum's face is crestfallen. She looks almost as gutted as I feel inside.

'Well, if you've made up your mind then I'm not even going to try and convince you to go to the party,' she says. 'But life has a funny way of coming full circle, Lou. I've always told you that if something is meant to be, it will find a way. If the time is right, you and Ben will find your way.'

I swallow hard. We both smile.

'We'll see,' I tell her. 'Thanks for listening, Mum. And I'm sorry I didn't confide in you more back then. I knew you were already heartbroken over me and Gracie leaving. You didn't need to know that I was heartbroken in many other ways too.'

Nana Molly's shrill splurge of expletives makes us jump to attention after our hushed heart-to-heart.

'What's going on in here?' she says, holding a huge bouquet I don't recognise as one of our own. 'Is this a private party or can any of us join?'

I feel a brief rush of excitement when I remember how Master Campbell is planning to ask Nana Molly to go with him to the Ballyheaney House party. I hope she says yes, even if she claims to have some sort of ill will against the whole thing.

'The strangest thing just happened,' Nana says, full of drama, just how she likes it. 'These flowers were delivered for you, Lou. I mean, who would be so cheeky as to deliver flowers to a florist in her own shop? There's a note too. Open it. The suspense is killing me.'

For me? Surely there must be a mistake.

I take the bouquet from Nana Molly, pausing to smell the deep red roses, so velvety and classic. Whoever ordered these has expensive taste. Nestled among them are creamy-white ranunculus and delicate paperwhites, with sprigs of evergreen scattered through.

'How about we leave her to it?' whispers Mum to Nana. 'I think I hear some customers.'

'Oh, all righty then,' Nana grunts, before she reluctantly follows Mum out to the shop floor.

My heart is going ten to the dozen as I open the small envelope that bears my name. It's addressed to me via Buds and Beans, which gets me all of a fluster. Who would do such a thing? But when I take out the fine, crisp white paper, I recognise the handwriting straight away.

Dear Lou,

This is a gesture to the woman who deserves flowers as much as the hundreds of people she makes happy with her deliveries and poems every day.

You have never once given me 'the ick' – I hope you know that. Well, apart from that one time when . . . I'm joking.

You see, Lou, there are a thousand things I've always loved about you – but it's the little, quirky ones that still sneak up and make me smile the most.

I love how you always talked to plants and flowers like they were old friends, or how you'd hum Sinatra while you were driving, even if it was through a thunderstorm, or how you danced in the kitchen at Ballyheaney with your socks on, sliding into my arms like it was a place just for you. Because it was.

I love how every year you'd make some crazy changes to our party plans, convincing us all it would work. You were always right. And that laugh – God, Lou, how I love to hear you laugh – sharp and sudden when we had a fit of the giggles, like it surprised even you.

These pieces of you and so many more are etched into me. They've kept me company all these years.

Now that I've found you again, I don't want just memories.

I want to laugh with you again and again. I want more chaos in the kitchen, your voice in my silence, and your hand in mine for as long as time will give us.

We have changed so much, but we still have so much more to discover together.

Let's not waste another year apart. We always said we'd get there when the time was right.

I believe our time is right now, Lou.

And true love is forever, not just for Christmas.

I still love you.

Ben

PS: Do you still bite your nails when you're nervous? Or forget to use your wing mirrors when reversing a car?

Please come to the party x

I can barely breathe. How did he even think of sending me a note with flowers, like I did with the young couple, Beth and Danny? I lift the letter to my face, close my eyes and I can smell his aftershave. I can see him putting pen to paper. I can imagine him thinking.

And I love that he did it all for me.

Nana comes back for a nosey, but I can't bring myself to tell her about any of this yet. I need to process it all in my own mind. I want to savour this moment. I want to read over his words again and again.

But I'll have to do all of that later, because duty calls, it seems.

'That cute puppy lady is back, so the customers are going gaga again,' says Nana, taking the bouquet from my arms. 'And that Mrs Quinn from the committee is here asking for you, Lou. She's younger than I thought, I must admit, and Master Campbell looks like he's going to spontaneously combust over something he won't tell me about. On top of all that, I've made a complete balls-up of one of those fancy lattes, and your mum is up to her ears in dishes. I need you to come to the rescue.'

Despite the romantic bubble I'm now in, I've a business to run, so I pat down my apron, fix my eyes with a touch up of make-up and a signatory sweep of lipstick, then make my way out to my shop floor.

I scout quickly around, wondering has Mrs Quinn given up waiting on me, but then I spot Beth with the cute sausage dog, Crumb. She's with another lady down by the vintage train set at the back of the floristry, deep in discussion as they admire my window display and what's left of the eclectic mix of ornamentals and gifts scattered around the shop.

She waves, so I wave back, doing my best not to drool over the puppy. The woman with her wears an expensive camel-coloured coat with flattering fitted black trousers. Her hair bounces on her shoulders as she turns around to the sound of Nana Molly's voice.

'Mrs Quinn, you were looking for my granddaughter?' Nana Molly says. 'This is Lou. Mrs Quinn is Beth's aunt, can you believe it? She's from the committee. You know, the one who wrote to Tilda Heaney . . .'

My grandmother's words trail off as the woman walks towards me, her hand outstretched to greet me, but I'm frozen to the spot.

'Lou, it's been years!' she says. 'And I know I'm the last person you want to see, but I've a lot of explaining to do. And apologising for some of my youthful decisions. I was a bitch back then. Can you please forgive me?'

I curse myself for giving in to her limp handshake, but I'm too stunned to do anything else right now. She smells of Chanel, her complexion is flawless, and her eyebrows are heightened by what looks like a recent dose of Botox.

Mrs Quinn isn't a fuddy-duddy little old lady with too much time on her hands, like I imagined her to be.

Mrs Quinn is my age or thereabouts. She is rich, she is glamorous, and she has a striking look with a voice that ties my stomach into knots in the same way it always used to.

Mrs Quinn is my nemesis. She is Olivia Major.

Chapter Twenty-two

Ben

One Day to Christmas Eve

Ballyheaney House is feeling festive and prepared. The fires are lit, the house is cosy, the trees are sparkling, but outside is a different story as the heavens have opened.

So much for the weather being on our side.

Raindrops bounce heavily off the patio area out the back, forming a flowing river that seeps on to the lawns while all five of us all stand at the long, tall windows of the ballroom, looking on with a sense of doom. Even Roly joins in. He whimpers pathetically with his front paws on the low windowsill.

'Maybe Dad's trying to give us a sign to say we should have let sleeping dogs lie,' says Cordelia, sipping her tea. 'I can almost hear him cursing us, even challenging his precious drainage system to make his point.'

None of us answers because none of us knows the answer, though we're probably all thinking the very same.

'The whole place is already a sodding mess outside,'

Uncle Eric moans to me. I do believe it's the first time he has said anything to me directly since I told him Lou wouldn't be helping us out any further. I wonder if she received my flowers yesterday. I've heard nothing from her as yet. 'We'll have a hundred dripping umbrellas in the hallway and muddy feet throughout the whole house. This is a disaster.'

Ava looks like she might cry. Mum looks like she's frozen to the spot. I'm the picture of misery for so many reasons that I've almost lost count, from Ava's upset to being separated again from Lou after everything was going so well.

Maybe we should have stayed in Dublin for Christmas after all.

'All right, team. Get it all out of your system once and for all,' says Cordelia, clapping her hands together.

'Eh?' says Uncle Eric.

'All of your moans, groans and worries,' she continues. 'Spit them all out now because in thirty seconds we're shifting this negative energy and getting back to what we do best round here.'

'What's that?' asks Uncle Eric.

'Very funny,' she replies. 'You know what I'm talking about. Shake off all those worries once and for all because tomorrow, on Christmas Eve, we are going to rock everyone's socks off with the best party this village has ever seen, rain or no rain.'

I like her thinking. I'm not usually a defeatist, but I have felt the mood slipping as the afternoon rolls in and the rain dances against the windowpanes.

'Remember the year we'd the crisp, fresh snow and

sunshine,' Mum recalls with a smile. 'That was such a wonderful party.'

'Or when it snowed so heavily one time, we had to clear the laneways with a snowplough,' Uncle Eric chuckles. 'We thought it would stop our guests, but no. Instead, it added to the fun and the atmosphere was the best I'd ever known.'

I put my hand on Ava's shoulder. She doesn't move away like I expected she might, which both surprises and delights me. I haven't been able to reach her properly since Uncle Eric's outburst in this very room the evening before last.

'That's the spirit,' says Cordelia. 'We can't control the weather, but we can take care of everything else, so let's go, family. Let's get this show on the road.'

Thank heavens for my sister.

Her upbeat vibe and uplifting energy is instantly contagious, and I feel my spirits rise a little as she clicks her fingers and sways to imaginary music. She takes Ava by both hands and swirls her around.

'OK, so it's time to check our to-do list,' I say, doing my best to match my sister's evergreen glow. 'Let's go over it so we know exactly what needs doing before we open the doors on the big day.'

I fetch a clipboard from the table, waiting for the inevitable groan from the others. We always joked how the person with the clipboard was the person wanting to be in charge, so I lovingly pass it to my sister with a smile.

'Ava, you're with me in the kitchen,' says Cordelia, running her eye down what's left to do today. 'Are you good at decorating pastries? I know that's a silly question. Of course you are.'

'I can try,' my daughter answers quietly.

'She is perfect for that job,' says Mum. 'What do you need me to do, then?'

Cordelia paces around the ballroom where chairs are stacked in corners and Dad's makeshift stage leans against the wall.

'Mum, we'll need you to keep an eye out for a delivery of leaflets and goody bags from the Daffodil charity,' says Cordelia, full of business.

'Uncle, we'll get cracking on these tables and chairs,' I say to Uncle Eric, doing my best not to think too much about how Lou would be taking over if she were here, dressing the tables to perfection like only she could. 'And we need to set the stage up too for the jazz band. If it crackles with thunder outside while we're doing so, then Dad is definitely sending us a sign. Though he did love jazz music.'

Uncle Eric rolls up his sleeves and chuckles. Joking aside, I do think my father would have more than mixed feelings about throwing the Christmas Eve party again, but despite his griping year after year, he always managed to enjoy it when it was in full swing.

Overall, he was often overwhelmed when it came to the upkeep of Ballyheaney House, having watched his own father and grandfather develop it over the years into what it is today. Dad believed each generation had a responsibility to pass on the house in a better condition than they found it, and I promised him that Cordelia and I would do just that.

We haven't quite figured out how yet, we haven't discussed where we'll find the money, but there's so much potential.

Cordelia and Ava head off to the kitchen to decorate pastries, while Mum goes to the drawing room to relax and keep watch for the arrival of the charity leaflets and gifts. As I watch Ava set off to help her aunt, my heart bursts with pride.

'You know I feel your mum so close to us every day, Ava,' I told her last night at bedtime, but she barely lifted her eyes from her iPad. 'She's never far away. I can still hear her voice in my head, I can still see her beautiful face, and sometimes when I walk into our bedroom, I even think I can smell her perfume.'

It was the truth. As much as I feel my father's presence here at Ballyheaney House, I often find Stephanie when I need her most.

'I wish that would happen me too,' said Ava, before turning away from me. 'Nothing like that ever happens to me.'

I sat on the edge of the bed, praying to Stephanie like I always do, asking her to help me find the words to guide our daughter as best I can. At times like this, I long for the warmth of her familiar wisdom or her gentle touch to get us through. It's like walking a tightrope, balancing my own grief for the loss of the life we'd planned, while doing my best to care for and protect our precious child.

'It's such a slippery slope, isn't it,' Cordelia said to me this morning over breakfast. 'The poor wee mite must be so confused. One minute she wants you to find someone to live happily ever after with, but then the guilt and sadness she feels when she realises nothing is going to fill that gaping hole her mother has left tears her apart. You're doing a great job, Ben. Don't be hard on yourself, and don't give up on finding love again either. You deserve to.'

But I'm not so sure any more. One minute I'm marvelling at how far Ava and I have come over the last six years since we lost Stephanie, and then, just when I feel we're steady, a tiny remark or a careless word can remind me that we've still a long way to go.

'Have I ruined everything for you?' Uncle Eric asks me as we unstack chairs in the ballroom. He can just about manage to lift one chair at a time, reminding me of how frail he is behind his bravado. 'I put my big size-ten feet in it with Ava, didn't I? Not once but twice since you got here. Me and my big mouth.'

He keeps glancing out the window. I know he's hoping that Lou will rock up any minute and declare she's back on board, not only for the party but for all of us.

'It wasn't the cleverest thing to say at the time,' I reply, 'but it's not your fault. Lou and I had a few heated words on Saturday night, which pushed the first domino on the whole tricky situation.'

He stops and leans on the back of a chair, clearly waiting for another 'but' to follow. I don't say a word.

'Well, that has made me feel like shit,' he says.

'Good,' I jest in return.

'So is that it, then?' he asks me. I'm not sure what he means at first. 'Lou has scuttled away from Ballyheaney again, and

Ava is miserable, so you're going to rush back to Dublin to get on with a lonely life there. Are you telling me we're doing all of this for nothing?'

Now it's my turn to stare at him and wait.

'Hang on a minute, I'm confused,' I tell him. 'What do you mean, "we're doing all of this for nothing"?'

'This,' he says, looking round the room.

'Do you mean the party?' I ask him.

'Yes, I mean the party,' he says. 'If Lou isn't here, you're unhappy, and Ava is unhappy at the mention of her name, so we've done all this for nothing.'

I pause from unstacking the chairs. 'Uncle Eric, is there something going on here that I don't know?'

He lifts the chair and shuffles across the room to put it in its place, muttering to himself, but I can't make out a word he is saying except for something along the lines of how he's said far too much again.

'I think I need to speak to my sister,' I say, bursting out of the ballroom and walking briskly down the hallway to the kitchen.

When I reach Cordelia, she and Ava are making up some sort of dance routine while holding wooden spoons to an earworm-type Christmas song I don't recognise at first.

'Dad, Dad, you should see some of Cordelia's sassy moves,' Ava giggles. 'She almost did the splits.'

'Accidentally!' says Cordelia. 'I slipped on some cream spilled on the floor. That would have been a disaster and a half!'

'Cordelia, can I have a word?' I ask.

She puts down the wooden spoon slowly. Ava does the same.

'Is something wrong, Ben?' she says. 'You've a face on you like thunder. It's worse than the weather outside.'

I don't want to say anything more in front of Ava.

'Darling, can you give me and your aunty a few minutes?' I ask my daughter. 'Maybe you can go and check on Grandma. She's in the drawing room.'

'She's probably fallen asleep waiting for the delivery,' replies Ava before leaving us to it in the kitchen. 'Are you going to talk about Lou again behind my back?'

My heart stops.

'No, I'm not going to talk about Lou behind your back.'

'Or should I say, the love of your life,' she replies. Why do I feel like I'm being attacked by my own family at every opportunity?

'Maybe I should tell you to go to your room for speaking to me like that?' I say to my daughter, the pain of being at loggerheads with her almost too much to bear. 'Look, Ava, go and check on your grandmother, please. I need to speak to Cordelia.'

'I'm so sick of you!' she says, storming off, while Cordelia turns her back to me, busying herself with her culinary creations. I'll deal with Ava later. In the meantime, Cordelia doesn't fool me. I know she's hiding something and it's time I got to the bottom of it.

'Cordelia, what's going on?'

'Sorry?' she says, genuinely puzzled. 'I've no idea where

that came from with Ava. She was dancing and singing a few minutes ago.'

'Are you Mrs Quinn?' I ask her. 'Was that letter a fake, or is there such a person in real life? What have you been up to?'

'Don't be silly, Ben,' she mumbles.

'Then can you shed some light on what the hell has been happening behind my back?' I ask her. 'Is the whole idea of throwing this party again some sort of deliberate matchmaking ploy to get me home so I'd spend time with Lou? What have you been up to? Talk to me!'

She puts both hands on the worktop, her head bowed and her eyes closed.

'You're making it sound like it was done with some sort of malice in mind,' she tells me.

'So it was! I can't believe it!'

'Yes, it was all my idea, but bringing the party back was meant to be fun for us all, Ben,' she says. 'It was meant to be a way of getting us all back together after far too long.'

I don't know whether to laugh or scream.

'Oh yes, how wonderful. Let's get the whole merry gang back together,' I say, doing my best not to raise my voice. 'Let's play with people's lives like they're puppets on a string. This is not a game, Cordelia! Maybe now you can see how it's not quite as simple as that, is it? Who else was in on the big plan, eh? Mum? Was Lou? Did you convince Ava? Uncle Eric certainly was, as he's just let the cat out of the bag and it's not the first time he's said too much since I got here.'

She turns to face me at last.

'No, Lou wasn't in on it and neither was Ava,' she tells me. 'You're already overthinking it, making it more about you than it was ever meant to be. I am not Mrs Quinn.'

'Then who is?'

'Olivia Major, but that's totally irrelevant,' she mutters. 'Quinn is her married name. Before you spontaneously combust, the whole thing has very little to do with her, believe me!'

I find a chair and sit down, putting my head in my hands.

'Is this some sort of bloody freak show?' I ask my sister. 'I haven't as much as thought of Olivia Major or Olivia Quinn since I was a twenty-something lovesick kid, so why would she want to have anything to do with my life now? What's in it for her? I don't get it.'

Cordelia sits down across from me. Her face is flushed, though her usual vibrant tone isn't quite dampened yet.

'Breathe, Ben,' she tells me, holding my gaze. 'Let me explain before you give yourself a heart attack. I've told you, it wasn't her idea. It was mine. I knew you wouldn't agree to the party if it came from the inside, but it all fell into place once I started to look into it. I was the one who got Olivia involved. It was coincidental that she was chairperson of that events committee in the village, and her letter, which was my idea, was a minor detail overall.'

'So you're telling me you orchestrated this all behind my back and pretended it had come from the village?' I reply. 'I'm sorely disappointed in you, Cordelia. Olivia Major of all people!'

She slowly blows out a long breath.

'This was never intended to be all about you,' she says, 'nor was it ever a scheme of any sort to push you and Lou back together, so please take about ten steps back in your overactive mind and breathe.'

I do my best to give her the benefit of the doubt.

'Go on,' I say, looking at my watch. 'This had better be good.'

The charity lady said she'd have the goody bags delivered by four-thirty and I've just heard a vehicle outside.

'I can explain,' says Cordelia.

The doorbell rings.

'Well, you'd better explain very quickly,' I say to her.

She takes a deep breath. 'With my convincing, Olivia agreed to write to Mum to see if that got the ball rolling,' she tells me. 'But once the letter was posted, she said she would step out of the way and leave it to me to do the rest. Which she did, over and out.'

I bite my lip. I hear Uncle Eric open the front door.

'It was all very innocent, Ben!' she continues. 'We talked only briefly about the good old days, the parties here year on year. She was asking about all of us. I said how I was worried that Mum had become reclusive and that Uncle Eric was lonely too. We never talked about involving Lou if the party was a goer, but yes, I was probably secretly hoping that it might happen. I hoped it would bring some joy back to these silent walls. I'm sorry if you think I was wrong.'

I open my mouth to respond, even though the words are stuck in my throat. My mind is replaying the events of the last two weeks in fast forward. The phone call from Cordelia, the speed at which everything had happened, the way I'd fallen for it all to make Ava happy. Yet here we are, it's potentially falling apart, and I was in the dark the whole time.

But before I can find what I want to say, I follow Cordelia's gaze to the kitchen doorway, where Uncle Eric looks like he has won the lottery.

'Look who I found on our doorstep almost drowning in the rain,' he announces. 'The First Lady of Bellaghy village herself. Mind you, Lou, you'd be forgiven if you thought we were planning a funeral or a wake rather than a Christmas party from the look on these two faces.'

'Hi, Ben. Hi, Cordelia,' Lou says, peeping round from behind Uncle Eric, who hasn't yet realised he is totally block-ing her way. He steps aside, his arm outstretched as if Lou is some form of royalty.

I suppose to him she is. And to me too, if truth be told. She looks exhausted under her big, hooded coat, her pale face accentuated by her damp dark hair and navy branded jumper over loose-fit jeans and trainers.

'I'd fully intended to stay out of your way today,' she tells us, her eyes darting around the kitchen. I've just realised that Cordelia and Ava's song has been playing on repeat. 'Feliz Navidad', that's what it's called. 'But then something changed my mind. Thank you, Ben.'

Cordelia glances from her to me then back again.

'Why aren't you all racing about to get everything ready?' Lou asks. 'The tables in the ballroom, the stage . . . anyhow, I've no doubt you've it all under control. Don't mind me.'

Cordelia speaks up before I get the chance to.

'I'm sorry, Lou,' she says, standing up to make her point. 'Ben has just found out that the idea for the party was instigated by me, but I made it look like it was a committee headed up by—'

'Olivia Major, now Olivia Quinn,' Lou interrupts. 'I know already. I spoke to her yesterday when she unexpectedly turned up to my shop, apologised profusely and told me she'd written the letter to Tilda under your guidance. Turns out her niece, Beth, is one of my favourite customers. I think I'll be over the shock of that alone by, say, next Christmas Eve? She's cool. We're all cool in that department.'

Cordelia walks towards her, helps her take off her wet coat and gives Lou a hug.

'Well, I'm glad someone's cool, cos Ben is still chewing wasps over it all. It might take him a bit longer to forgive me,' she says, 'but please know it wasn't in any way an attempt to push you two together. Can I get you anything? Tea? Coffee? Whiskey?'

Lou laughs at the suggestion of whiskey at this time of the day, holding up instead a bag of what I assume are her famous Colombian coffee beans. I'm tempted to ask for a brandy for medicinal purposes myself.

'How have you been?' I ask Lou as Cordelia fixes a pot of coffee.

She smiles and shrugs in return.

'Not bad,' she tells me. 'I've been feeling a bit like the Grinch, if truth be told, no matter how I try to shake it off. Gracie not coming over for Christmas has been difficult for me, but your gift yesterday made my day. Thank you for your words. And the flowers are stunning, even if you gave your business elsewhere.'

I pull out a chair beside me.

'I didn't want to make it obvious by ordering flowers from you,' I explain, even though I know she's joking. 'I'm so glad you liked them.'

She sits down.

Uncle Eric muddles past us, saying something about making a start on the stage, even though I know he has no intention of any manual labour. Still, he disappears nonetheless, singing as he goes, seemingly unaware of how in his old age he has somewhat lost the filter between his brain and his mouth. In a way, I love him even more for it.

'My God, it's good to see you,' I say, losing my own filter for a moment too.

Cordelia pours us a coffee.

'I'll just go and check on Ava,' she says. 'Won't be long.'

I can hear my own heartbeat thumping in my ears when it's just the two of us again. Lou stares at her coffee cup, then looks up at me with a smile.

'It's good to see you too,' she says.

I put my hand on top of hers.

'I've missed you.'

'It's only been a day or so since I saw you last. You've got it bad,' she jokes. 'I'm so sorry, Ben. I'm sorry for all that's happened between us now and all that happened when we were younger. We're not the same people any more, but there's no denying how I long to get to know you again.'

Butterflies dance around inside of me. I lean across and

lightly brush her hair from her eyes. I want to kiss her, I want to hold her and tell her how, yes, we've changed, but the chemistry between us has never gone away and never will.

'I'm sorry too for the part I played in stopping us from having what we both wanted more than anything,' I tell her. 'Let's draw a line under it all if we can?'

But our bubble bursts when Cordelia comes racing back into the kitchen out of breath, her cheeks reddened and panic in her eyes.

Lou and I both jump up from our seats.

My first thought is Uncle Eric or Mum. Has something happened to one of them?

'I can't find Ava!' she cries.

'What do you mean, you can't find her?' I shout.

My heart rate goes through the roof in an instant.

'I've checked the whole house, Ben,' says Cordelia. 'She's not in her room, she's not with Mum, she's not with Uncle Eric. It's raining buckets out there still and she's nowhere to be found. Ava is gone, Ben. It's already getting dark outside. Come quick! We need to find her.'

Chapter Twenty-three

Lou

Ben searches the grounds of Ballyheaney House with a fine-tooth comb, scrambling through the stable stalls while calling out Ava's name. The rain is persistent, loud and unforgiving, making visibility even poorer, not to mention heightening the fear that she might be out there somewhere huddling for shelter.

Cordelia has gone into the village, pledging to check every nook and cranny on the streets as well as the shops and restaurants, while I've told Mum and Nana Molly to let us know immediately if she turns up at Buds and Beans.

'Edward and I are going to take a drive around while Nana minds the shop,' Mum tells me when I call her in a state of despair. 'We've been so busy since you left, but this is much more important.'

'Edward?' I ask her.

'Master Campbell,' she replies. 'He's waiting on me outside already, so I'll keep in touch.'

Good old Edward. He really is a decent sort. I just hope Nana Molly hasn't knocked him back if he's finally asked her to the Christmas Eve party tomorrow. I still haven't had a chance to ask him if he plucked up the courage or changed his mind.

'I didn't even hear her leave the house,' says Tilda. 'Please God, let her be safe. It's going to be dark very soon. I'll never forgive myself for not hearing her leave if she's come to any trouble.'

We estimate Ava had left the house no more than fifteen to twenty minutes before Cordelia discovered her missing, which gives her a fairly decent head start to make an escape, but I do my best to play it down to Ben, who's gone so pale with worry.

'She's a child, she's only a child,' Ben keeps repeating before we go our separate ways again to continue searching. 'She thinks she knows this area, but she doesn't at all. And for a twelve-year-old, she isn't streetwise. She'll panic once she strays too far and can't find her way back.'

'We'll find her,' I promise him. 'You and I grew up here, so we *do* know the area. So does Cordelia. I'll go down to the strand boardwalk and search there. She can't have got too far.'

We are crippled with fear, but adrenaline has kicked in and we've developed a plan at lightning speed, agreeing that Tilda and Uncle Eric will keep checking the house and alert us if Ava returns.

'Be careful,' Ben tells me as I leave him at the gates of Ballyheaney House. 'I still have some parts of the grounds here to check. You will let me know as soon as you can if you find her?'

I nod in response, my heart bleeding for him as he sets off with Roly towards the outhouses, hoping to find his precious girl.

'We'll find her!' I shout out to him again. He doesn't hear me as he's too busy calling for Ava through the relentless wind and rain. I jump into the car and drive as fast as I can down to the village, where I park up on the Ballydermot Road and get ready to face the elements. At least I know this area like the back of my hand.

Lough Beg in winter has always been breathtaking, but my mission here today isn't to admire the scenery, which is slowly disappearing into the evening mist, but to search it instead.

With the hood of my waterproof coat dipping over my forehead, I scour the landscape as best I can through the sheets of icy rain. The shades of green that usually frame the strand boardwalk are now muted to greys and browns, the water on the lake is calm with small ripples forming across its surface, and the bare branches of the trees are silhouetted against the dull sky.

'Ava!' I call out, treading carefully along the slippery boardwalk, but my voice goes nowhere. The air is damp. It catches my breath as the smell of burning peat fills my nostrils from chimney pots in the distance. It's already gone five o'clock, so the dark clouds and the mist in the air make it hard to see the spire on Church Island, never mind help me to find a runaway child.

My stomach clenches. I say a prayer as I leave the boardwalk and walk towards the woods, using the torch on my phone as I approach, though it doesn't make much difference in the murky light. My gut knows that Ava won't have ventured too far, nor would she want to feel scared, but I keep on walking, something telling me to do so.

'Ava!' I call again. 'Ava, darling, are you out here? Can you hear me?'

My phone bleeps as a text message arrives. It's Cordelia. I stop in my tracks, my fingers shaking as I open the message after wiping raindrops off my screen.

She isn't in the village. I've checked everywhere. Oh Lou, this is so frightening.

I double-check to see if there's an update from Ben, but no. There's nothing.

I close my eyes and do my best to think straight. A twelve-year-old girl, confused and angry at her father, overwhelmed with feelings of guilt, fear and longing, a little girl who only wants to be loved. Where would she go? How much does she know about Lough Beg? What did I know when I was her age? Where might I have run to?

I have an idea. It's a long shot, but it's worth a check.

I start walking again. My pace quickens so much I'm almost jogging, until I slip and fall, catching my hand on a sharp bramble.

'Ouch!'

I clamber back to my feet and brush the dead leaves from my legs, allowing myself a moment to get my breath back. I see a dog walker in the distance, someone out for a rainy walk completely oblivious to the terror I'm feeling as the clock ticks away. No word from Ben. No word from Tilda or Uncle Eric either, who are keeping watch at the house.

I can't see the hut in the distance, but I head right towards it, only because I know what I'm looking for. It's so well camouflaged, nestled in nature and almost invisible to a casual observer in daylight, never mind the dark of winter. Hundreds and hundreds of people will have passed through this dense woodland patch, never noticing the result of hours of labour by a group of young teenagers in the nineties who longed for a hideaway from the big bad world.

We called it the Shepherd's Mud Hut, even though there was more chance of seeing cattle round here than sheep back then. Some said it had been built by the British army years ago for shelter, but I knew different.

I straighten myself up and take a deep breath, but this time I don't call her by name.

Instead, I go to the entrance of the man-made shelter, twigs snapping under my feet and the wind whipping up a storm, though it doesn't mask the sobbing sound from inside.

I crouch down, holding on to the sodden, weathered wood while doing my best to avoid jagged nails above me. I peer through the branches.

And then I see her.

'Oh, Ava!'

She is a tiny and pitiful sight, tucked up against the far wall of the grubby hut. She doesn't look at me, nor does she answer at first.

'Ava, darling, it's Lou,' I say softly. 'Are you OK? I've been looking for you. We all have.'

She still doesn't look at me directly, but I can see her deep brown eyes, so full of fear.

'What time is it?' she asks me, sniffling as she speaks. 'Is my dad really mad? I heard what he said to Uncle Eric about you. And then when I saw you arrive at Ballyheaney I couldn't stay there, so I ran, but I'm sorry, Lou. I'm scared and I'm sorry.'

I crawl in beside her, hoping that if I stay calm then she will too. The hut smells of damp earth and pine, and the ground is not as dry as it used to be in here. It's covered in soggy leaves and mossy branches. A couple of sun-faded beer cans are neatly stacked in the corner, telling me Ava isn't the only one to have found my once-secret hiding place.

'He isn't mad at you, honey. He's very worried, so why don't I tell him I've found you, eh?' I say to her. I sit down on the damp ground, trying to stay composed as I find her dad's number on my phone. 'Everything's going to be fine, Ava. You've nothing to worry about.'

I call Ben rather than message him, knowing he'll want to hear her voice to reassure him.

'I've found her,' I tell him, smiling at her in a bid to ease the fear in her eyes. 'Yes, yes, she's absolutely fine. She's safe, she's dry, and she's OK. I'll bring her home straight away. You go inside and get warmed up and we'll be right there.'

Ava reaches for my phone, so I give it to her, noticing how shaky, bright red and bitterly cold her hands are. I take off my coat and tuck it around her shoulders. My coat may be dripping wet on the outside, but inside it's cosy, soft and warm.

She doesn't object.

'I'm so sorry, Dad,' she tells him, her little voice all aquiver. 'I'm sorry for worrying you. I thought you were mad with me, so I ran. I know it was stupid. I'm sorry.'

I can hear Ben's voice, but I can't make out what he is saying so I close my eyes, savouring the relief I feel inside while knowing it's not even a patch on what he's going through.

'How did you know where I was?' Ava asks me when she ends the phone call.

'Because I've been here before too, many times,' I tell her.

'Really?' she asks in bewilderment. 'Roly found this place when we went walking with Grandma. She said I'd found a secret hideout never discovered before.'

'Well done, Roly,' I whisper. 'He has been helping your dad look for you too.'

She sniffles loudly and gasps.

'I wasn't going to stay here for long though,' she says quickly. 'I only wanted to get away from everything and have a think. I'm not sure what's going on with you and my dad and it scares me.'

I remind myself how Ava doesn't know me very much at all yet. To her, I'm the florist in the place that makes nice hot chocolate, I'm the family friend who helped a bit with the party. I'm the one who was once in love with her dad, though I don't know how much of that she's heard so far.

'When I was about thirteen, not much older than you,' I

tell her, 'me and my friends would come down here in the summer. I wasn't allowed out this far, so I didn't dare tell my parents or Nana Molly where I was going. Some local boys gathered wood, we found some rubber coverings in my dad's shed to make a patchwork roof, and soon we had our very own place to play card games, listen to music on our battery radio and hang out together away from it all. I'd sometimes come here alone too when I was confused or scared, to think, just like you were doing. We called it the Shepherd's Mud Hut. It's cool, isn't it?'

She nods, looking around her, wide-eyed in wonder.

'So, you built this?'

'Yep,' I say, feeling a pinch of nostalgia for innocent days gone by. 'With a little help from my friends. But see that patch of rubber right above you? If you look really closely, you can see where I wrote my initials in permanent marker. It was my thirteenth birthday, and I thought it was the coolest place in the whole world.'

I point my phone torch towards it to show her.

'Impressive,' she says, taking in her surroundings.

We sit side by side, shoulder to shoulder, and suddenly I'm hiding here at the age of thirteen again, caught up in tangled emotions. One minute bold and confident, the next full of fear and frustration.

'Ava, I know that Christmas can be hard when you've lost someone special, especially your beautiful mum,' I tell her, hoping I haven't crossed a line by bringing it up. 'You see lots of friends your age with both parents, and it makes you feel very lonely and very different.'

She wipes away some fresh tears from her eyes, staring at the ground with her knees huddled under her chin.

'No, you don't know,' she replies. 'How would you know what it feels like? You're a grown-up, so you can't know anything about it. You all think you do, but you don't.'

I take a deep breath, understanding how isolated she is feeling right now.

'You're right, I don't know fully what you're going through, but I can understand a little because my daddy died very suddenly when I was a teenager,' I explain.

'Oh,' she replies.

'Very suddenly,' I reply. 'He was killed in an accident at work. I was so angry at myself for a long time. I was angry at everyone, to tell you the truth. I ran away too. Not in this way, but I ran away to America for the summer, as I couldn't bear to be at home without him.'

'Sorry to hear that,' she mumbles.

'And even though I was quite a bit older than you were when it happened, it hurt like nothing had ever hurt before,' I say, doing my best not to well up. 'I still feel very sad when I think of him and how much he missed out on. And then when I think of my mum, who really misses her husband, that can make me sad too. It wasn't fair. It still isn't fair, even though I'm a grown-up now. It still hurts. I still miss him.'

Ava stares at the ground. I realise I need to get her home quickly to the cosy fire in Ballyheaney House, but I also need to let her air her feelings now that she's away from it all.

'I don't remember her all that much,' she gasps.

'Oh, Ava.'

'It scares me,' she says, her chin trembling and her shoulders shaking as she speaks. I could put my arm around her, but I don't want to interrupt what she's saying. 'I'm so afraid I'm forgetting her that it keeps me awake at night. And now I'm afraid that Dad will forget her too.'

'Your dad could never forget your mummy,' I say.

'He will now that he's found his one true love again,' she tells me.

My heart skips a beat.

'His one true love?' I ask her. 'Who said that?'

'Uncle Eric said that you are Dad's one true love, so he needs to be careful not to lose you again,' she sobs. 'If that's the case, then why did he marry my mummy? Why didn't he marry you instead? Hearing that makes me think he didn't love her in the first place. He loved you more.'

I shake my head, wanting to shake Uncle Eric too for putting such notions into a child's head, even though I'm sure he didn't mean any harm. Well, this changes things entirely. No wonder the poor child is confused.

'Let's start walking home and we can talk more,' I suggest. 'Would that be all right?'

She nods, her little face furrowed into a frown. I attempt to crawl out of the hut without scraping my knees or grazing my hands again. Thankfully, when we get outside, the rain has subsided into a light drizzle, leaving the ground mulchy and slippery beneath our feet.

'I think us grown-ups have some explaining to do,' I say as we walk side by side towards the boardwalk. 'Ava, your daddy found his perfect life partner when he met your mum.

Cordelia was telling me all about her and she sounds so wonderful. Please don't listen to what Uncle Eric said. The whole family were utterly heartbroken to lose her, which says a lot for how much she was loved by you all.'

She fixes my coat against her chin, still too cold to brave the elements without it.

'Dad says he feels her near him sometimes, but I never get that,' she says when we're about halfway across the boardwalk. She stops, then bends down and lifts a twig before throwing it into the lake.

A pair of swans fly above our heads, so closely that we duck down to avoid their swooping wings from brushing our heads.

'Wow!' she says. 'Did you feel that?'

This makes her giggle. It makes me laugh too.

'Did you know that when two swans fall in love, they mate for life?' I say to Ava as we watch them land on the lake under the moonlight, their huge grey-white wings flapping until they find their balance. 'Watch how they glide together, almost synchronised in every way as a sign of their deep love. They are fiercely protective of each other, especially when they've a young cygnet. And that baby becomes the most important thing in the whole world for them. The swan mum and dad would do anything for her. Anything.'

Ava's eyes flicker back and forth as she concentrates. Her head tilts slightly and she purses her lips in deep thought.

'Your dad has told me how happy he and your mum were together, Ava,' I continue. 'He didn't want anyone else but his very beautiful, caring wife. He chose to marry her, and they pledged to be together for as long as they both lived, which they did, just like the swans do.'

I watch as Ava's eyes follow the gracious birds until they almost disappear into the distance.

'But what if one of the swans dies?' she asks me. 'What does the other one do then?'

I thought she might say as much.

'When one swan dies, the other grieves for a very long time,' I explain, glad that I'd heard all about this from Nana Molly when I was a child. 'The other swan will usually be extremely sad and lonely. He or she will have a broken heart.'

'Forever?' she asks me.

'Sometimes forever,' I tell her. 'Though sometimes he or she might meet a new mate, meaning they get to be happy again, sometimes for the rest of their life. It doesn't mean they didn't love the first swan, of course. Or that the first swan will ever be forgotten. Our hearts are made for lots of love, Ava. Even when they're broken.'

She takes a deep breath.

'So he won't ever forget her?' she asks me.

'Never,' I say straight back. 'And you won't forget your mum either, because she can't be too far away when you are here. You are part of her. Ava, your precious young mother left everyone who loved her one of the favourite parts of her behind. You.'

Ava puts her hand to her chest, then looks up to the sky as the moon shines brightly through the clouds. We both stare in wonder at the drastic change in weather, then our eyes meet for the first time since I found her huddled in the hut.

'Look, it's her!' Ava tells me, her face now full of hope. 'She loved the sun and she loved the moon so much. Not as much as she loved me and Dad of course.'

'That's her saying hello,' I whisper, putting my hand on her shoulder. 'See? You only have to look or ask, and she'll be right beside you every step of the way.'

Ava beams a smile almost as bright as the moon above us.

'So I've nothing to worry about,' she says, but I think it's more to herself than it is to me. 'There's enough love for everyone, even when a heart is broken.'

'You'd better believe it,' I tell her.

We walk along the rest of the boardwalk in silence, and when we get to the car park at the Ballydermot Road, Ben is there waiting for his number-one girl, with his arms outstretched and tears in his eyes.

Ava points up to the bright, shining moon, showing her dad with delight.

'I see her, baby,' he tells her. 'I told you I see her everywhere we go.'

I watch on with the strong feeling that the fuzzy joy of Christmas might be a bit closer now at long last. We deserve this and we need this.

And I think I can say that now for all of us.

Chapter Twenty-four

Christmas Eve

Shimmering baubles glisten under the chandeliers in the huge hallway, fairy lights twinkle and dance above the glow of flickering church candles on every surface, and the smell of spicy mulled wine mixed with fresh pine fills the air.

Everyone is dressed for the occasion already, except Ava, who is upstairs with Cordelia trying to choose between an outfit all the way from Madrid, or a sparkly dress she claims is 'a bit last year'.

I think the Spanish option might win.

I also imagine that Cordelia will be itching to get back to the kitchen to put the finishing touches on her culinary delights in time for serving. My mouth waters at the thought of it all.

'Excuse me? Over this way, please,' I call out to the leader of the jazz band, who is heading in the wrong direction with what looks like a large trombone. 'Yes, follow me and I'll show you where to set up in the ballroom. Thank you so much. I can't wait to hear your music. What a treat!'

The jazz musician and his fellow band members follow as Ben brushes past me, barely time to stop, though he touches my arm briefly before making his way to the front door to greet some of the villagers who have volunteered for car-park and waitering duties.

I shiver beneath his touch, remembering how hard it was for him to leave me last night after we'd spent a snatched couple of hours together in my cottage once Ava was tucked up in bed, fast asleep and full of excitement for everything that today will bring. We lit the fire in my bedroom for the first time, we talked through the whole event from start to finish, and we made up for our last attempt at romance by lying in each other's arms. It was heavenly.

I tiptoe into the ballroom for a final look and my heart swells with pride. It truly is a sight to behold. The long, snow-white table is laid with fine china, while shining cutlery and crystal glasses all gleam in the soft light.

My harp sits tall and strong, waiting for me to bring it to life again, a request from Tilda I couldn't possibly refuse and a nice way of me remembering my dad, who bought it for me all those years ago.

In the corner just like before, Jack Heaney's stage is already filled with musical instruments and a sound system to get the party started.

I only wish Gracie was here to see it all. I wish Nana Molly was coming too, but it turns out old Edward didn't invite her after all, and Nana laughed at the suggestion when I mentioned it, so it's probably a good thing he didn't.

'Lou, he's far too young for me,' she said. 'I wish you all well with the event, but I won't be attending. I burnt my bridges with the Heaneys long ago, and I'd rather spend the afternoon in front of the telly with a sherry in peace, no harm intended.'

'Jealous,' whispered Mum, who to the contrary was buzzing even more than I'd anticipated. She couldn't wait for the clock to turn two so she could show up in her new emerald-green dress and matching shoes. But I was baffled by what Nana said about burning bridges. It seems there is more to her avoidance of Ballyheaney House than she's been letting on, but she refused to comment any further and I got tired of asking her. Maybe she'll tell me when it's all over.

'Thank you, Lou,' Tilda says, coming up behind me as I take a moment to double-check the ballroom set-up before our guests arrive. 'I'm not sure I've said it to you enough, but despite whatever hiccups may have arisen over the past few days, we couldn't have created this magic without you. The whole house is like something from a fairy tale.'

'It really is,' I agree. 'It not only looks like a fairy tale, but it feels like a fairy tale too. What a team. There's no way I can take all the credit. It's your beautiful home, after all.'

Tilda looks around in wonder. It really is a sight to behold, from the crackling log fire in the grate to the snowflake-shaped napkin holders, which add a playful touch to the elegance. The flowers are exquisite, if I do say so myself, with the white roses looking particularly beautiful against the gold ribbon.

'I think Jack, grumpy as he may have been, would be very proud of us today,' says Tilda. 'You have really made him part of it all with your finishing touches and finesse.'

My eyes fill up when she puts her arm around my shoulder,

a gesture that I know is way out of her comfort zone. Tilda is a warm and loving mother and grandmother, but outside of her immediate family circle she is reserved when it comes to showing emotion.

'Even the weather is on our side,' I say, nodding at the long windows to acknowledge the crisp, dry afternoon we've been blessed with. 'A far cry from yesterday's torrential downpour. Yes, I agree. It sure does look like Mr Heaney might approve after all.'

Out in the hallway, Ben is organising the small group of schoolchildren, who are impeccably dressed in Christmas jumpers, ready and eager to greet our guests with Christmas carols. He looks dashing in his tuxedo, another subtle nod to his father's absence. Despite his reluctance to embrace the party, Jack Heaney would always turn up on the day looking fresh and dapper in black and white, his dicky bow perfectly tied beneath his chin. Uncle Eric has followed suit in similar attire, and with Cordelia's help his usually wispy white hair is slicked to the side. If I'm not mistaken, I believe he may even have allowed her to trim his bushy eyebrows.

'There she is! My golden girl,' Uncle Eric says to me in the hallway, looking in admiration at my black, sequinned jumpsuit and killer heels, which I know I'll regret wearing very soon. 'Is it too early for champagne? I feel incredibly nervous, Lou. Maybe it's my old age but I'm shaking.'

'Same,' I say, linking my arm through his. I lean my head on his shoulder. 'Uncle Eric, did you open your Christmas present early?'

I'd left him a sneaky present under the sitting-room tree which he seems to have found already.

'I have absolutely no idea what you might be talking about, but boy, I smell good,' he laughs.

'You rascal,' I say. 'Our guests will be here any minute, so I reckon it's the perfect time for a glass of champagne, though that display looks almost too good to touch.'

A pyramid of champagne flutes on the round hallway table is a striking centrepiece, but I can't take credit for it. Olivia had the idea when she came round earlier, armed with a magnum of champagne as a contribution from the committee, though I've a feeling it has come from her own pocket, if truth be told.

'I'll wait a few more minutes, then,' says Uncle Eric, licking his lips. 'Whoever thought we'd see the day that witch would be back through the doors of Ballyheaney. I hope she doesn't upset you.'

I throw my head back in laughter.

'No, she doesn't upset me at all any more,' I tell him. 'She's a much humbler version of herself now that she's in her forties. I haven't told anyone yet, but this morning I agreed to take one of her gorgeous puppies after Christmas. He's the last of the litter. I'm going to call him Jingle, as a reminder of the year we all got back together.'

Uncle Eric doesn't know whether to look puzzled or impressed at the revelation.

'As long as he reminds you of happy times. You always did like a festive name for the animals,' he says, in recognition of Little Eve. 'Maybe one day we'll have dogs and ponies and ducks back here at Ballyheaney.'

'Well, Alexander the Great is a good start,' I say. 'A Christmas party in full swing again and a peacock strutting around the courtyard are two bold steps in the right direction.'

Ben swoops in to join our conversation, but we don't take it too far as he's keen to make sure we're all in place to welcome the first of our guests, who are trickling into the car park already.

'Mum, Uncle Eric, make sure you're close by the front door,' he says. 'Cordelia! Ava!'

He calls up the stairs to where his sister and daughter seem to be taking ages to get ready. Cordelia is confident that all is under control in the kitchen, so she didn't mind taking the time to help Ava. We've all been keeping a close eye on her since yesterday's escapade, and when she asked me to stay for an early-evening Christmas movie once we were all warm and dry, I couldn't refuse such an endearing invitation for the second time.

'All set?' says Ben.

'All set,' I reply, my very toes tingling with anticipation.

As the clock strikes two, I let the schoolchildren's teacher know that their singing can begin, and when they strike up 'Let it Snow', jingling little sleigh bells in their hands, I have goosebumps.

Ben catches my eye again. We both break into a huge smile. This is it. We've made it happen, and it already feels even more special than we could have imagined.

I look to the left towards the staircase where Cordelia,

looking a vision in a white tailored trouser suit, makes her way down the stairs holding her niece's hand. Ava isn't wearing the Spanish outfit she'd almost settled on, nor is she wearing the sparkly dress which is too last year.

Instead, Ava is wearing a red dress which clashes fashionably with her auburn hair and fits her like a glove. With fine black buttons up the front, a flared skirt and neat collar, she looks like she's stepped out of a different era, with all the grace of the beautiful young lady she is becoming.

'Surprise!' says Cordelia when she reaches the bottom of the stairs. 'Wearing her grandmother's precious Christmas dress from 1960, please welcome our very own belle of the ball, Miss Ava Heaney.'

Ben bursts into applause, his face a picture of wonder while Tilda wipes tears from her eyes. Uncle Eric puts his hand on his chin, shaking his head with delight.

'Well, I never,' he says. 'What a spectacular touch to an already spectacular afternoon. And it looks like our first guests have arrived.'

Ava makes a beeline for me, her face bright and cheerful. This time I don't hesitate to give her a hug.

'I saw the framed photos of Mum and Grandpa you arranged in the drawing room,' she tells me, her voice full of delight. 'When the lady from the cancer charity asked who they were as she was setting up her information, I didn't even cry. I just told her all about them both and she was such a good listener.'

'See?' I say to her, squeezing her tighter. 'You'll never

forget your mummy. Never ever. Now, how'd your drawing-room playlist turn out?'

'Really cool! I even included 'Last Christmas' for Mum, and Bing Crosby for Grandpa Jack. I'd better go put it on before Cordelia asks me to help with more kitchen duties,' she says, a fresh sparkle in her eye and a spring in her step.

I look on in wonder from my position beside Olivia's magnificent champagne display, watching the Heaneys greet each and every guest with laughter, handshakes, hugs and enthusiasm. Declan the delivery guy is here with his mother, who is thankfully feeling well enough to attend.

'I've an extra donation for the charity,' he tells me, holding out an envelope stuffed with cash. 'Some of my clients around the village couldn't get tickets as it's sold out, so they asked me to pass these funds on instead. And there's something in there from me and Mum too as a thank you. We couldn't have got through her illness without the support of the community and the charity.'

I direct him to the drawing room, watching how he is so patient and attentive to his darling mother, the centre of his whole world.

'Lou, you look delightful,' I hear my mum say. 'Is there anything I can help with? Is this dress OK? I wasn't sure if it was a bit over the top, but Edward says it's perfect.'

'Ah, Edward!' I say as the penny drops.

I spot Master Campbell making his way towards us through the gathering crowd.

'He asked me to accompany him here today,' says Mum,

'and, well, I couldn't say no. I was quite honoured, to be honest. I used to fancy him lots back in the day.'

Well, I got that one wrong entirely, I think to myself. Today is already full of surprises. We pose for photographs, I check in with Cordelia, who has everything under control, and then I scan through the guest list to see that a couple of people are still due to arrive, including a few names I don't recognise as local. Soon it will be time for the food to be served, the jazz band will strike up, and everyone will mingle and chat over the sounds of laughter and the clinking of glasses.

Everything is running like clockwork. Everything is perfect, even if a claw in my gut still grabs me every now and then when I wonder if Gracie is missing me as much as I am her.

'When everything settles, how about you and I take a walk outside for old times' sake?' Ben whispers to me from behind my back.

'I like your thinking,' I say to him, turning to face him. I don't think I will ever tire of seeing his face or hearing his voice, not to mention feeling his touch. We haven't yet talked about our future, but we both know we're going very much in the right direction. 'Once the final guests arrive, everything should tick over nicely when the music kicks off and the food and drinks are served. Are you happy so far?'

'I'm ecstatic so far,' he says before sneaking a kiss on my forehead. 'I think that must be the last few people in now. Wait a minute, is that your grandma? She looks a million dollars.'

I slowly turn around again to face the front door, my jaw dropping at the sight of Nana Molly, who follows a few people I've never seen before, then politely air-kisses Tilda Heaney when she steps over the threshold. She looks dazzling in a royal-blue dress and silver flat pumps. Her hair is smoother than usual, and I believe I might be able to smell her perfume from here.

'Nana?' I say in disbelief. 'I thought you weren't coming.'

Uncle Eric catches my eye as he watches her like a love-struck puppy, waiting on her attention, but she casually ignores him.

No.

Surely it can't be.

'I'll admit it, I had FOMO,' she says to me with a shrug. 'Isn't that what the young ones say? Fear of missing out?'

'That's it,' I reply, leaning in for a hug to welcome her. 'I'm sure you know my good friend Eric Heaney?

I lightly pinch her arm in a bid to provoke some manners towards our host, but she defiantly puts her nose in the air.

'My one true secret love,' says Uncle Eric. 'Molly, my beautiful Molly. How I've dreamed this day would come.'

If it weren't for the schoolchildren singing 'White Christmas', you could have heard a pin drop here in the hallway of Ballyheaney House.

Nana Molly purses her lips tightly, but she can't hold back her giddy side for long before she starts to giggle.

'Bet you say that to all the girls, Heaney,' she says, giving him a look from the side of her eye and a friendly swipe.

'Now, any chance you might get me a champagne? I didn't come here for the good of my health, you know.'

Uncle Eric dances on his toes as he leads her across to the drinks display, which is more a lopsided rectangle now than the pyramid it was before, while Ben and I shake our heads in disbelief.

'Did you know about this?' I ask him.

'No,' he says, his eyes wide.

'Did you even have an inkling? I can't wait to tell Cordelia!'

'I had absolutely no clue,' he says, distracted it seems by some new activity by the front door. 'Oh, look. I thought your grandmother was the last to arrive going by our ticket numbers, but it appears we've another unexpected guest.'

'Then we're closing the doors,' I say to him without looking. 'We need to get food served before Cordelia has a fit, and rightly so. She doesn't deserve the pressure of trying to keep her canapés warm for people who can't be bothered to get here on time.'

Ben turns me around by the shoulders so I can see our late entry. My hands go to my mouth. My skin goes cold.

'Sorry to gatecrash,' I hear an all-too-familiar American accent. 'I don't have a ticket, but I'd really like to be here for my mom. She has no clue I'm coming, so I hope to surprise her for Christmas.'

My legs almost buckle beneath me. I stand, frozen to the spot, as I'm caught up in a true-life Christmas miracle. My eyes fill with tears of pure unfiltered joy.

'Gracie!' I whimper in a sound that's somewhere between

shock and joy, then the floodgates open and I race towards her, wrapping my arms around her in a tight, almost desperate hug.

'I couldn't do it,' she cries into my shoulder. 'I couldn't stay away from you on your first Christmas back here, so Dad and I did the whole presents-and-dinner thing yesterday and I got the very last seat on a flight into Dublin this morning. Happy Christmas, Mum. It's so good to be home.'

I hear the smooth, velvety tones of jazz music seep through the open door of the nearby ballroom. I smell the tantalising aromas waft through the air as the canapés are brought in from the kitchen under Cordelia's careful guidance, with Olivia holding one of the trays. She isn't afraid to get her hands dirty this time round it seems, but I'm not focused on her at all.

I'm too busy absorbing the delight on Ben's face as he introduces himself to my precious Gracie with a warm handshake and a dimpled smile.

'The last time I saw you, you were a tiny babe in arms,' he says to her. 'And you're the image of your beautiful mother in so many ways. Aren't you lucky.'

'I'm told that so much these days,' says Gracie. 'I'm very, very lucky and I'm so glad to be here.'

Most of all, I feel like my heart might burst with the joy of every single precious moment I'm experiencing. And the party is only starting.

'Now I know why you kept rabbiting on about Ballyheaney this and Ballyheaney that,' Gracie whispers as I lead her into the ballroom to find Nana Molly and Mum, who are about to get the shock of their lives in the best possible way. 'It's because of him, isn't it?'

I stop and look my beautiful girl, my best friend, who is now a thoughtful, sensitive and caring young lady.

'It's because of him,' I tell her, tears pricking my eyes again. 'Yes, it's all because of him.'

As our guests sway to the music, talking and laughing with old friends and new, I see Tilda look around her with such joy and pride. Cordelia, with the bulk of her job done, nudges her mother playfully and hands her a drink. Mum and Master Campbell are locked in conversation, while over by the window I see Uncle Eric and my grandma outside, laughing merrily as he shows her the new prize peacock.

Then, when I think I can't take any more happiness, I feel Ben's arm drape around my waist as Ava invites Gracie on a tour of the house.

The Christmas spirit seeps into every crevice and every corner of Ballyheaney House once more. The walls are no longer silent. The rooms are no longer still.

'I love you, Lou,' Ben whispers, his words making my heart swell. 'I hope you know now that you made the right decision to come back here. I know I have.'

I lean my head on his strong shoulder, wondering if life can get any better than this. Then the band strikes up a thumping version of the song 'Feliz Navidad', and the whole place is rocking.

'That song is going to haunt me forever,' laughs Ben. Cordelia is already on the dancefloor, followed by Ava and a much more reluctant Gracie, who does her best to copy their dance moves.

'Will we join them?' I ask, but Ben is already leading me by the hand to where even Tilda is dancing along. I wave outside to call Uncle Eric and Nana Molly in, though I'd no need as they're already behind us, shimmying and swaying to the music.

'By the way, I love you too, Ben Heaney,' I say to him when we're strutting our stuff on the dancefloor. 'Same time next year, then?'

'Same time *every* Christmas Eve from now on,' he says, kissing my cheek before twirling me under his arm.

'Every Christmas Eve,' I agree. 'Every single one of them.'

Chapter Twenty-five

Christmas Eve, Two Years Later

As the snow falls on to the streets of Bellaghy village, I take one last glance at the sign on the window of Buds and Beans that says we're closed for a family wedding today at Ballyheaney House. My skin prickles with excitement at what lies ahead.

'Your chariot awaits,' Uncle Eric calls from the chauffeur-driven shiny black Bentley on the kerbside by the shop. 'Did you get everything you need?'

I place the paper bag of Colombian coffee beside me in the back seat, a last-minute contribution to the menu of the day, which has been planned with precision down to the very last detail. Except for the coffee. I can't believe we forgot the coffee.

But truth be told, I wasn't only there for the coffee. In my hasty fluster the evening before, I'd left something much more precious behind. I reach for it round my neck, knowing I had to have it with me today of all days.

'That's everything,' I say breathlessly to Uncle Eric. He insisted on coming with me, even though the ceremony is due to start in ten minutes, and our morning Bucks Fizz toast meant I couldn't drive to fetch it myself.

'Are you sure no one else could have run such an errand on a morning like this other than your good self?' he asks. 'Talk about being fashionably late. Thank goodness there's no traffic to battle through on the road out to Ballyheaney.'

'You're becoming as grumpy as your late brother,' I joke with him. He doesn't have an answer to that, but I get his point. It was a rather radical detour to make on such a big day when we should be there already.

The ever-so-patient uniformed driver shuttles us down the country lane out of the village, then through the gates of Ballyheaney House, where hundreds of guests tiptoe carefully along the frosty pathways towards The Stable Room, where our ceremony will be held. We will party afterwards, not in the blue ballroom as before, but in a spectacular custom-built wedding marquee Cordelia invested in when she took over as general manager of the newly named Ballyheaney Park.

Since Ben and Ava moved in to Katie's Cottage with me, Cordelia has put her heart and soul into making Ballyheaney bloom again, while we help her out as much as we can around Ben's new village vet practice and Ava's schooling. Gracie, who is home for the wedding, has already been headhunted by Cordelia to help with event management should she ever feel the desire to settle down in Ireland, though I don't see that happening for a very long time.

Today's wedding is extra special for more reasons than this, however.

It's the first time that guests will be able to stay in the new luxury accommodation, designed by Ben, in what were once the outhouses that lined the courtyard. It's also the first time that Cordelia has opened the doors of The Stable Room, now a high-end venue for fully licensed ceremonies and where the vows will be pledged today.

And most importantly, it's the first time that a Heaney family member will be married at the place they grew up in.

Alexander the Great meets us as soon as we step out of the car in the courtyard, his sixth sense knowing it would be us, it would seem. He struts around my feet, his beady eyes shooting me a look to warn me how time is ticking on.

'Even the bloody peacock is concerned,' Uncle Eric says, jutting out his chin. 'Or he's jealous of your fancy frock. All that over coffee. I still can't believe it.'

'Oh, give over and give me away already,' I say to Ben's uncle. 'You and Nana have become so insufferable and bossy since you reignited your friendship. I thought reuniting with your one true loves would make you both happier, but all you two do is vent and moan. You're rubbing off on her. Stop it.'

He staunchly offers me his arm. I hook mine into his, knowing he has more to say still.

'We're more than friends by now, if you know what I mean,' he says, with a playful nudge in my direction. 'We may be in our early eighties, but as the saying goes, the older the fiddle, the finer the tune.'

'You are bold as brass, Uncle Eric,' I tell him. 'Never change though. It's why we all love you so much.'

I feel chills run right through me as the sound of the

bagpipes announces our arrival, bringing guests to an immediate hush inside.

'Let's do this,' I say aloud.

'Let's get my two favourites married,' says Uncle Eric. 'My nephew is waiting for you. What a lucky man he is.'

'And what a lucky woman I am too,' I whisper.

Cordelia's new Scottish fiancé, Angus, taps his foot three times when he sees us, then pipes us through the snow, past the decorative display of white roses in Jack's walled garden, which I've placed there in his honour.

'Now, that's what I call an entrance tune,' says Uncle Eric. 'I hope the piper isn't wearing shiny shoes. You know what they say about a Scotsman and his kilt.'

'It was my dad's favourite lilt,' I reply, having to dig deep to control my emotion as Angus belts out 'Highland Cathedral'.

We carefully climb the couple of steps to reach The Stable Room, where Cordelia, Gracie and Ava await us in the doorway, all wearing smiles as beautiful as their rich green bridesmaid dresses. I can't help but smile when I see Jingle and Roly dressed for the occasion too, sitting most obediently by their sides.

I spot Mum and Nana Molly in the front row, craning their necks like I told them not to, while Edward (we're definitely not allowed to call him Master Campbell now) obediently sticks to the rules and looks straight ahead. Ben's good friends from Dublin, Matt and Vic, are there too along with their three very handsome boys, who are acting as Ben's ringbearers.

I take a deep breath.

So this is it.

This is the moment I've dreamed of since I was a fresh-faced sixteen-year-old girl who melted at Ben Heaney's kiss and yearned for him year after year after year.

And then I see him. The man of my dreams, waiting for me in front of our nearest and dearest, where today we'll pledge to be together not only every Christmas Eve but every single day of our lives from now on.

Ben Heaney. Love of my life, holder of my heart and keeper of my dreams.

Angus leads us up the short aisle in The Stable Room, his kilt swinging as we pass rows of guests who await us in the eighteenth-century former coach house. It's a true credit to Cordelia, who has transformed every inch of the stable while keeping features such as the arched recesses which were once stalls for the carriage horses. They now hold vases of white hydrangeas and twisting ivy, which I was delighted to arrange myself.

'Look after each other,' says Uncle Eric, his voice choked up as he gives me away to his nephew. 'You two are precious to me. You're precious to all of us.'

Ben takes my hand and kisses it lightly. He looks more handsome than ever in his navy tailored suit, and he smells like a dream. His eyes widen with delight when he notices the turquoise gemstone round my neck, on the chain he bought me all those Christmases ago.

'You really do think of everything. Are you magic, Lou Doherty, soon to be Mrs Heaney?' he asks me, his voice making my knees go weak already. 'I think you could be magic.'

I do my best not to cry as we recall one of our very first conversations we had in this very room.

'Being with you is magical, Ben Heaney,' I whisper to him in return. 'It always has been, and it always will be.'

We are declared husband and wife as the snow falls gently outside, right here in the stable where Little Eve was born, and the place where Ben and I shared our first kiss on a cold Christmas Eve, many years ago.

And when the sun peeps through the clouds after the ceremony as we make our way together across the snow-covered lawns to the marquee for food and celebration, I catch Ava looking up to the heavens with a smile.

'A broken heart still has room to love again,' she reminds me. 'I've never forgotten that, thank you. Welcome to our family, Lou. You and Dad are a match made in heaven.'

'Maybe we are,' I say to her, feeling the winter sun on my face. 'Maybe this was all very much meant to be. Two less lonely swans in the world, eh?'

I take my new husband's hand, our fingers entwining so easily as we step inside the warmth of the marquee, where under twinkling lights the band is ready to start a celebration with a difference.

It's Christmas Eve again. How blessed are we to have another one.

How blessed are we all to have found our way home, safe in the knowledge that true love is forever, not just for Christmas.

Acknowledgements

One year on from writing my last acknowledgements, it feels both humbling and heartwarming to look back and reflect on the continued support and kindness that has come my way. My diagnosis of Multiple Myeloma in March 2024 was a showstopper. At the time, I didn't know if I'd have the strength to deliver another novel, especially after undergoing a stem cell transplant in October/November, but here it is!! It was a huge challenge. I won't pretend otherwise. Every health hurdle imaginable came my way, but thanks to the love and support of some truly special people, I found a way to keep going.

I can say with complete confidence that I have the best literary agent in Sarah Hornsley at Peters, Fraser & Dunlop. Thank you, Sarah, for guiding me through the stormy waters of the past eighteen months, for making me feel safe, and for always believing in my writing, even on the darkest of days. Your faith has helped me keep moving forward when it mattered most.

It was a real pleasure to meet Caroline Michel, CEO of PFD, in person this year. Caroline, thank you for your words of encouragement, your warmth and your kindness. Meeting you reminded me just how honoured I am to be represented by your agency.

I'm also so grateful to the International Rights Team at PFD, especially Alice Thornton-Dorkofikis, Zara Petranova and Antonia Kasoulidou, for helping my work reach new readers in Russia, Hungary, the Czech Republic and Ukraine. Thank you to Gillian Harris for keeping all the finances on track, too!

Alongside a wonderful agency, I am truly fortunate to be working with an exceptional publishing team at Penguin Random House. Huge thanks to my new editor, Susannah Hamilton, who helped shape this story. It's been such a joy collaborating with you on Lou and Ben's journey. Your vision, creativity and patience, especially around flu viruses, hospital stays and all the chaos this year has brought, mean more than I can say.

Writing a novel is one thing, making it into the book you see on the shelves is another, so a massive thank you to Sarah Hulbert (Acting Managing Editor), Caroline Pretty (Copy Editor), Rosie Grant (Marketing) and Aoifke McGuire-France (Publicity); to Olivia Allen, Evie Kettlewell, Mat Watterson and Jess Ferrier (Sales); to Richard Rowlands and Barbora Sabolova (International Sales); to Jade Stratton (Production) and Lizzy Moyes (Inventory). And, as always, heartfelt thanks to Lucy Thorne (Designer) and Jennifer Costello (Illustrator) for their beautiful cover design. The depiction of Ben, Lou and Ballyheaney House (with Jingle!) truly brought the story to life. Isn't Ben handsome?

Thanks to Michael McLoughlin and all at Penguin Ireland, especially the ever-brilliant Leonora Ararújo, who is an absolute star when it comes to publicity. I can't wait to see you all again in Dublin to celebrate *Every Christmas Eve*.

To all my incredible readers, both at home and around the

world, thank you from the bottom of my heart. Your support during the most difficult chapter of my life has been overwhelming in the best of ways. From kind messages online to thoughtful comments, and even gifts in the post, each gesture has lifted my spirits and reminded me that I've never been alone.

A warm thank you to those who've subscribed to my Facebook page, an exciting venture where I hope we can grow our book club and share more slices of life together. And to those of you taking part in my *Write with Emma* novel-writing video course, your creativity inspires me. Hearing your ideas and watching them come alive on the page fills my heart with pride.

I'm always so excited to bring new parts of the island of Ireland to readers, so it's a joy to introduce readers to Bellaghy, Co. Derry, the village where Ben and Lou are from. I chose this location out of lifelong admiration for our Nobel Prize-winning poet Seamus Heaney (RIP), with whom I share a birthday. As a devoted fan of Heaney's poetry, it was a gift to write about the places he once roamed, including Longpoint Wood, Church Island and Lough Beg.

Locals will recognise landmarks like Katie's Cottage, where Lou lives. Huge thanks to Mary McGeough for allowing me to feature her lovingly restored sixteenth-century ancestral home. Mary, your guided tour was delightful. The cottage, with its Irish charm, culture and heritage, is a true treasure. (And yes, readers, you can even stay there!)

Then there's Ballyheaney House, a name inspired by Seamus Heaney's legacy, but mostly based on the stunning

Ballyscullion Park, owned by the incredible Mulholland family. Thank you to Rosalind Mulholland, whose vision and creativity is limitless. Ballyscullion Park, overlooking Lough Beg, is a jewel of Bellaghy, and it hosts the brilliant Ballyscullion Book Festival every May, a festival I'm honoured to be part of.

My regular readers know I love getting little signs while writing, and you might not believe this, but I thought of the name *Cordelia* for Ben's sister in a very specific moment, and only later discovered that Rosalind's daughter, raised at Ballyscullion, is also named Cordelia. Another magical, serendipitous moment. That's three books in a row where something like this has happened! I like to think it means I'm on the right path.

A big thank you to Will Scholes and Jenny Lee of the *Irish News*. Your support over the years has meant so much, and I'll miss working with you. Thanks to Gemma Fullam at the *Irish Examiner* for her sensitive interview about my cancer journey, and to all at the *Claire Byrne Show* on RTÉ Radio 1. I'll never forget speaking live on air the morning of my stem cell transplant, an unforgettable moment that connected me with so many others who shared their stories in return. Thanks also to Eddie Rowley (*Sunday World*), Áine Toner and Niamh Campbell (*Belfast Telegraph*), Kat O'Connor (*Her.ie*), Thomas Maher (*Ulster Herald*), Conor Coyle (*Belfast Live*), Maureen Coleman and Anna Curran (*BBC Radio Ulster*).

To all my fellow writers, especially Claire Allan, C. J. Cooke and Fionnuala Kearney, thank you for the camaraderie. Special thanks to Madeline and TP at Sheehy's Cookstown,

Lesley Price at Bridge Books Dromore (what a book festival! Thank you for having me and Claire!), and all the booksellers and librarians who recommend my novels (thank you, Pete and Jillian at Libraries NI). I'm also grateful to all the bloggers and influencers, with a special shout-out to Izzy at The Reading Room, who hosted an online read-along during my hospital stay. Since I couldn't see my last book in real life, huge thanks to everyone, including staff at Waterstones Derry and Forestside, for sending me photos.

Speaking of my transplant, I'd like to publicly thank Dr Donaldson and every single staff member on Ward 10 of Belfast City Hospital. For four weeks, you were my lifeline in isolation. You are not just medical professionals, you are heroes. Thank you for your expertise, your care, and for creating a space where people like me could feel safe and less afraid. I promised one of my doctors I'd put his name in a novel, so Shaheer, there you are! A special shout-out to Jane, who shaved my head when the time came, and to Crawford for his daily chats, *'maidin mhaith'* wishes and trips to the shop for goodies when I couldn't eat much but had a random craving.

I'm also cared for monthly by the phenomenal team at Craigavon Area Hospital, under the guidance of Dr Foy, who monitors my condition with precision. The Mandeville Unit has become a second home, and a place where I always leave feeling reassured that I'm in the best hands. You all have been by my side since day one. Your kindness, strength and familiar faces have been a constant comfort, and you've come to feel like family in the truest sense.

To my friends and family, you know who you are. Your

love has been a lifeline, and I'd be lost without you. To the strangers who've checked in, prayed for me, or sent words of comfort, thank you for reminding me that kindness still runs deep in this world.

Thanks as always to my wonderful daddy. Your quiet, unwavering support is unconditional, and I am truly grateful.

Every Christmas Eve is dedicated to my fiancé Jim McKee and our wonderful children – Jordyn, Jade, Adam, Dualta and Sonny. You make me proud every single day. Thank you all for your endless love, strength, and for the magical memories we create together. Jim, I couldn't have got through the past year and a half without you. Thank you.

And finally, to anyone wading the waters of their own cancer journey, or caring for someone who is, I see you. I won't offer empty advice, but I've hope you've found that, even in the hardest times, there are still days when life is quietly beautiful.

Unti next Christmas, please God, take good care.

Emma x

Read on for an exclusive Q&A
with the author . . .

Q&A with Emma Heatherington: Writing
Every Christmas Eve

Where or how did you find inspiration for *Every Christmas Eve*?

Every writer has their own unique process of how to start a novel. While I don't claim to have a specific formula or pattern, I do find lately that once I've decided on a setting, the characters grow out of it and the story quickly comes to life.

My brother David and his wife Sarah Jane were married a few years ago in a stunning place called Ballyscullion Park in Bellaghy, County Derry, right in the heart of Mid Ulster where I'm from. It was a beautiful sunny day, there was dancing on the lawns, music around a firepit and to me it felt like something from a movie, so when I was contacted by Rosalind, owner of Ballyscullion, in early 2024 to take part in the first Ballyscullion Book Festival I had one of those moments where the pennies were dropping into my head and by the time I came off the phone, not only had I said a big 'yes' to the festival but I knew I'd the tiniest seed of my story in place. I had the perfect setting, now I needed to flesh out the story. Who lives in the 'big house' in my fictional version? What's their background? How did the people in the house relate to the people in the nearby village? I imagined a winter wonderland Christmas party where everyone came together. And so, it all began.

I love period dramas, so I jumped on the idea of mixing something almost old worldly with modern-day village life. Soon, characters like Ben and his uncle Eric, his mother Tilda and of course young Ava all sprung to life, as did Lou and her wonderful girl gang who support her in Buds and Beans.

And by absolute divine timing, I was scrolling through LinkedIn one day when I came across Katie's Cottage in Bellaghy. My jaw dropped, and I rushed to ask the owner Mary if I could use it as Lou's home in *Every Christmas Eve*. Mary kindly gave me a tour of the cottage, I fell madly in love with it and the rest is history!

Also, Bellaghy is the home place of my favourite poet, Seamus Heaney (RIP). It was deeply inspirational to discover more about the village he grew up in and the places that inspired his poetry. My personal favourites are 'Scaffolding' and 'When all the others were away at Mass'. Both poems make me cry, in a good way.

Some of your supporting cast members have become almost as popular as the leading protagonists. Why do you think this is?

Perhaps these characters are relatable to us all, or at least to a part of us that would love to know someone like unpredictable Uncle Eric, or quirky Granny Molly, or endearing old Master Campbell.

Lots of readers still get in touch to say how much they loved Aunt Nora and Leroy in *Maybe Next Christmas*, or Rusty in *This Christmas*. I must admit, I do too.

It's a bit of a cliché, but I do feel like they're real people by the time I've finished a book. I find myself thinking I'm missing someone, or something, then I realise it's the world I've created, and I remind myself they aren't real people.

So, to answer the question, I do think these characters spark off a memory or a longing or a connection to the reader. I like to surround my leading protagonists with people who bring out all sides of their character – their passions, their weaknesses, their vulnerabilities. Maybe by doing so, the supportive cast shine brighter.

Readers have also contacted you to say they've planned to visit some of the places featured in your novels. How does that feel?

I honestly think this is so cool, and it's something I always love to hear. For anyone who fancies doing the same, here are some of the places I recommend from my recent works:

Fanad Lighthouse – This iconic landmark on the northern tip of Co. Donegal is breathtaking in all seasons. I never tire of a visit to the lighthouse when I can. Don't forget to pop by the Lighthouse Tavern where Charlie and Rose from *This Christmas* spent time together.

Glenveagh National Park – While I only touched on this spectacular forest and nature reserve, it's a landscape like no other in the very heart of Co. Donegal. Mountains, pristine lakes, rugged and wild walkways to suit all abilities, it's like stepping into an Irish fairy tale under the watchful eye of a castle. Readers might remember this is where Charlie took his dog for a walk in *This Christmas*.

Benburb Priory, Co. Tyrone – This serene haven is on my doorstep in my native part of the world. Walk around the grounds along the foaming River Blackwater, see the cute railway-style cottages where Bea's family lived, and spend time in the chapel to quiet your heart. The Priory also runs some fantastic events, and it became a place of deep solace for me during my illness.

The Slieve League Cliffs – This is the perfect day trip to see some of southern Donegal's finest landmarks and cute fishing towns, including Killybegs (fun fact – Killybegs is where I imagined my very first novel, *Crazy for You*, was set, though I changed the name at the time to make it more fictional). When I was researching *Maybe Next Christmas*, I took a spin up to see the cliffs with my two daughters and my youngest son. We thoroughly enjoyed a boat trip around the cliffs, where dolphins followed us along the way! It was magical. Afterwards, you can whet your whistle and fuel up in my character Ollie's local, The Rusty Mackerel.

Silver Strand Beach – Now this is a real treat! The horseshoe-shaped beach in Malin Beg has golden sands, best viewed from the top of 174 steps, so if like me you're not up for climbing up and down (I would *love* to have been able to), you can still take it all in. This beach featured in *Maybe Next Christmas* when Ollie and his dad were making precious final memories.

Bellaghy, Co. Derry – Check out Katie's Cottage (or even better, stay there!), catch the Ballyscullion Book Festival in

May, be inspired by our Nobel-winning Poet Laureate Seamus Heaney at the Seamus Heaney HomePlace and walk in his footsteps around Longpoint Wood, from where you can view Church Island in the very near distance. And of course you've a choice of restaurants, pubs and coffee shops to follow the path around places where Lou and Ben fell in love.

How does it feel to have *Every Christmas Eve* featured as part of ASDA's Tickled Pink campaign for the second year in a row?

Having my book selected for Asda's Tickled Pink campaign for the second year in a row is deeply meaningful to me, not just as an author, but as someone living with cancer. This campaign goes far beyond book sales. It raises vital awareness and funds for breast cancer charities that are doing incredible, life-changing work. To be part of that effort, through my writing, is both humbling and empowering.

Living with cancer brings so much uncertainty, but moments like this remind me that stories have power, not only to entertain but also to connect us, comfort us, and sometimes even help us feel seen. Being chosen again is a reminder that my voice matters, and that even through illness I can contribute something positive to a much bigger cause.

What's a pleasure you turn to when not writing?

Reading, always! When I'm in the middle of writing a book, I find it hard to switch off from the world I'm creating, so once the work is done, I really look forward to getting lost in someone else's story.

I also love slow, gentle walks on the beach in my beloved Downings, Co. Donegal, where I try to spend as much time as I can. Living with illness has slowed everything down (in its own strange way, a silver lining) and it's made me appreciate life's quieter, simpler pleasures more deeply than ever.

Spending time with my partner, our eleven-year-old son and our young adult children is what fills me up the most. My energy is limited, so I've become more intentional about how I spend it, and with whom. That kind of clarity has been a gift. Life has never felt more precious.

More from
Emma Heatherington

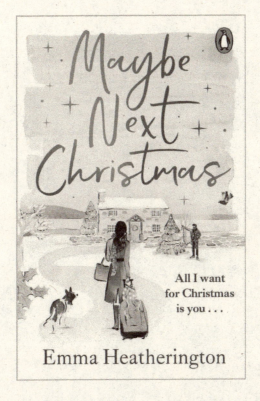

'A Christmas hug of a book' and 'the perfect
festive romance' from the bestselling author of
Every Christmas Eve

More from
Emma Heatherington

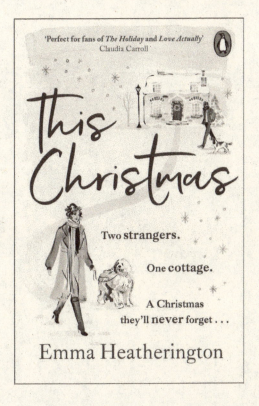

'Perfect for fans of *The Holiday* and *Love Actually*'
Claudia Carroll

this
Christmas

Two **strangers.**

One **cottage.**

A Christmas
they'll **never** forget . . .

Emma Heatherington

Discover the heartwarming cosy Christmas
romance to curl up with this winter from the
bestselling author of *Every Christmas Eve*